I enjoy it,

Blood Like Poison:
For the Love of a Vampire

M. LEIGHTON

M Leighton

ISBN: 1463597665
ISBN-13:978-1463597665

The murmur of death, a dark shadow overcast,

Ringing long and eternal as life slips slowly past,

It breeds the unthinkable and touts the unknown,

It begins at the end, on a whisper, a moan.

PROLOGUE

Bo was on his knees in the center of the concrete floor, kneeling on a black towel. He was shirtless and covered in blood spatter. Under the slimy red sheen, I could see a sickly greenish black color seeping across his chest, radiating from the left side outward. It was darkest over his heart and it pulsed as if gangrenous death was being pumped throughout his body with every slow squeeze of the muscle. That, however, was not the most alarming part. The thing that caught and held my attention was his face.

As always, when I thought of Bo, my heart clenched painfully. I remember seeing him that day, the horror of it and how terrified I was. But even now, I can't bring myself to regret stumbling upon him like that. I might've gone through the rest of my days in a selfishly numb state of hiding if I hadn't met him, hadn't known him for who and what he was. He taught me so much about a world I didn't know existed and so much more about a life I hadn't been living.

He taught me to stand up for what I believe in, to shout it out at the top of my lungs. He taught me to feel—the deep, gut-wrenching, heartbreaking, soul-singing kind of emotion I had avoided for so long. He taught me about the importance of life. He taught me about the beauty of death. He also taught me about love.

This is our story.

CHAPTER ONE

Drums blared from the radio, but even over the loud music, I could still hear Izzy's bell-like voice as she sang along. She knew every word to the song. She bobbed her head and wiggled her shoulders, tapping her thumbs rhythmically on the steering wheel.

Her dark auburn hair was pulled back in a French twist at the back of her head and the dashboard lights illuminated her heart-shaped face, making her silvery blue eyes look even paler. Her cheeks were a little fuller than usual and her skin had an uncharacteristic glow.

I wondered about her weight gain, had my suspicions, but I said nothing. If she had something to tell me, she'd get to it in her own sweet time. That was Izzy's way.

She slid me a sidelong glance. "What are you staring at, Perv?"

"Those man hands," I replied teasingly. "You could palm a grown man's head with those mitts."

"Hey," she said, glaring at me. "Do you want to walk home?"

"Yeah, like—"

And then, as I'd done hundreds of times in the last three years, I awoke in a cold sweat. Heart racing, chest aching, I lay in bed and struggled to catch my breath. I squeezed my eyes shut against the last few seconds of the car crash, but that didn't stop me from seeing it. It never did. The awful crunch of metal rang in my ears and I knew what was coming after that—the same images that always did, the ones that only got more confusing with time.

Memories of a deer and a boy tangled together in my mind. I'd told the authorities of a person I'd seen as the car spun off the road, about the pale face of a stranger that had flashed in front of the headlights just before my recollection went blank.

I assumed we'd hit him, but they'd found no body, no evidence of blood or tissue on the blackened remains of the front bumper. They'd assured me that no one could've survived being struck by a car going over fifty miles per hour. They'd concluded that, since they hadn't found a body, the boy must've been a figment of my imagination, born of terror and trauma.

But I wasn't convinced, and after three long years, I hadn't forgotten him either. Though the details of his face had faded over time, there was something about his eyes—a soul-deep agony, a burning self-loathing—that I'd never been able to get out of my head. It had stayed with me since that night. I was drawn to that kind of suffering, almost like a kindred spirit.

Slowly but surely, as I stared at the ceiling, reality returned, settling over me like a blanket of blandness. The television played the early morning news reports, as it did every morning.

I was probably the most well-informed kid in school, mostly because I went to sleep every night with the television on and woke up every day listening to the most recent happenings as they echoed through my room.

I listened with half an ear to the Channel Six anchorman as he talked about the top story.

"Another body was found late last night in Arlisle Preserve, near the area police have dubbed the 'Slayer's Slaughterhouse'." The body was positively identified as seventeen year old Jolene Turner of Falls Town. At this time, police are not able to divulge all the details surrounding her death, though they did confirm that she was killed in a manner typical of the Southmoore Slayer, including the animal attack-like markings on the neck, a fatal chest wound and exsanguination. Turner makes victim number twenty-seven of the Southmoore Slayer and, unless he's captured, police fear that her death will not be the last.

Southmoore Chief of Police Edwin McDonnahough has teamed with local authorities from four neighboring towns to form a task force dedicated to the identification and apprehension of the Slayer. Law enforcement officials from Harker, Columbia, Camden, and Sumter have devoted at least one officer to the team in hopes of bringing the Slayer to justice before the violence spreads across the borders into their townships.

In other top news, The Center for Disease Control in Atlanta still has not been able to confirm that the mysterious illness plaguing now thirty-one Southmoore residents is Mad Cow Disease. Authorities have yet to lift the quarantine that has been imposed on the sale of local cattle…"

I let the reporter's voice fade into the background as my breathing returned to normal and then, with a sigh, I smacked blindly at the television's remote control until I found the power button. Without the noise of the TV, an uncomfortable silence filled my bedroom. It was the kind of quiet that always led to troubling thoughts. It was the kind of quiet I avoided like the plague. Already, my mind was wandering back to the dream.

With another sigh, I rolled over and turned off my alarm clock, even though it had yet to buzz. I knew from years of experience that I wouldn't find sleep again. Resigned, I threw back the covers, got out of bed and went to take a shower.

****

I shouted at the tiny, dark-skinned blonde at the top of the pyramid. "Trinity, you're wobbling!"

"I can't help it. Aisha's moving. If I fall off, I'm gonna kick her- ahh!"

And just like that, the pyramid came tumbling down. Actually, it was more like a gentle folding, thank God. But I knew that just because no one was hurt this time didn't mean it wouldn't end badly next time.

"Aisha, I'm switching you to the shoulder stand on the end."

"Thank God," she muttered, angrily flipping her long, intricately braided hair.

Ignoring her, I directed my attention to the slightly stocky brunette with the pigtails at the other end of the formation. "Carly, can you help hold Trinity for the center?"

With a snort and a roll of her eyes, Carly agreed, albeit ungraciously. "I guess," she said weakly.

We looked at each other expectantly—me waiting for her to move and her waiting for...I don't know what *she* was waiting for, but it was obvious Carly had no intention of moving whatsoever.

Carly was my whiner. I wanted to slap her. I wanted to slap her *a lot*. Seriously, I did, just not as badly (or as often) as I wanted to punch Trinity. And I mean really punch her. Hard. Right in her pouty mouth. Trinity was the type of personality that would've brought Gandhi himself to violence.

I was rarely ever surprised by the behavior of the other cheerleaders, only irritated by it. After all, I understood them better than anyone. Until three years ago, I was fundamentally the same as them—shamefully selfish, vapid, useless and vicious. But when tragedy strikes, it leaves no part of your life, of your being, untouched, unscathed, unscarred. No, tragedy had carved a whole new person out of my less-than-ideal former self, and in a way, I'm thankful for it.

Now my eyes are open and I'm content, at least for my soul's sake, to be growing more and more different, growing further and further apart from them. It does make things more difficult, though. Much more difficult.

Pushing both the violent and the troubling thoughts from my mind, I simply smiled sweetly and asked Carly, "Then how about getting over there so we can try it?"

With a loud, exaggerated sigh, Carly obliged me by moving toward the other end of the line.

"Ridley, you better not get me killed," Trinity said theatrically as she followed Carly into position.

"Don't be so dramatic, Trinity. Just keep your balance and you'll be fine."

"I don't see you up here, risking your life for a pyramid, Moby Dick" Trinity mumbled under her breath.

Her comment was point in case. Trinity was convinced that anyone who wore a size greater than a four was a cow. Or a whale in this case. She was unbelievable.

Though the barb rankled, I ignored her. As always. She assumed that I didn't hear her, but she couldn't have been more wrong. I simply disregarded her remarks because anything less than that was like pouring gasoline on a fire.

If her nastiness was given the tiniest bit of attention or credence, she just acted out all the more.

So, as I'd done a thousand times before, I swallowed my anger and my retorts, opting for a future at Stanford instead. My college dreams, my *life's* dreams were riding on a scholarship and Trinity was a great flyer for the squad, just another reason not to rock the boat.

My biggest goal was to keep my nose clean until graduation. The end. And if that included ignoring Trinity so as not to get her too riled up, then so be it.

"Alright, let's see it from the ground up with the music," I shouted, hitting the play button on my iPod's docking station.

Usher blared from the speakers and the cheerleaders began to move in time with the beat. Steadily, they climbed and built the pyramid until Trinity was once more perched on top, a foot in each of two girls' palms. Then, right on cue, they lifted her until she was standing high in the air, atop their extended arms.

"Perfect," I said, clapping excitedly. "Now we can work that new toss in from right there." I approached the girls as they dismounted. "Let's take five and then we'll work on flying for the rest of the afternoon."

Shorts-clad cheerleaders disbursed to the bleachers to get sips of their bottled waters and complain about what a slave driver I was. Same drill, different day.

After a couple of minutes, I heard Trinity say, "Stalk much?"

A few seconds after that, several of the others chimed in.

"Hell-o, Sexy!"

"He can stalk me any time."

"That's just creepy."

"He looks weird. And dangerous."

I looked up to see who was causing such a commotion. All the girls were looking back toward the fence that surrounded the practice field. Curious, I turned in that direction, too.

The setting sun was right in my eyes, but if I squinted, I could see a guy in a black hoodie, standing at the fence. Since I hadn't seen him around school before, I could only assume that he was new. He was leaning against the metal chain link, one arm draped casually across its top, watching us as if we were shiny new things that puzzled him.

I held my hand up to my eyes, shielding them from the bright light so that I could get a better look at him. When I met his eyes, I realized that he wasn't watching *us*; he was watching *me.*

"Got a new admirer, huh Ridley?" Carly liked to tease. Carly also liked to spread rumors.

"And you've got a great imagination, Carly," I said lightly, not wanting to make a big deal of it. I was dead set against my name being bandied about in typical cheerleader fashion so I made sure to give her as little ammunition as possible.

A masculine voice interrupted our rude staring.

"Hey, T!"

It came from somewhere behind me. I recognized the voice of course, but even if I hadn't, I still would've known who was hailing me. It was Drew. For some unknown, inexplicable reason, when he didn't call me Ridley (which was most of the time), he called me "T".

Some of the cheerleaders gossiped that it stood for "tease" because I didn't put out, but I doubted Drew was that crude. If I really thought he was, I wouldn't be with him.

Reluctantly, I turned from the stranger to find Drew. He was coming across the field, decked out in his football pads, looking attractively sweaty and mussed.

"Hey, babe, can you get a ride home with Trinity or Summer today? Josh wants me to go with him to pick up some parts for the Mustang after practice," Drew explained.

"I'll just walk," I said, swallowing my frustrated sigh. "No biggee."

That was the one bad thing about letting Drew drive me to school. If he changed his plans, I got screwed. Luckily, I didn't live far and I never minded walking when the weather was nice. It was like a mini vacation.

"You sure?"

"Yep." I nodded to further reassure him and reinforce my answer.

"You're so awesome," he said, winding one arm around my waist to pick me up and smash his lips playfully to mine.

"I am?" Even as I so coyly—teasingly—asked the question, I thought of my nickname, "T". Maybe the girls were right. I couldn't help the frown that accompanied the thought.

Setting me back on my feet, Drew just grinned mischievously and shrugged. "That's what they say," he taunted as he turned and jogged back across the field to his own practice.

Turning back toward the bleachers, I wiped the frown from my forehead and forced my mind to return to the task at hand. "Alright, let's get this toss down."

Grumbling and complaining, the girls reluctantly descended the stands. I watched in wonder as they dragged themselves to the field. It was probably a mystery to almost everyone how such a motley crew managed to make it so far in competitions. We didn't look very dedicated or energetic.

As the last of the girls walked past me, heading back out onto the grass, I couldn't stop my eyes from flickering back to the fence. I was curiously hungry for one more peak at the stranger. He was still standing there, too. He just stared at me, as motionless as a statue.

Though he was backlit by the setting sun, I could see his eyes clearly. They were a dark, rich brown that seemed almost black in his pale, pale face. The spark of interest shone in their depths, but beyond that, there was something else. Danger? Determination? Sadness? Fear? Satisfaction? Was it him, or was I simply seeing a reflection of my own inner demons? After all, I'd always wanted but never found someone with whom I could share the real Ridley. Was I imagining that I saw such a person in the face of the stranger? I couldn't be sure what it was, but something in those eyes felt strangely familiar.

The longer he held my eyes, the more I felt like he was touching me in some way, almost physically, tangibly. Much to my surprise, my belly did a little flip, excitement dancing along my nerve ends.

We watched each other for a second or two longer and then, dismissively, he turned and walked away.

****

Later that evening, Summer and I sat cross-legged on my bed, making flash cards for our Anatomy and Physiology test. We were both taking college preparatory classes and Mr. Richardson, our A&P teacher, gave us only four grades in the whole year. We had two major tests, a mid-term exam and a final exam. If you bombed any of the four, you really didn't have a snowball's chance in Hell of fully recovering your grade.

Summer was probably my best friend, though that didn't mean as much as it used to. Much as had happened with almost everyone else, I'd grown apart from her over the last three years. But still, she was the lesser of the evils as far as friends went. I mean, confiding in Trinity was completely out of the question. Having her as my best friend would be like keeping a pet barracuda in my bathtub.

"If I tell you something, will you promise not to tell?" Summer didn't look up at me, just kept writing on the back of the card marked *Alveoli.*

"Of course."

"Trinity wants me to help her get revenge on Devon. Well, sort of."

Devon was Trinity's ex. If she had anything close to a weakness, he'd be her Achilles heel.

I put down my marker. I could sense a storm on the horizon, a nasty plan birthed in the sick mind of Trinity and it deserved my full attention. They didn't call her *The Unholy Trinity* behind her back for nothing.

"By doing what?"

"She wants me to get Devon to take me out and then post on Facebook that he's really, really tiny so that no one else will want to go out with him."

"Ahh," I said, immediately understanding her end game in such a plot. "Then Trinity will be the only one gracious enough to date him despite the vicious rumors."

Summer shrugged. "I guess." She still hadn't looked up to meet my eyes.

"Summer, you're not considering this, are you?"

She shrugged again.

"But why? Why would you do that? To Devon or to yourself?"

She looked up at me, frowning. "Oh, I wouldn't actually have sex with him. I'd just tell people that we did."

"But everyone would think that you just went out and slept with him. Do you think they won't be calling you a slut by lunchtime if you do this?"

"You know how Trinity is. If I say no, it's hard to tell what she'll do to me."

I growled, sliding off the bed to pace the floor. Everyone was afraid of Trinity, afraid of what she would do if she was angered. Trinity was smart, though. She never pushed the wrong people. She always picked the weakest ones of the herd to do her dirty work. She would never ask me to do something like that. I might bite my tongue a lot, but she knew I wouldn't go along with something so deplorable. It was times like this that made me wonder if Stanford was really worth it.

"Summer, you can't do this."

"I have to," she said miserably.

I paced the floor, thinking. I stopped when a possible solution occurred to me. "Devon's a nice guy. Let me talk to him. If he refuses to take you out, problem solved, right?"

Summer's eyes lit up and she clapped excitedly. Though this disaster was averted, I knew it was just a matter of time before Trinity thought of something else, some other despicable way to win Devon back.

I called Devon and, as I suspected, he was more than willing to go along with our counter-Trinity plan and keep it hush-hush.

****

The next morning, I decided to drive to school. There was an away game that night and I didn't want to get stuck riding home with somebody else when the bus dropped us back off at school. Since I could never count on one of my rogue parents to be a reliable back-up plan, I tried always to make other arrangements—me. As usual, I was my own plan B.

I pulled my old Civic into a parking spot and grabbed my duffel from the back seat. I had to hurry. I was running late.

I scurried into Home Room and scooted into my seat, dropping my bag quietly onto the floor. Mrs. Dingle was going over the local news, as she did every morning. She felt it was her duty to keep us informed of what was going on around us, as if we were all so oblivious we wouldn't find out otherwise. But then I realized something. She was probably right. The only reason I knew what was going on was because I went to sleep with the television on. I couldn't tolerate silence. Or, better yet, I couldn't tolerate the places my mind went in the silence. Either way, I heard the news whether I wanted to or not.

The first tidbit she force-fed us was the increase in the number of animal deaths. Farm animals were being mauled and brutally killed all over the area. The Wildlife Officers had neither confirmed nor denied speculation that there might be a pack of wolves or even a mountain lion terrorizing livestock in the region. As an avid animal lover, topics like that disturbed me, even more than those involving the Slayer, which was what Mrs. Dingle moved on to next.

Southmoore was a thriving city that lay just north of our small South Carolina town, Harker. For that reason, citizens and reporters alike had all been closely following the killings there. As a community, we hadn't been put on lockdown yet, but if things got much worse up north or, heaven forbid, moved down south to us, our freedoms would be quickly and severely curtailed.

As she droned on, I let my mind wander. For some reason, it meandered straight down a path that led to the guy I'd seen at the field the day before. I could picture his face with perfect clarity, as I'd done countless times since yesterday. There was just something about those eyes.

Just then, as if a light tap had sounded on the inside of my skull, I looked up. There, standing in front of the lockers outside my classroom, was the object of my ruminations. He had obviously been walking somewhere. He had stopped, mid-stride, right in front of my Home Room door. He just stood there, staring at me with those hauntingly dark pools of chocolate.

I was immediately captivated. Looking into his eyes was like standing at the edge of a deep pond and gazing down into swirling, hypnotic waters, becoming mesmerized by them, trapped in them. I felt as if I couldn't look away, not even if I had wanted to.

I have no idea how long we stared at each other that way, but when the bell rang, I jumped, blinking and looking around guiltily. When I looked back out into the hall, I was deflated to see only a row of gray lockers. There was no intriguing stranger standing in front of them anymore. He was gone.

I hopped up out of my desk and hurried to the hall, hoping to catch another glimpse of him, but I wasn't fast enough. Floods of bustling bodies were already pouring out of all the classrooms. I scanned the sea of faces, but among them, I didn't see the pale face for which I was searching.

Inordinately disappointed, I slowly made my way down the hall to my locker. I couldn't help but ask myself why I was so interested in him, why it mattered where he went, why I cared.

With no answers rising to the surface, I put my duffel away and put books into my messenger bag to carry to class. I tried to convince myself that it was just curiosity that made him so noteworthy—normal, healthy curiosity—but in the back of my mind, I kept seeing his eyes. There was just something about those eyes.

The rest of the morning was nothing short of excruciating. The minutes of each class seemed to tick by at a snail's pace. I caught myself watching the hallways more than the teacher and, between classes, watching every face that I passed, looking for a pair of compelling black-brown eyes. I never did find them, though, and the whole hide-and-seek thing just left me frustrated to the point of a headache.

Lunch was something of a reprieve, thank goodness, but only because I was surrounded by people who required an incredible amount of focus and attentiveness from everyone else around them. They were like solar panels and attention was like the sun. They absorbed it, absorbed us, and trust me, it's not easy being the sun.

At our table on the covered concrete patio just outside the cafeteria, Drew sat on one side of me and Summer sat on the other.

I saw Trinity lean around Summer to address me. "Are you and Drew going to Caster's party this weekend?"

The way she was eyeing me said she'd had to repeat herself, something Trinity found intolerable. There were few things that got under her skin more quickly than being ignored. I didn't do it on purpose, of course. I was just preoccupied. But I knew that in a thousand years, Trinity would never understand how anything could be more interesting than our group discussions at lunchtime. She didn't ask what I was thinking about and I didn't volunteer.

"Caster's party," she snapped.

"Oh, sorry," I said.

Trinity always gave the final say on social events, like what the group was doing, when we were doing it and who we were doing it with. She was like the popularity godmother. When she tapped her wand on a particular person or activity, it took on a life of its own. With her approval, the sky was the limit, a reputation could soar into the limelight. But with her disapproval, she could squash a person's spirit under her heel like it was nothing more than a bothersome ant.

If I weren't the captain of the cheer squad who happened to be dating the quarterback of the football team, she wouldn't have given my input a second thought. But I was both of those coveted things, and it was my status—and my status *alone*— that prompted her to care what my plans were. Besides, she knew that my plans would likely include Drew, which in turn would likely include Devon.

One more year, one more year, one more year, I reminded myself, sick to death of all the high school games and drama.

"I don't know," I answered, turning to Drew. "Drew?"

"What?" He hadn't been paying us the least bit of attention.

"Caster's party. Wanna go?"

"Maybe," he shrugged.

I turned back to Trinity. "Maybe."

Her expression showed frustration and I knew she was reaching her patience threshold.

"How am I supposed to make plans if you two won't make up your mind?"

"Go if you want to go. We're not stopping you," I reminded her casually.

It was like poking a bear and I knew it. I suppose it was my passive-aggressive way of lashing out. Whatever. It felt good.

Trinity growled in response. She didn't need to say it, but we were both thinking to ourselves that *that* would never happen. She turned to pass what she'd learned down the lunch table and I could almost see the indecision spreading across faces like wildfire. No one's plans would be concrete until Trinity gave the go-ahead that we were all going to Caster's party.

I sighed and thought again how I couldn't wait for high school to be over.

I didn't let my exasperation show, however. I'd long since discovered how to live inside the shark tank without getting eaten or becoming a shark: never let 'em see you sweat. Don't show any emotion, no matter how many you're feeling. It just reveals your weaknesses and, to them, weaknesses are like blood in the water.

I try never to let them see me get angry, upset, defensive, flustered, uncertain, *anything.* I'm sure that, to them, I seem somewhat robotic, but it keeps *me* out of trouble and keeps *them* at arm's length. And that's how I survive.

Spearing a cucumber with my fork, I nibbled its crisp edges while I listened with half an ear to what was being said all around me.

Drew and Devon were talking to Josh about how to get more horsepower under the hood of the Mustang they were working on. Trinity was whispering to April and Aisha so quietly I couldn't hear her, which invariably meant she was talking about me (Trinity was rarely ever so quiet). Summer was regaling Carly and Shana with her personal success stories of pairing ankle-high boots with a skirt. Chace and Minty were arguing over which freshman at the table next to ours had the nicer rack.

All their talk jumbled in my head as my mind strayed once more to a pair of the most intense eyes I've ever seen. I was both intrigued by my unusual reaction to him and aggravated by it. I mean, it's not like he's Damon Salvatore hot or Keith Stone smooth. But regardless, he'd certainly managed to work his way into my head with absolutely no effort on his part whatsoever.

What's worse is that I have a boyfriend. I shouldn't even be giving him a second glance, much less thinking about him so much, and yet I just couldn't seem to escape those eyes.

Shaking off thoughts of him—again—I looked out across the campus. As if they were drawn by some invisible magnetic force of nature, my eyes collided with the very ones I was trying to forget.

There he was, sitting beneath a tree all the way on the other side of the green expanse of grass behind the school, and just like before, he was simply staring at me.

I shouldn't say "simply." There was nothing simple about the shower of chills that rained down my back and arms. There was nothing simple about the flutter in my chest that made me feel short of breath.

Instantly, I forgot all the reasons I was avoiding him, all the reasons I was trying not to think about him. At that moment, I just wanted to hold his gaze as long as it would hold me back.

Penetrating, unwavering and extremely unsettling, his boldness was probably wildly inappropriate, but not in a stalker way. It was bold in a good way, in an exciting way. The way he looked at me, I felt like the only girl in the world.

He didn't smile and he didn't move a single muscle. He just stared at me, like he was seeing right into my soul. I sat perfectly still and let him.

"Ohmigod, Ridley! Could you be more obvious?" Trinity's tone was a little louder and sharper than need be and it carried all the way down the table. I knew she was trying to get Drew's attention.

I jerked my eyes away from the fathomless brown ones and turned a frown on Trinity.

"Obvious? About what?" I assumed my most casually confused expression.

It was important to remain calm and appear casual no matter how *not* casual I was feeling. I hid every iota of emotion behind a carefully schooled mask of confident nonchalance. It was essential.

"Who's that?" At Drew's question, I felt like sneering. Her plan had worked perfectly.

"Who?" I looked up questioningly. I didn't need to ask to whom he was referring; I knew, but I did so just to prove my point: that I had no idea who they were talking about.

"That guy over there," he said, tipping his head toward the stranger. "The one that's about to get his teeth handed to him."

My eyes darted back to the mesmerizing ebony ones, but I looked quickly away before I fell into their depths again. Then, with a shrug that belied how jittery I was, I said, "I don't know."

"Hey," Summer said, throwing her two cents in. "That's the guy from yesterday, the one who was totally stalking you."

"No one's stalking me, Summer," I snapped. The look of shock on every face in my line of sight had me instantly regretting my impulsive display of emotion. "You watch too much Gossip Girl," I added with a carefree laugh.

Faces relaxed somewhat, but I knew it wasn't quite enough.

"So who else is going to Caster's party?" I asked, knowing that was the only thing more interesting than me having a stalker. If I didn't nip it in the bud, something like that would be fodder for the gossip mongers for weeks, maybe months.

Everyone but Trinity and Drew fell right into party talk, just as I'd hoped they would. Trinity was too sharp for that, though. She's got a nose for deception. She can smell evasiveness at fifty paces. And Drew, he was a naturally jealous guy, so they were both a little harder to throw off the scent than the others. Finally, though, after a few tense seconds, my casualness won the day and they took the bait. Much to my relief, they pitched in with everyone else on the subject change.

Mentally, I sighed and tried to put lingering obsidian orbs out of my head—*tried* being the operative word.

****

Chemistry: the last class of the day and by far the most boring. You'd think Chemistry would be one of the most interesting subjects and, really, it should've been. In this instance, the problem was the teacher. We had a mind-numbingly boring one named Mr. Dole. I pondered the incongruity of it on the way to class; anything to keep my mind off of *him*.

With a sigh, I turned in through the door, taking my usual seat at the second long black science table beneath the window. I threw my messenger bag up on the table and slouched down in my chair. I just wanted it to be over so we could go to Norton, cheer at the away game and get home. I was in no mood for extra time on my hands and that's what I'd surely find under Mr. Dole's tedious instruction.

In Mr. Dole's class, no one sat at the front two tables in the room. It was a well known fact that they were semi-dangerous. Mr. Dole spit a lot when he talked and it was nothing to get sprayed in the eye or, heaven forbid, in the mouth if it happened to be open. We all kept a good distance whenever possible. One of our best defensive measures was boycotting the first two tables.

Today, however, there was a black messenger bag lying atop the table to the right and in front of mine, at one of the off-limits tables. I looked at it curiously then put my head down on my crossed arms. My temples were throbbing.

I heard Mr. Dole slam his book down on his desk, just like he did every day, and I raised my head attentively. My expression was immediately one of interest, or so it would seem to the casual observer. I could fake it with the best of 'em.

My pretense was soon to be genuine, however, when I spotted a familiar dark head directly in front of Mr. Dole. It caught my attention so quickly and held it so completely it might as well have been a flashing neon sign.

He didn't have to turn around for me to recognize the stylishly disheveled practically-black hair. Or the charcoal hoodie. I'd have spotted it anywhere, probably even at a store that sold black hoodies. It drew me like gravity. *He* drew me like gravity.

The material was stretched taut over broad shoulders as he leaned forward on his elbows. It hugged his back all the way down to his trim waist and narrow hips. My eyes were lingering on the way his jeans strained over his butt when I saw his head turn.

Our eyes met and, for an instant, I wondered if he could feel me looking at him. But then, just like before, I fell into the sparkling onyx and was lost to the world.

In them, I thought I could see a thousand emotions, all twirling restlessly in the dark. Some of them were painful, some bewitching, some haunting. All of them were thrilling.

Mr. Dole's voice penetrated my thrall.

"Class, let's give a warm welcome to Mr. Jonathan Bowman. He's a transfer from Southmoore," Mr. Dole said in his bland monotone.

The new guy turned to Mr. Dole and I heard a husky rumble, but couldn't make out the words. Mr. Dole quickly assuaged my curiosity, however, when he announced, "And he goes by Bo."

"I hope he's not the Southmoore Slayer," Troy Dennison said from the back of the room.

Troy was a snot and, though I think he just couldn't help himself, it didn't make it any easier to tolerate him. I usually just ignored him, but for some reason, his making fun of the new guy, Bo, made me angry.

Everyone snickered. Tight-lipped, I wanted to make a comment, but, as per my usual, I refrained. Nevertheless, I felt stirrings of strong emotion bubbling just beneath the surface.

I tossed a withering look over my shoulder at Troy and when he saw it, he stopped smiling and muttered a quick "sorry", casting his eyes down at his book.

When I looked back toward the front of the room, Bo was watching me and I smiled uncomfortably. He looked at me for a moment longer, straight-faced and serious, and then turned his attention to Mr. Dole who was ready to begin the lesson.

I got absolutely nothing out of class, although I could hardly have called it boring today. I was on pins and needles the entire hour. Though he didn't make eye contact with me again that period, I saw Bo turn his head numerous times, as if glancing at me via his peripheral vision. My heart stopped each time he did it, thinking he might turn all the way around and look at me, let me melt into those striking eyes. But he never did. He just teased me.

When the bell rang, I was usually the first one out the door. Today, however, I dawdled as much as possible. I watched Bo from beneath my lashes and he didn't seem to be in any hurry either. I matched my pace with his, wondering if he was waiting to talk to me, hoping that he was.

I got the feeling by watching him that he never hurried, that very little bothered him or ruffled his feathers. I don't know what would make me think that, but I was almost certain of it. He carried himself with a languid ease that said he had all the time in the world, and therefore felt no need to rush.

With my books secured in my messenger bag and nothing left to linger over, I made my way to the front of the class and walked in front of the Bo's table, heading for the door.

I didn't look his way. I thought for sure he'd say something, *anything,* as I passed. I mean, he had been watching me an awful lot. But he didn't say a word. I thought I saw his head come up briefly when I walked by, but otherwise he didn't move.

I hesitated at the door for a heartbeat, giving Bo one last chance to say something, but he didn't. So I left.

At my locker, I threw my books inside and took out my duffel then slammed the thin metal door shut. I was feeling prickly and irritable and, though I was loath to admit it, it had everything to do with Bo.

I was really disappointed that he had turned out to be such a dud. I mean, he didn't speak to me, didn't even acknowledge me, like he hadn't been watching me like a hawk for two days. What's up with that?

Determined not to think about him any more, I sought out Trinity and Aisha and we made our way to the bus. We had a long trip ahead of us.

****

Several annoying hours later, the bus was pulling back into the lot at the school. Maintaining my usual ambivalence had been a true test of my resolve. I felt itchy all night and had to make a concerted effort not to snap at anybody or let on that I was out of sorts. I knew that if I did, the inevitable questions would follow and that would've been a disaster.

So, I smiled and cheered happily, all the while seething inside. I messed up three different cheers. After the third one, it wasn't difficult to conclude that I needed to stop thinking about Bo and his eyes. It was becoming glaringly obvious that he was not doing my life any favors.

On the way home, it seemed I was constantly pushing thoughts of him out of my mind. The problem wasn't in getting him out; it was in keeping him out. He just wouldn't stay gone, at least not for very long anyway.

I knew that I needed to be persistent, however, to resist thinking about him. It's what needed to be done, so I told myself that's what I'd do. Simple as that. The funny thing is that, at the time, I thought it would be easy. Turns out resisting Bo was anything but easy.

"Ridley, you need a ride?" Trinity was calling to me from the rear of the bus. We were back at school, unloading people and equipment into the parking lot.

"No, thanks. I drove. I'll just see you tomorrow night," I replied, lugging my duffel to my car way out at the end of the lot.

"T," Drew hollered from behind me. I stopped and waited for him to catch up. "Why don't you leave your car and I'll take you home tonight. I can bring you back over tomorrow before the party to get it," he suggested.

"My mom will worry if she doesn't see my car in the driveway."

"You can call her when you get home," he said. He stepped closer to me and rubbed my arm suggestively. "We can take a detour on the way to your house."

I looked up at Drew, at the wholesome, handsome face of the most popular guy in school, and for the life of me I couldn't remember why I liked him. I mean, he's occasionally funny, fairly smart, sporadically thoughtful and he used to turn me on, but now it seemed that whatever was between us was just gone.

Unbidden, luminous coffee-colored eyes drifted through my mind. Angrily, I swept them aside. Again.

"No. I'm tired. I'm going home. I've got plans in the morning anyway," I fibbed.

He sighed deeply and gave in. "Alright. So I'll pick you up for Caster's party tomorrow night?"

I briefly considered making up some excuse, but I knew that would sound suspicious. I'd wait and see how I felt tomorrow. Maybe I was just having an off day. Maybe the demise of our relationship wasn't really as imminent as it felt.

Come tomorrow night, though, if I still felt the same way, I'd have to have a talk with Drew. At least he'd be loose and happy after a party and a few beers. It might actually work out better that way. Maybe he'd take the news a little more gracefully.

Though I already dreaded the fallout, I felt like there was no sense in pretending that I liked Drew when I didn't. I wouldn't string him along; it wasn't right. Unlike some of the other girls, I wasn't so obsessed with being popular that I would date a guy I'm not even interested in just because he has great social standing.

Drew prompted me. "T?"

He looked irritated that he'd been forced to bring me back to the present when I'd drifted off into my own thoughts.

"Sorry. Uh, yeah. Pick me up at nine?"

"Good deal," he said, taking me into his arms to kiss me goodnight.

I could tell by his effort that he was trying to get me to change my mind, but it was *so* not working! In fact, I could hardly wait for it to be over. What's worse is that I don't think he even knew that I wasn't into it.

"See you tomorrow night," he said and then turned to walk back down to the front of the lot where he'd parked.

I proceeded on to my car, unlocked the door and slid my bag inside before dropping my tense body into the driver's seat. I pulled the door shut, leaned my head back and just sat there for a few minutes, thinking about the strange details of my day. I really did feel out of sorts. Even when I tried to describe it in my own mind, that was the most accurate label I could come up with: out of sorts.

I listened to the sounds of my friends' voices as they giggled and whooped, making their plans and saying their goodbyes. I felt sure that many of them would gather at Trinity's house later for a small party. But tonight, I just wasn't in the mood to be a joiner.

When all the lights had faded and my car was the only one left in the parking lot other than the empty bus, I leaned forward to start the engine. Only it didn't start.

"You've got to be kidding me," I growled into the silence.

I turned the key again and pushed on the gas pedal, but it only made a tired whirring sound. The dash lights were noticeably dim and when I turned on the headlights, they barely dinted the darkness in front of the car.

While I'm no mechanic, I have enough sense to know when the battery's dead. And that battery was dead.

I shouted out in frustration. "Crap!"

Options, options, options, I thought to myself, hating to call Drew, but unable to readily think of another choice. After all, I was my own plan B.

I stared out into the night, racking my brain for a person to call that could help me. I doubted Trinity even *had* jumper cables and most of the other girls probably didn't even know what they were. Mom was out, as usual, and Dad was gone, as usual. That left me. And since I wasn't much help to myself at this particular juncture, I was left with Drew.

Frustrated yet resigned, I looked up and out into the night as I rooted around in the console for my cell phone. It startled me when I caught a hint of movement in the gloom. My heart picked up the pace, pounding in my chest like the hoof beats of herd of wild Mustangs. Frantically, I searched blindly for my cell phone, afraid to take my eyes off the windshield for even one second.

A disembodied hoodie materialized in front of my dim headlights and my runaway heart jumped up into my throat. But just before panic could officially set in, I saw a hauntingly familiar pale face come into view. Though my pulse slowed somewhat, all the excitement seemed to transfer to my stomach, where a nest of butterflies fluttered anxiously.

Some part of my brain warned me that I should be scared, that this was creepy and that I should lock my door and call for help. But it was a small part, one quickly silenced by the voice of my growing attraction. Even more bizarre than that, though, was the feeling in my gut, the feeling that said I could trust him with my life. Now *that* made no sense *at all*.

Hands resting casually in the pockets of his jacket, Bo approached my window and sank down into a squat. Obligingly, I reached to lower the window. My fading battery didn't have enough juice to work the mechanism, however, so I had to open the door in order to address him.

Bo rose and shifted to the side to let me push the door wide. When it was open as far as it would go, he stepped into the V and squatted down right in front of me.

Up close at night, his eyes appeared to be endless wells of inky liquid. The low light shone on their glassy surfaces and sparkled. His hair was the rumpled mass of jagged peaks that it always was and his jaw was dark with five o'clock shadow.

He smelled wonderful, too. I could tell it wasn't cologne. He just smelled clean, like soap and something tangy, spicy.

"Need some help?"

Though his voice was not much more than a whisper, I heard him clearly. It was as if his soft words resonated somewhere deep inside me, causing a little thrill of pleasure to vibrate through my body like a tuning fork.

I could've just answered his question. I *should've* just answered his question. But I had questions of my own and they seemed far more important at that moment.

"What are you doing here?"

"Watching you," he confessed, as if that was the most natural thing in the world, to be lurking in a dark parking lot in the middle of the night.

"Why?"

"Why what?"

"Why are you watching me?"

"Why does everyone watch you?"

"Everyone doesn't watch me," I rebutted.

"Yes they do."

"No they don't."

"You just don't see them watching you. But they do," he said, his lips twisting up into what might've been a tiny grin. I couldn't be sure since the shadow of the door frame fell across part of his face.

"But why? Why would anyone watch *me?"*

"Come on. You have to know how beautiful you are. You don't need me to tell you that," he said, making it sound as if I was fishing for compliments.

"I guess that's just your opinion," I responded sharply.

He eyed me suspiciously, determining whether or not I was being sincere.

"You really don't know, do you?" He seemed genuinely surprised.

I shrugged, wishing that I could tear my gaze away from his and look anywhere but into those eyes.

"But you are," he declared softly. "You shine like the sun and you move like water. Your eyes are the perfect mix of gray and brown, like fog in the woods, and you smell like lilacs in the summer. I think if you laughed, it would sound like music."

If anyone else had said something like that to me, I probably would've smiled and written them off as either a total dork or a total nut job. But not with him, not the way he said it. He was enchanting and I was enchanted.

Even though his poetic words stirred something inside me, bringing long dead things to life, it was his eyes that told the real story. They promised that he meant everything he'd said and that he was just as intrigued by and attracted to me as I was him.

My lungs seized, trapping air inside the painfully tight walls of my chest. I didn't know what to say. I had no such elegant prose to explain the way he made me feel when he looked at me with those hypnotic eyes. I couldn't even really make it make sense to myself, so telling someone else was hopeless.

But I could feel it. Oh, how I could feel it.

"Your battery's dead," he stated flatly.

"I-I know," I admitted.

"Let me walk you home. You can get it fixed tomorrow." He stood, holding the door open wide.

He held out his hand and I took it. It was cool and a little rough, but attractively so. When I stood, we were less than a foot apart. The words of gratitude I'd been about to speak died on my tongue. My insides were warm and tingly and tightly focused on him, and I fell mute in the face of his nearness.

Though he was a few inches taller than my five foot six frame, he was not so tall that I would have trouble touching my lips to his. All I'd have to do is stretch up on my toes and lean forward just a little bit...

Logically, the thought ended with our mouths locked in a kiss, a fiery one that made my knees weak. Shaking off the image, I was flustered by how much I wanted that kiss to happen, exactly as I'd seen it, passion and all.

As if he could read my thoughts, his eyes dropped to my mouth and stayed there for a nerve-racking minute before they rose once more to meet mine.

"Let me get your bag," he said, leaning past me to reach inside the car.

His body brushed mine and gooseflesh broke out all along my arms and legs. I held my breath and closed my eyes against the onslaught of sensation that followed the simple contact. But closing my eyes was not the wisest choice.

On the backdrop of my lids, I had no trouble imagining where a kiss like that could lead—his endless eyes staring down into mine, his bare skin pressed to mine, desire rising hot and wild between us. It was so clear, this scene, that I might've seen it before in reality. Only I hadn't.

Embarrassed, I forced my eyes open and shifted to the side so he could pass without touching me. When he straightened, duffel in hand, he was grinning.

He tipped his head and said, "Come on."

When I turned back to the car and hit the lock button on my remote, I caught sight of my reflection in the driver's side glass. For the first time since I-don't-know-when, I didn't see the too-pointy chin or the too-thick hair. Instead, I saw something else, I saw some*one* else. I saw what Bo saw, like a curtain had been drawn back and she'd been magically revealed to me.

My sable hair had fallen from its confines and hung in wisps around my face. My lips were partially open, full and trembling. I looked like I'd been kissed already.

"You coming?"

Bo's voice startled me into action. I closed my car door and we set out across the parking lot.

"Aren't you afraid to run around by yourself at night like this? I mean, Southmoore's not that far away," I said, referring to the Southmoore Slayer.

"I like the night."

I resisted the urge to comment on his answer, which was not an answer at all. Instead, we walked in silence for a ways before the need to speak overwhelmed me.

"So, how are you liking Harker?"

Bo looked over at me before he responded, his eyes scanning my face. "Much better than I thought I would."

I felt my cheeks heat and I was glad that he couldn't see my reaction in the darkness.

"What brings you here?"

He shrugged. "It's a long story."

Though we obviously had plenty of time, I figured that was his way of saying he didn't want to talk about it, so I didn't press.

He fell quiet again.

"You don't talk much, do you?"

He shrugged again. "Don't have much to say."

We walked in silence the rest of the way to my house. As much as I normally hated the quiet, ours wasn't the torturous silence that I'd detested for so long. No, it was quite the opposite. Our silence was highly charged, full and alive, though not with words. It crackled with electricity and hinted at dark and dangerous things, secret things. Passionate things.

I could never remember wanting to reach out and touch someone so badly in all my life. My fingertips literally tingled with the desire to run them through his hair and test the muscles of his thick chest.

With his wide shoulders and trim waist, he looked like an athlete and I wanted to ask him about his time at Southmoore, whether or not he played sports, but I'd apparently have to wait until he was more inclined toward loquaciousness, if ever there was such a state for him.

I was disappointed to see my house come into view and even more so to see my mom's car in the driveway.

"This is me," I said, turning to step up onto the walkway that led to the front door.

He nodded and stopped on the sidewalk.

"Well, um, thanks for walking me home," I said, suddenly feeling nervous.

"No problem."

I felt silly waiting, but I was hesitant to leave his quiet company. I was hoping he'd have something else to say, anything that might prolong the night.

"Ok, so, um, I guess I'll see you at school," I said, taking a slow step backward.

Again, he nodded.

I nodded, too, turning to walk to the house. Then it occurred to me that, since he was new, he might be looking for some social interaction. Granted, he didn't seem like the social type *at all,* but who was I to judge or make assumptions like that? The right and proper thing to do would be to invite him to Caster's party. So what if I was reaching. Sue me.

"Hey," I said, whirling around and stepping back toward him. "There's a party tomorrow night at Caster's cabin in the hills. You should stop by."

The invitation was out before I could even think about how fraught with problems a situation such as that would be. After all, I was going with a date, and not just any date. I was going with the same date I'd had for over a year, the date that I had semi-concrete plans to break up with.

He sort of wagged his head in a way that was neither positive nor negative. "Maybe I will," he said, but to my ears it sounded like a platitude.

"Unless parties aren't your thing," I offered, giving us both a way out. I wasn't sure who needed one more—him or me.

"Actually, they're not," he said, stepping up onto the walkway. "But I can think of one really good reason that this one might be more to my liking."

Before I could stop myself, I raised my hand to my chest, as if to still the erratic beating there before any of my organs flew from my body. Bo was standing so close to me, his jacket brushed the backs of my fingers. I was struck by the thought that all I'd have to do is to turn my hand over and I could feel the thump of his heart. The desire to touch him was nearly overwhelming. We were so close, but I wanted to be closer still.

The world came to a breathless halt when I saw his hand come out of his pocket. As if it happened in slow motion, it rose toward my face and my eyes locked on his. He swept the backs of his fingers down my cheek in a feather-light caress.

"I want to kiss you," he whispered.

Spellbound and tongue-tied, I just nodded, hoping he understood that I was granting him permission.

"And you want me to kiss you," he continued.

The only thing I could've added to that was, *More than anything.*

"But I shouldn't," he said, a frown wrinkling his otherwise smooth, pale forehead. "It's not a good idea for you to be involved with someone like me."

Someone like me.

A warning bell rang somewhere in the back of my befuddled mind. In a way, I knew, had known from first that first day, that he was dangerous. I didn't doubt what he was telling me was true, and that he was right. I should probably turn and run. The problem was, I didn't want to. I didn't care how dangerous or how ill-advised being with him was. I didn't care about warnings or caution. I didn't care about consequences or rationale. I only cared about this—this night, this moment, this kiss.

When finally I found my tongue, I asked, "Then why are you here?"

To this, he smiled. It was a wry, self-deprecating twist of the lips. "Because I just can't seem to stay away, no matter how hard I try."

Though it was hardly a compliment, pleasure blossomed in my belly anyway. He couldn't stay away and I knew how that felt.

"What if I don't want you to stay away?"

I knew I was playing with fire, but I couldn't help it. I could only pray that the end result wouldn't be a heart burned up beyond all recognition.

"You'd be a fool."

"Brains are overrated," I quipped.

For the first time, he really smiled, a spread of the lips that revealed straight white teeth and caused his eyes sparkle. It was a gesture that made my legs feel like melted butter.

"You should at least think about it," he said, holding my chin still between his thumb and forefinger. "The only problem is, you might decide I'm right." His smile dissolved into another frown, his eyes darting between my lips and my eyes. "And just in case you do, just in case you want me to stay away, there's one thing I need to do before I go."

With a tug on my chin to part my lips, Bo bent his head and kissed me.

It was over almost as quickly as it had begun, but somehow it still managed to turn my stomach inside out. Even after he'd lifted his head, I could feel the imprint of his mouth. It was etched onto my mind and burned onto my lips.

I opened my eyes in time to see his tongue sneak out, as if he was savoring me.

"Mmm. You taste like candy, like strawberries and sugar."

"It's my lip gloss," I said automatically.

He grinned again, but it didn't quite reach his eyes. They were steamy and intense. "No, it's not. Trust me."

He bent his head to mine again and dragged his lips from the corner of my mouth, across my cheek to my ear.

"Goodnight, Ridley."

Mesmerized, I stood absolutely still and watched him go.

CHAPTER TWO

I stared into the empty darkness for several minutes after Bo left. I relived that kiss over at least three times before I could bring myself to go inside. I think I hesitated for so long because turning away was like an admission that the night was over and he wasn't coming back, something I desperately wanted *not* to be true.

But, alas, reality waited, quickly making itself heard via the shrill voice of my mother. She called to me from the living room as soon as I opened the front door.

"Ridley, is that you?"

"Yeah, Mom. It's me," I answered, closing the door behind me and snapping the locks into place.

"Well get on in here and give your momma a hug," she slurred.

I rolled my eyes and dropped my duffel by the door, resigned to a long night of babysitting.

When I walked into the living room, Mom was struggling to sit up on the couch, her royal blue dress a tangled mess around her legs.

"What the—" she exclaimed, pulling at the wispy material in obvious frustration.

"Here," I said, rushing to the sofa to help her before she tore her new dress. She wouldn't remember doing it, but she'd be mighty upset in a few days when she found it laying in the bottom of her closet, trashed.

I moved her legs and leaned into her, pushing her up on one hip so I could gently extricate the material from under her butt. It was wound around her like a tight blue cocoon.

"Alright, now you can sit up," I announced once I'd freed her from the fabric.

Mom clumsily resituated herself on the couch and then patted the cushion beside her.

"Sit with me, tell me how's your- how's your life is," she said, her tongue tangling over the words. She frowned, knowing something didn't sound right with that phrase, but unable to figure out what it was. She closed her eyes in concentration. "How are you?"

When she opened her eyes, she looked satisfied with the less confusing sentence structure.

I sat down next to her and she put her arm around my shoulders and pulled me against her side.

"I'm fine, Mom."

She smiled down at me. "My baby's going away soon. You'll be in Stanford and I'll never get to see you," she whined, her voice quavering.

"Yes, you will, Momma. You just won't see me every day."

That thought always brought me a sense of relief and anticipation, which was then always followed by guilt for feeling that way about leaving home, about leaving my mother.

Attending Stanford was my goal, my one true dream in life. It was just about the only thing that I truly looked forward to. It kept me going when I wanted to give up and run away. That's why I put up with so much in cheerleading, and in life for that matter. Going to Regionals would win me the athletic scholarship that would help pay for school. My parents couldn't afford to send me otherwise. To me, that scholarship was worth whatever I had to endure for the next nine months to get it. Whatever and whoever, Trinity included.

"I love you so much, Ridley," she declared, giving me a hard kiss on the forehead.

"I love you too, Mom."

"Now help me to the bathroom," she groaned. "I think I'm gonna be sick."

Pulling her to her feet, I shuffled Mom to the half bath as quickly as her unsteady legs would allow. I deposited her in front of the toilet and grabbed the bucket from under the sink.

When Mom gets sick, she gets clingy and doesn't like me to leave her sight. That's why I started keeping a mobile medicine cabinet (i.e. the bucket) close at hand, always stocked and ready to go.

I kept it filled with supplies in case of emergencies of the inebriated variety. The bucket itself was invaluable, especially when we couldn't quite make it to the bathroom in time. But inside it was a washcloth, some baby wipes, Tylenol, a bottled water, a sleeve of saltines and some mouthwash, all things she'd likely need and all in one container that I could grab on the fly. Sadly, it had served me well on far too many occasions.

I wet the washcloth as she vomited into the commode. Her brown hair was short so I didn't have to worry about holding it out of the way. I just wiped her face and forehead with the cool rag until she was finished.

When it seemed she'd gotten it all out, I helped her stand, got her cleaned up and took her to bed.

"Don't go, Ridley. Stay and rub my back. Just for a minute," she pleaded.

"Ok, Momma," I said, crawling over her to lay down behind her.

I rubbed her back until I heard her breathing become deep and even. Slowly, gently, I crept off the bed and tiptoed to the door.

Just as I was pulling it shut behind me, I heard her stir.

"Ridley," she called, struggling to roll off the bed.

"I'm right here, Momma," I whispered, hoping she'd quiet and go back to sleep.

"Help me to the bathroom."

Hurrying back to the bed, I draped her arm over my shoulders and supported her as we made our way to her en suite bathroom. Unfortunately, we weren't fast enough, though. Mom started throwing up just before I got her head in front of the toilet. As luck would have it, it landed right on the *H* in the middle of my uniform. The *H* happened to be white.

After I got Mom situated in front of the commode again, I went to the sink to put soap and water on my top. It was no use, however, as she must've had red wine. I knew I'd have to treat the stain and wash it right away or it would never come out, and the origin of the stain was something I didn't feel like explaining to every Tom, Dick and Harry at school.

Dreamy thoughts of escaping to Stanford rolled through my head for the thousandth time. Although I worried about what would happen to Mom when I went away to school, it always made me feel better to visualize that tiny ray of light at the end of the tunnel, and at times like this, that speck of hope far outweighed my guilt over leaving.

With a sigh of resignation, I took Mom's dirty clothes hamper out of her closet then stripped off my cheerleading uniform and tossed it on the pile.

Might as well do a full load while I'm at it, I thought, carrying the basket down the hall to the washer.

I poured some detergent under the stream of water and loaded Mom's clothes, paying special attention to treating the new spot on my uniform. When the lid was closed, I made my way down the hall to my room to put on some pajamas and collect my dirty colored clothes. I'd do them as well.

My hamper sat just inside the door of the jack-and-jill bathroom connected to my bedroom. I dumped its contents onto the floor and separated the whites, putting them back into the basket.

With my arms full of colored jeans, shorts and t-shirts, I turned to walk back the way I'd come. I had only gotten a few steps when the nightlight in the next room caught my attention as it so often did.

Shifting directions, I went on through the bathroom and walked into the adjoining bedroom on the other side. I took a deep breath. It still smelled of gardenias, but just barely. The scent was fading. One day, it would be completely gone.

A poignant feeling of melancholy washed over me. I looked at the perfectly made bed and the perfectly placed vanity items. It was almost as if Izzy still slept in there every night and got ready in there every morning. It didn't look as if she'd been gone for three years. But she had.

In a way, it felt like she was just there, like I'd seen her only yesterday. But in another way, I could feel her fading, like the gardenias. It was getting harder and harder to remember what her laugh sounded like, what exact shade of blue her eyes were. In a dimly lit corner of my mind, I feared that one day her memory would be nothing more than a whisper, nothing more than a faint bittersweet smell.

****

The next morning, I woke up at 7:45 and squinted angrily at the sun peeking through my fuzzy pink curtains. My head started to throb immediately, so I rolled over and buried my face in the pillow. I knew Mom would be sleeping off her hangover and Dad's flight wouldn't get in until 3:30 so I went back to sleep.

Three hours later, I forced myself to get up. Mom's day-after drama would be starting any time now and I wanted to be—needed to be—energized with some coffee before that happened.

After using the bathroom, I padded into the kitchen and started a pot brewing before I went out to get yesterday's mail. As I walked back to the house after collecting the mail, I unrolled the paper to see what the headlines were.

The front page read, "Community Rallies around Recovered Attack Victims." I scanned the first paragraph.

"Friday evening, following a miraculous recovery, the two surviving victims of a recent Southmoore Slayer-type attack were released from the hospital. Doctors say that both David Hale and Jarrod Brown made a stunning and sudden recovery from the unknown anemia that had plagued them since the grisly attack earlier this month. Though authorities were pleased with the victims' speedy recovery, neither Hale nor Brown was able to provide any information helpful in the apprehension of the perpetrator(s). Police are still working around the clock to…"

A pang of sadness shot through my heart so I folded the paper back up and carried it to the house with the rest of the mail. I had just laid it on the counter and was pouring myself a cup of coffee when Mom stumbled into the kitchen.

She eyed me blearily and ran a hand through her hair. "How long have you been up?"

"Just a few minutes. I just went out to get the mail," I said, pushing it toward her, hoping she wouldn't see the paper.

She asked wryly, "Anything that's not a bill?"

"Not that I saw," I said, leaning on the counter to obscure the newspaper from her view.

"Is that the paper?" She was craning her neck to look around me.

"Oh, yeah," I answered casually, not offering to get it for her. "How'd you sleep?" Subject changes never worked out well for me, but I thought it was worth another try just this once.

"Ridley Elizabeth Heller," she said, using her most maternal tone. "Give me that paper."

I handed the paper over, hoping that I'd be wrong and that it wouldn't cause the outburst that I suspected it might. Only it did.

Mom unfolded the paper and immediately began to read the same article I'd just read, only her interpretation of the news would be much different than mine. It always was.

"Oh," she cried, putting her fingers to her trembling lips. "This is what should've happened with Izzy. She should've had a write up in the paper about her miraculous recovery. If only those doctors had—"

"Mom, Izzy died. The doctors had nothing to do with it," I reminded her gently.

"But maybe they—"

"It happens all the time to people in a coma, Mom. Remember what the neurologist said?"

Mom glared at me with her teary hazel eyes. "You're just like your father. You both gave up too easy," she spat hatefully.

"We didn't give up, Mom. Izzy did. She just couldn't hang on any longer. Her body gave out. You *know that.*"

"But—"

"No buts, Mom. You're just torturing yourself. She's gone. There's nothing anybody could do."

"And the baby," she sobbed.

"Mom," I said, stepping over to hug her. "This is why I didn't want you to see the paper. I knew how upset you would get."

"Don't treat me like an infant, Ridley," she hissed, pulling away from me. "You have no idea what it feels like to lose a child, to bury your daughter."

If I didn't see it for what it was, bitter anguish, I would almost have sworn that there was hatred in her eyes. But she didn't hate me. She was just trying to make it through life with a part of her heart missing. We all were.

"I know, Mom. I'm sorry," I said, casting my eyes down.

After nearly a full minute, Mom turned and walked away. I breathed a sigh of relief. It wasn't as bad as it could've been, as it had been in the past. Maybe she was finally coming to terms with it. Surely that would happen eventually. Wouldn't it?

"You need to go to the store sometime before your father gets home," she called back from the living room.

"I'll get ready and go in a few minutes," I said, more than happy to oblige. It would be a welcome respite.

I went straight to my room and showered. Rather than putting on makeup and worrying about my hair, which I would do after I showered to get ready for the party later, I simply ran a brush through my long brown waves, swiped on some mascara and lip gloss. I slipped on some cut off jeans and a red t-shirt that read "Got Milk?" across the front then pushed my feet into some flip flops.

I carried my purse down the hallway, walking softly, listening for Mom. I heard the quiet sounds of weeping from behind her closed door so I grabbed the list off the refrigerator door and left.

It only took me a few steps to remember that I wasn't going far. My car was not in the driveway, which was a dead giveaway. I stomped my foot in frustration and headed back inside.

I knocked softly on Mom's door. "Mom, my battery's dead and I had to leave my car at school last night. Can I take yours?"

Sniffle, sniffle. "Yes."

"Thanks," I said, turning to grab Mom's keys off the top of her purse where she always left them.

I hit the button to unlock the door of her Maxima and ducked in behind the wheel. It was always a treat to take Mom's car. It was brand new and loaded with every available bell and whistle. My Civic was neither new nor loaded. I don't think bells and whistles were even invented when my car was manufactured.

The engine purred to life and I shifted into reverse and backed out of the driveway. I cracked the windows, opened the sunroof and turned up the radio.

I sang along with lyrics that felt as if they were written for me, *about* me. I often felt like a plastic bag, nearly transparent and light as air, being whipped around aimlessly by the wind. But sometimes I felt like the plastic bag was my life, surrounding me tightly, stifling and hot, suffocating me.

With every mile I drove away from my house, with every street that separated me from my home, from my family, I felt lighter, brighter, more like a firework. Away from all the bitterness and turmoil, from all the painful memories and heartache, I felt like a different person.

My usual determination poured through me. It brought with it a confidence that my future was bright and happy and well within my control.

I decided that since it was such a beautiful day and I was driving such a beautiful car, I was going to take my time and enjoy it. I could see no reason why her funk had to be my funk, so I drove to the store all the way across town. I usually went to one closer to the house, but I was in no hurry to get back.

I pulled into the shopping plaza and slowly made my way around the store fronts, in the direction of the supermarket. As I casually scanned the people milling about on the sidewalk, a familiar dark head caught my eye when I passed the rare books store. Shamefully, despite every*thing* and every*body* else in my life, my heart soared.

I slowed and did an embarrassing double-take. Then, just as quickly as it had taken off, my heart came crashing back down to earth with a dull thud.

It was Bo. There was no doubt about that. But he wasn't alone. He was with a girl I recognized, a sophomore named Savannah. I didn't really know her per se, but I knew *of* her. Trinity absolutely despised her because Devon had once made a comment about her.

If I remember correctly it was something fairly innocuous, something about her being nice or funny maybe. I couldn't recall exactly, but that's all it took to get Trinity's ire up. After that, the full weight of The Unholy Trinity's angry social power was turned on the poor girl. Now, she was basically exiled, forbidden entry into any and all decent parties and events.

Watching her laugh with Bo, however, caused me to see things from Trinity's perspective for one jealousy-induced, temper-flaring minute before I reminded myself that I was nothing like Trinity (a secretly insecure, cripplingly envious psycho). Besides, I had no claims on Bo, and that was that.

I must've gawked too long because Savannah noticed me and said something to Bo, who then turned to look back at me.

Humiliated, I sped up, racing to the supermarket lot and turning into the first parking spot I came to. I got out and hurried into the store, mortified that he'd caught me staring.

My pleasurable outing had taken an unfortunate turn for the worse. Evidently, I wasn't the only one at school that he had an interest in. All those flowery words and all the sincerity that gushed from his eyes had scrambled my brain. How could I have been so wrong about him?

You don't even know him, that's how, Ridley. It doesn't matter what you thought you saw in his eyes. You were wrong, I told myself.

Irrationally aggravated and disproportionately disappointed, I went rushing through the aisles, picking out items on Mom's list and throwing them into the basket, all the while slapping deep brown eyes out of my mind. I'd probably get home with broken eggs, smooshed bread and bruised fruit, but at that moment, I couldn't have cared less.

When I got through the checkout line, I remembered (too late) that I hadn't gotten money from Mom. Choking on the scream of frustration that simmered in my throat, I pulled out my debit card and swiped it. There went a little bit more of my summer money. It was the second time this month this had happened. At this rate, I'd be destitute in no time.

Carrying the bags to the car, I quickly stuffed them into the back seat and climbed in to speed away, taking a different way around the lot than the one I'd used coming in. I didn't want to risk seeing them again or, worse yet, them seeing me.

At home, I put the groceries away and then went back to my room for a healthy dose of focus. I put my ear buds in and picked out angry white female music to listen to while I flipped through my Stanford brochures. I pictured myself among the happy students on campus, living a life totally different from this one, accomplishing great things and making my dreams come true. My biggest goal in life was to become a whole person again, and a new start at Stanford seemed to be the most promising way to achieve that.

I didn't intend to fall asleep, but that's exactly what happened. Dad woke me up when he got home and, at his insistence, I went out to spend some family time with him and Mom.

When Dad was home, we all pretended that we were once again a normal, average, Leave-it-to-Beaver kind of family. We pretended that tragedy hadn't struck, that Mom wasn't an alcoholic and that Dad wasn't running away. We pretended that I was a typical teenager with typical teenage problems. We pretended that our lives were still our lives from three years ago, only minus one family member, one we never spoke of.

It was exhausting. By the time dinner was over and I'd cleaned up the dishes, I was more than ready to escape to my room and get ready for Caster's party. The only good thing I could say about the time spent with my family was that they'd managed to take my mind off Bo, but that was like saying that someone cut off my leg to take my mind off the hole in my chest—simply a trade of one painful thing for another.

After finishing my second shower of the day, I flipped idly through my closet looking for something to wear. The nights were starting to get a little cool, feeling more like fall, so I dressed in jeans and a light sage-colored sweater that made my skin look like rich, gleaming bronze.

I waited in my room until I saw Drew's lights as he turned into the driveway. I virtually ran out the door to meet him, a fact that was not lost on him. He mistook it for excitement to see him in particular rather than just excitement to be rescued from Hell House.

"You sure you want to go to this party? We could always skip it and go to my uncle's cabin instead," Drew suggested, always thinking with his little head.

I was instantly irritated and I snapped. "Can't you, just for tonight, not be a typical guy?"

Drew rolled his eyes and backed out of the driveway. Neither of us said another word until we got to Caster's.

"Looks like a good turnout," Drew said as he cut the engine once he'd found a parking spot.

He got out, as did I. A remake of an old Def Leppard song, *Photograph,* blared from a stereo somewhere inside the cabin and people milled about in the front yard, laughing and talking, drinks in hand. A bonfire burned to the left of the structure and beside it, staying cool in a barrel of ice, was a keg. We made our way in that direction. Drew never turned down free beer.

Trinity was the first to greet us. She had managed to drape herself all over Devon. By the look on his face, the party was not going at all according to his plan, but he knew, as we all did, that Trinity was someone that you just had to humor. Her claws and forked tongue left vicious wounds and even Devon avoided making her angry whenever possible.

"Ridley! Omigod, you will never believe who is here," Trinity said excitedly as we stopped in front of them. "Do you remember Bobby Knight? He was a year older than Izzy," she explained.

Even after three years, I still felt a small stab of pain every time someone mentioned Izzy.

"I remember," I replied.

"He's here with LeAnne Warner," she said, as if that was the juiciest gossip ever.

"I thought she—"

"Exactly," Trinity said, raising her eyebrows suggestively.

"Ew," I said, wrinkling my nose.

We stood and talked for a while. Trinity was having the time of her life and you could tell. Devon was having probably one of the worse nights of his. You could tell that as well. Drew was waiting for something, but I didn't know what and I was…I don't know what I was. I wouldn't call my mood happy per se; I would just stipulate to being happy that I wasn't at home. That was a certainty.

In a way I'd become adept at, I was listening to Trinity without hearing a word that she said. She did manage to grab my attention when she stopped mid sentence and exclaimed sharply, "You have got to be kidding me!"

We all turned to see what had made such an impression on her. When I saw that it was a *who* rather than a *what*, my heart sank into my sandals. Walking up to the cabin was Savannah Grant, Trinity's arch enemy, and she was not alone. She was with Bo.

I was first struck by how different he looked. Gone was the dark hoodie. Instead, he wore a gray and white

Abercrombie and Fitch rugby shirt that made his shoulders look devastatingly wide and his hair look black as the night around him.

Trinity reached between us and grabbed Drew's arm, doing her best to turn him to face her.

"Are you just gonna stand there? That's the guy that's been stalking your girlfriend," she said, her first attempt of the night to stir up trouble. Sadly, even if Savannah left, it wouldn't be the last.

"He's here with someone else, Trinity. I don't think—"

"That's not the point. You need to set him straight about keeping his eyes to himself."

"He hasn't even—"

"Oh, come on, Drew!"

"Trinity, I—"

"Am I the only one at this party with the balls to ask them to leave?"

No one answered her. I knew she was going to go off, and while normally I would've done something to try and avert a disaster, all I could think about was how Bo's eyes made me feel and how they were now turned on Savannah.

Numbly, I watched the scene unfold.

"Fine," she said, stomping off. "I'll just take care of it myself."

Trinity marched right up to them and said as loudly as she could, "You need to leave."

She was standing directly in front of Savannah when she said it, staring right at her, so there was no doubt to whom she was referring.

Savannah looked confused and taken aback. "Me? Why?"

"Because no one wants you here. I don't even know why you came."

"I came because I was invited," Savannah said, straightening her spine defiantly.

"No one invited you to come here," Trinity spat.

"It's an open party and I came with Bo."

"I don't care if you came with Mother Teresa, no one wants you here. We all want you gone. Now leave!" Trinity's decibel level had risen to the point that everyone at the party could hear the spew of her venom. After all, no party was complete until Trinity had shown her butt at least once.

Across the bonfire, Bo's eyes met mine for a split second before he looked away, turning his attention back to Trinity. In that moment, I saw something flicker in his eyes, something that made me feel small and ashamed, spineless and cruel. I never wanted to see that look again.

"Why don't you just go back over there with your friends and enjoy the party? She's not hurting anyone," Bo chimed in amicably.

"Why don't you stay out of this? It's not you that I have a problem with. It's her," Trinity said, poking one bony finger at Savannah's chest.

"Hey, hey, hey," Bo said, stepping between the two girls. "We don't want any trouble. Everybody's here to have a good time. Don't ruin it."

"I'm not ruining it. She is," Trinity shouted.

"Bo, let's just go," Savannah said, tugging at his arm. "I didn't realize that this party was reserved for jealous skanks. My bad."

"You b—" Trinity began, darting past Bo to lunge at Savannah.

Bo grabbed Trinity around the waist, easily setting her away from Savannah. Over the top of her head, our eyes met again. They burned through me like hot pokers of disappointment and then he looked away.

"Alright, we're going," he said quietly. If there hadn't been utter silence at the party, I would never have been able to hear him. But as it was, all eyes and ears were tuned into what was going on around the trio and no one was moving a muscle. You could've heard a pin drop.

Bo released Trinity and turned to take Savannah's elbow and guide her back the way they'd come. As I watched them walk away, I was torn between shame that I didn't intervene and hurt that he'd actually shown up with a date.

As was usually the case, the party quickly resumed as if nothing had happened, but the night was a total loss for me. The more I thought about it, the worse I felt for letting Trinity treat Savannah that way.

"Drew, can you take me to school and jump my car off? The battery's dead."

"Now? Can't it wait?"

"I just want to leave. You can come back after you help me start my car."

With a sigh, Drew turned and walked away, back in the direction his car was parked. I hurried to follow. When we were both in the car, he turned to me and said, "I don't know what your deal is lately, but it's getting old."

It was my turn to sigh. "I don't know either," I said softly, leaning my head back against the headrest and staring out the window. That was a lie, though. I did know what was wrong. Bo was ruining my life, plain and simple.

Almost an hour later, when my car was purring quietly, I thanked Drew with a chaste kiss, told him I'd talk to him later and rolled the window up. Before he was even back in his car, I shifted into drive and turned the car toward home.

Once there, I sat in the driveway looking at the house, dreading going inside. I needed a few more minutes, so I turned the ignition switch over to where just the radio would work. If my battery died now, at least I was at home and there'd be someone around to get it going again in the morning.

I closed my eyes and listened to a song about how to save a life. A soft knock at my window startled me and my eyes flew open.

There, standing on the other side of the glass, was Bo.

CHAPTER THREE

A myriad of emotions played through me when I looked out and saw him. His eyes were dark shadows in the pale angles of his face. They gave away nothing. It was something about his posture that told me he wasn't very happy, but I didn't care; neither was I.

Angrily, I pulled the keys from the ignition and got out of the car. Crossing my arms over my chest, I leaned back against the closed door and waited. When he spoke his voice was low, neutral.

"What was that all about tonight?"

"Trinity hates Savannah. I thought that was fairly obvious," I said curtly.

"That's not what I meant and you know it."

I cast my eyes down, knowing exactly what he meant, but not sure how to respond.

Bo stepped toward me until he was close enough to touch my face. With a finger beneath my chin, he lifted until my eyes met his, until I saw his confusion.

"I know that's not who you are. What happened?"

I shrugged, staring over his shoulder, out into the night, unable to bare the look on his face. His disappointment was crushing.

"Look at me," he demanded gently.

Grudgingly, I did.

"You're not this person. I can see it. Why do you give in to them like you do?"

I felt tears threaten and I willed them back.

"I don't know what you mean."

"Yes, you do. You go along with them when I can see that you don't want to. You want to fight against them, to say what you feel, but you don't. Why?"

"It doesn't matter."

"It does to me."

"You wouldn't understand."

"Try me."

"I just can't."

"Can't what?

"Can't fight them."

"Yes, you can."

"No, I can't," I spat angrily. "I have a future to think about. I *need* cheerleading to help me get into Stanford. If I don't get into college, I'll…I'll…" I didn't even know how to explain what would happen to me if I was forced to stay here. I shook my head in frustration. "It is what it is, and there's nothing I can do about it."

"So you'd compromise yourself for a scholarship?"

There was no accusation on his face, no judgment. He was simply bewildered by my behavior and he was trying to reconcile the person I actually am with the person he thought I was. Somehow, that made me feel much, much worse.

"It's not that easy. And I don't look at it as compromise. I ignore a lot and bite my tongue to keep peace. Why is that such a bad thing?"

"When you want so badly to do otherwise, that's compromise."

"Well, call it what you will. This is the only chance I have to get out of here," I explained.

I didn't want to admit that another reason I hadn't helped derail Trinity was because of my ridiculous jealousy of Savannah.

Bo watched me intently for several minutes before he spoke again.

"Why did you invite me to that party?"

His question took me off guard and I stammered a little. "I, uh, I thought you might like to come."

"And yet you didn't even speak to me," he reminded.

Again, I found that I couldn't look him right in the eye.

"You weren't there long enough," I prevaricated.

"But that's not the only reason," he stated.

Bo shifted his head to be in my line of sight, forcing me to meet his eyes. When I did, I felt like I'd stepped in quicksand.

"Ridley," he prompted.

"I just wasn't expecting you to show up with Savannah."

"But you were there with a date," he pointed out.

True, but rather than say that, I shrugged again.

"I just met her," he clarified. "She lives near me. She seems like a sweet kid and she didn't have plans, so I thought she might like to go, get out of the house for a while."

As much as I hated it, I felt relief wash through me. I was so eager for an explanation that didn't break my heart, I barely questioned it.

"She's just a friend," he assured me with a small smile.

I nodded my acceptance, staring at Bo's throat, afraid if I looked up he'd see my shame and humiliation.

"I went there to see one person," he said.

When my eyes darted up to his, I found that they were as velvety and absorbing as his voice. They made me feel so many things, all at once, that I was overwhelmed by sensation.

"You don't love him, do you?"

Bo didn't need to include any names in his question. I knew exactly who he was talking about, and without hesitation, I shook my head in answer.

"Good," he said, bending his head to mine.

When he kissed me this time, it was with passion. His mouth devoured mine and I thought there was probably nothing more I wanted in the whole world than to be consumed by him. I gave myself up to it. I'd wanted this since the first time I'd laid eyes on him. I wanted his lips on mine, his hands in my hair, his focus on me and nothing else.

My fingers were fisted in his shirt, hanging on for dear life when Bo lifted his head with a quick jerk. Out of the blue, he whispered, "We'll talk tomorrow."

And then he was gone. I didn't even see him go, something I attributed to my spinning head and clouded senses. I just looked around and he was nowhere. Just gone.

A fraction of a second later, I heard my dad's stern voice at the door. "Ridley, get in the house."

The brisk winds of reality quickly blew the fog right out of my mind. If it hadn't been for the cool moisture on my lips from his kiss, I might've wondered if Bo had been a figment of my imagination. But when I touched my fingers to my mouth, I could still feel him there.

With a smile of satisfaction in place, I made my way inside and back to my room where I laid down and fell immediately into a sleep that was filled with dreams of Bo and his breathtaking kisses.

****

The next morning, we went to church, making our weekly foray into the spiritual realm. What used to be a family that enjoyed a close relationship with God was now one that observed nothing more than the appearance of clinging to religion. All three of us were about as hollow, as wounded and as far from God as we'd ever been.

Church was always a tense experience, tense and draining. The effects of it were emotionally staggering. Afterward, as I did every Sunday, I spent the rest of the day in a delicate tap dance of evasion, determined to avoid another energy-sapping family performance. I stayed in my room the entire afternoon, coming out only for food and drink.

It affected Mom and Dad, too. They pretended to be engrossed in any number of consuming projects, anything to avoid…life.

There was only one problem with staying in my room: it brought other unsavory issues to the forefront. My phone rang way too much to allow for a peaceful day. Drew called several times, as did Trinity, neither of whom I was particularly anxious to talk to. I got calls from numerous other people, none of which I answered, all wanting to talk about what happened at Caster's.

The only person that I really wanted to hear from was the one person that had yet to make an appearance, physical or electronic, and it wasn't doing good things for my mood.

By the time darkness had fallen, I was as prickly as I could ever remember being and I was suffering from a severe case of cabin fever. Cutting off my light, I yanked up my blinds and threw open the window then pulled a chair up in front of it and made myself comfortable.

I loved the night—the peacefulness of it, the smell of it, the sounds. It was about as close to being alone in the world as I ever felt. Not that I really strived for solitude. It was more that I was always in the company of some person or persons that drained me in some way or another, like they were sucking the life from me. Sometimes I just wanted to be *left alone;* sometimes, I needed time to heal.

Movement in the side yard caused my heart to leap in my chest. My first alarming thought was that someone was trying to break into the house. I was literally unfolding my legs, preparing to get Dad or get a gun or get *something,* when a familiar pale face materialized in front of the window.

"You scared me half to death," I scolded, my fingers still fisted over my runaway heart.

"Sorry," Bo said casually, coming over to lean up against the side of the house right next to my window.

"What are you doing here?" My tone was much more reasonable once my initial fear had given way to the pleasure of Bo's presence.

"I'm part of the neighborhood watch and I thought I saw some suspicious activity around your yard," he claimed.

"Do what?" I moved to stand against the window as well, choosing the side opposite Bo so I could face him. Through the window, I could smell him and I wanted to take a deep breath and hold that scent inside.

Bo's face was serious for another few seconds before it melted into a heart stopping smile.

"Are you really that gullible?"

I felt a little dazed by that smile and it took me a minute to recover enough to answer.

"Oh. Yeah, pretty much," I admitted with a self-deprecating smirk.

"That should be fun," he teased, his smile fading into a lopsided grin.

"Taking advantage of my infirmities and/or weaknesses is strictly off limits," I warned lightly.

"Really," he said, leaning in to my side of the window. "What other weaknesses do you have?"

At that moment, I could only think of one and it was less than a half a foot from me, standing on the other side of a brick wall.

"Too many to name," I finally managed, shrugging offhandedly.

"Mmm," he said, and then he straightened. "Hey, can I see your phone?"

I'm sure I frowned a little at the odd request, but I agreed, seeing no reason not to let him have it.

I walked back into my room to grab my phone off the dresser. When I turned around, I barely managed to smother a gasp when I ran right into Bo's chest. I don't know how he got through the window so quickly or so quietly, but there he was, standing in my room, big as life.

He was looking down at me with those fathomless eyes and I found it suddenly hard to breathe. All the skin that my short shorts and tiny tank top left exposed felt ultra sensitive, like my pores were opening up to him somehow, craving his closeness—flower petals spread wide to receive the wet kisses of the rain.

I swallowed when Bo reached toward me, but he only took the phone from my fingers. He fiddled with it for a few seconds, punching in numbers and making selections.

The bright screen illuminated his face and I was content to watch him. I didn't care what he did to my phone as long as he didn't stop biting his lip in concentration. I was sure I'd never seen anything sexier.

When he handed me my phone, I took it, albeit reluctantly. I could still feel the cool imprint of his fingers on the cover.

"Now, you have me on speed dial. Call me any time," he said, reaching up to push a stray hair from my face where it tangled in my eyelashes. "Day or night," he finished softly.

I was totally prepared for him to kiss me, wanted it more than anything, wanted *him* more than anything, but a dark spot on his white t-shirt collar caught my eye.

"You've got blood on your shirt," I blurted.

It was obvious by his expression that my question not only took him off guard, but that it ruined the moment. I could've kicked myself for my impulsiveness.

Had I not been so aggravated with myself, the shocked look on his face might've been comical. It was gone in a flash, though, quickly replaced by a frown.

"Where?"

"Right there," I said, indicating the spot with my fingertip.

Bo tugged his shirt down until he could see the spot to which I was referring. His frown eased and he shrugged nonchalantly. "Oh, that. Cut myself shaving. Must've been worse than I thought."

When he turned away from me and walked back to the window, I knew the moment wouldn't be recovered tonight.

I followed him over and stood behind him while he crawled through.

"I'll see you tomorrow," he said from outside, just before he turned to leave.

I felt bereft for some reason. I wanted to ask him to wait or to stay or to do anything except leave, but I didn't. Instead, I stood quietly by and watched him walk away.

He hadn't taken more than six or seven steps, however, when he quickly turned on his heel and came back to the window.

He leaned his head through the opening and crooked his finger at me. When I leaned down to him, thinking he was going to tell me something, he pulled me in for a quick kiss. He left again after that and I smiled as I watched him go, feeling much more satisfied with his exit.

My smile widened when I heard a faint whistling drift through the window on the gentle night breeze. I felt like whistling, too. Or singing. Or flying.

****

Monday's post-weekend conversation still revolved around Trinity's brutal rejection of Savannah Grant at Caster's party. I thought it was telling that no one seemed to want to rehash Savannah's brave rebuttal, only Trinity's vicious attack.

As I looked at the faces of the brainwashed followers that hung on Trinity's every word, I saw, probably for the first time, the true weight of what I'd done by turning a blind eye to her antics all these years.

There was no one to defend the people that Trinity walked all over, no one to call her out about her cruelty and nastiness. There was no one to stand up to her, no one willing to risk the distasteful consequences.

A bold voice sounded in my head, telling me that I should've done something, that someone had to. But then another voice spoke up, this one whiny and selfish, reminding me that few others had their entire future riding on it like I did either. I *needed* to be a part of the squad. I *needed* cheerleading. I *couldn't be* the one who stood up to her.

Ignoring both voices, I headed for class.

"T, wait up!"

"Ugh," I murmured under my breath.

Drew. I'd forgotten all about him.

I turned and saw him jogging to catch up to me. When he reached me, I plastered a smile on my face, as natural a smile as I could muster.

"Hey."

"Where were you all weekend? I tried to call you," he said, frowning. "Did you get my messages?"

"Sorry, I haven't even had a chance to check them yet," I confessed, which was partially true. More to the point, I hadn't *taken* the time to check them. I'd wanted to put it off as long as possible. "Dad was home. You know how that goes," I said, rolling my eyes dramatically.

"Oh, yeah," Drew said, curling his lip sympathetically. "So, what are you doing tonight after practice?"

Bo's face flashed through my head. I was hoping to hear from him, but even as the thought ran through my mind, I felt guilty, like I was betraying Drew. Even though I knew in my head and in my heart that it was over, I'd been remiss in not letting Drew in on that little fact. I'd been so consumed with Bo, Drew just hadn't crossed my mind, and that wasn't right. He deserved better than that.

I didn't want to make up an excuse. He might see right through that. But I also didn't want to keep going on as if nothing was wrong. Thankfully, the bell rang, saving me from having to make any kind of decision until later.

Drew bent to kiss me and I gave him a quick peck and dashed off, calling over my shoulder, "I gotta go. I'm gonna be late."

As I settled into my desk in Calculus, I was sort of amazed at how much Bo had affected me in a few short days. He took up a surprising amount of my available brain space and was apparently working his way into my heart space as well, pushing out people I'd thought were firmly entrenched there.

I used to really like Drew and, until Bo's arrival, I had thought things were going well. I mean, it's not like I saw us getting married or anything, but I figured we'd probably date for the rest of the year. I had no idea how weak my feelings for him really were until Bo came along. I felt like Bo had taken my life by storm and now nothing was the same. Somewhere deep down, I knew it never would be again.

At lunch, I sat in the same place I'd sat for a little over a year: sandwiched between Drew and Summer, with his friends beside him and mine beside Summer. I'd never felt more out of place.

Listening to them talk about the same things over and over again was getting on my nerves something fierce. It further aggravated my already sour mood, a mood which I knew was in direct correlation to Bo's curious absence. I hadn't seen him all day, not even a glimpse in the halls, and now he wasn't anywhere to be found at lunch either.

I felt like a drug addict in need of a fix, and knowing that he'd upset my life to this point only added to my irritation.

I saw Savannah sitting by herself at a picnic table out on the lawn. She was reading something, munching on a carrot and I took the opportunity to discreetly observe her.

She was striking in her appearance. She had vibrant red hair and I thought probably soft brown eyes, though I'd never really been close enough to see for sure. Like most redheads, her complexion was fair, but where others were plagued with freckles, Savannah's skin was creamy. She reminded me of a beautiful china doll.

Someone called to her and her head shot up. She waved and laughed and then put her nose back in the book she was reading.

I looked around for the person she'd responded to. It was a guy. Another sophomore I think, one that plays basketball. I searched my mind, but couldn't readily retrieve his name.

Still looking for Bo, I glanced all around the covered eating area, as well as the grass and picnic tables. In my sweep, I noticed that there were several people eyeing Savannah. It was plain to see that she was getting lots of appreciative looks. I wondered how I'd never noticed that before, but then remembered that my friends were so high maintenance, it was a miracle I ever noticed anything. The world was passing me by and I was quietly letting it.

Reluctantly, I returned my attention to those very same high maintenance friends. I craned my neck to look down the table. My eyes stopped on Devon. Like so many others, he was staring at Savannah, too. There was a longing look on his face, one I recognized because it mirrored the way that I yearned for Bo. It was then that I realized Trinity's jealousy of Savannah was justified. Devon definitely had feelings for her and they were anything but innocent.

At that moment, I felt a kinship for Devon that I'd never felt before. Like me, he was trapped behind the glass.

The rest of the day was a depressing blur. All day long I watched for Bo and all day long I was disappointed. He never showed up at school.

That night, I took turns between pacing my bedroom floor like a caged animal and lolling lifelessly on the bed. I tried to make my way through French homework, but I kept picking up my phone and scrolling through the numbers until Bo's number was highlighted. Each time my thumb would hover over the call button, I'd throw the phone down in frustration. I couldn't call Bo. What would I say?

A little after 1:00, I got tired of waiting—and wanting—and I fell asleep on top of my covers, unable to hold my eyes open any longer.

Later, something woke me. I looked first at the television, but its face was blank. Strangely, I hadn't even turned it on. I'd left my window raised and the room quiet just in case Bo made an appearance.

I listened, but it wasn't a sound that had stirred me. It was a smell, a teasing scent that had me sitting up to look around. My befuddled mind was slow to clear, but I would've sworn that I smelled Bo's tangy soap. It swirled in my nose, making my stomach flutter, just the reaction I'd have had if he were standing right next to me.

The clock read 3:30. I glanced at the window. Strangely hopeful, I got up and walked over to it. I looked out into the inky darkness and inhaled deeply. Not surprisingly, there was no one there, but still, I could detect a faint hint of Bo. I listened and heard nothing but the sound of my own heartbeat and the crickets singing in the night.

With a deep sigh, I walked back to my bed, pushed the pillows aside and crawled beneath the covers. After only a few minutes, the silence began to play its usual tricks on me, preying on my mind, so I used the remote control to turn on the television.

The familiar sounds soothed me, but it still took me forever to fall back to sleep and when I did, I didn't sleep well.

I woke before my alarm went off. As I'd done on so many mornings, I lay in bed and listened to the news.

Another body was found by Southmoore Police last night. The victim was identified as John Robert Gibbs, last year's primary suspect in the Southmoore Slayings. Discovered in Arlisle Preserve, Gibbs was killed in typical Slayer style, though authorities are awaiting official word from the medical examiner before releasing cause of death.

Last year, Gibbs was arrested for the 2008 murder of Travis Alan Bowman. Bowman, originally thought to be the victim of an animal attack, died of blood loss after his throat was torn out nearly three years ago today. Gibbs was later released on a technicality and his case was never presented to the grand jury…

I grabbed the remote and turned the television off. On a good day, I could only take so much news about what a crap hole the world was becoming. This morning, my threshold was even lower than usual.

At school, Drew was waiting for me at my locker. He asked again if I had any plans for after practice. I think on some level he knew something was wrong and he was trying to overcompensate by paying me lots of attention, even more than usual.

"Actually, I was going to see if you wanted to meet up on the field about seven or so. We've got a two-hour camp that we're holding for the junior high. We're teaching them some new basket tosses. Want to meet me at the bleachers after?"

"Mmm, bleachers," he said with a suggestive smile. "You know I do."

Drew and I had never had sex. We'd come close several times and now I was more grateful than ever that it had never progressed to that point. Drew, on the other hand, was bound and determined to push it until it happened. Typical.

He swooped in for a peck on the lips and I ducked as if looking for something in my bag. When I raised my head, I quickly pressed my lips to his cheek and rushed off again, promising I'd see him at lunch.

I didn't see Bo again all morning. I wondered what could've been keeping him from school again today. He'd seemed fine when I saw him Sunday night, and his continued absence was making me crazy. I was ready to bite somebody's head off by the time lunch rolled around.

I was chomping angrily on a celery stick when, much to my relief and chagrin, I caught sight of Bo sitting down at a picnic table out on the lawn. He was joining Savannah.

Although he'd all but assured me that they were just friends, I watched them with nothing short of envy. They talked easily and Savannah laughed a lot. I tried to push down the green wave of jealousy that rose inside me, but the more I watched them, the harder it got.

"What's so interesting over there?" Drew tipped his head toward Bo and Savannah.

I shrugged. "Everyone's talking about Savannah. I was just wondering what the big deal was."

Devon leaned around Drew to look me in the eye. "Have you ever even met her, Ridley?"

His tone and the firm set of his jaw and mouth reeked of defensiveness. He'd obviously decided he wasn't going to stand by and listen to another attack on Savannah, even though that's not what I meant at all.

"Not officially, no, but—"

Devon cut me off. "She's a nice girl. She's funny and smart and she plays the bass guitar, which is awesome."

I quirked a brow at Devon. I wanted to continue the conversation, but I was all too aware of our surroundings and that Trinity was only a few feet away. As if he'd suddenly realized the same thing, Devon's ire visibly waned and he turned his attention back to his tray. By silent agreement, we both let it drop.

Luck had apparently deserted us, however, because Trinity, with her ears like satellite dishes, had picked up on our quiet conversation.

"That's it," she yelled, pushing her chair back from the lunch table and turning a furious glare on Devon. All eyes shifted to Trinity, everyone curious about her sudden outburst. "If you've got a thing for white trash, then have at it," she spat, her eyes flashing angrily at Devon.

"Trinity," Devon said, pushing his words through gritted teeth. "That's enough."

"Don't you tell me wh—"

Devon cut her off, standing to his feet so quickly that his chair nearly toppled over. "Trinity! How long is it gonna take for you to realize that it's over? *We're* over? I don't know, but I hope this sinks in a little better because I'm only gonna tell you this one time: stay away from Savannah."

He turned around and stomped off.

Most mouths agape, nearly the entire lunch crowd watched him go. Devon didn't have much of a temper and I'm sure everyone else was as surprised as I was to finally see it. I could tell by the look on her face that Trinity was the most stunned of us all.

"You won't think she's so special when I scratch her frickin' eyes out, will you?" she asked, though Devon was already long gone. "Come on, Summer."

Before anyone could recover, Trinity had grabbed a shocked Summer by the hand and was dragging her across the grass. As they neared the picnic tables, I saw Bo and Savannah look up. Bo's face was a blank mask, but I could see tension in the stiffness of his body.

I thought of Savannah's words to Trinity at Caster's party. Obviously, she wasn't afraid to stand up for herself, but I wasn't sure she knew what a handful Trinity could be when she was really riled, and this time Bo couldn't run interference. He couldn't step in between the two girls on school grounds. If he so much as touched Trinity, even if it was just to subdue her, he'd be in a world of trouble.

I knew I had two options. Since Trinity was already gone and I could no longer stop her, I could let the scene play out, as was my habit. I could silently root for Savannah, hope that she had her brave-girl hat on today, and watch what happened along with everyone else.

Or I could get up and, for the first time, *do something*. I could intervene on Savannah's behalf, take a stand for once, and feel better about the person I saw in the mirror.

My most egocentric inner voice spoke up, reminding me that if I did that, I'd be basically sticking a sword into the heart of my cheerleading career and, therefore, my scholarship and future at Stanford.

With longing, I thought of all my plans. I thought of my much-needed escape from this life and, for a moment, I considered taking the selfish route.

But then, unbidden, I saw Bo's face when he came to me after Caster's party. Somehow, when he looked at me, he saw the better person that lives inside me, the person I quell every day. He could see her, but I couldn't. Today, I wanted to see her, too.

Nothing was worth selling my soul for, and that's what I felt like I'd been doing all this time by going along with Trinity. I was as guilty as she. Though she only physically took Summer with her, by sitting back and doing nothing, it was like we all went with her, supported her.

I, for one, didn't want to sit idly by any more. I was nothing like her and it was high time I stood up and let that show.

Without giving it any more consideration, I raced across the grass after Trinity. She had just opened fire on Savannah when I reached them. Summer was standing back, trying to be involved as little as possible.

Trinity was bent over Savannah, jabbing a finger in her face. Though Savannah looked positively mortified, behind that, I could see a spark of anger lighting her eyes, too.

"And if you so much as look at Devon, I'll kick your—"

"Trinity," I shouted.

Trinity's head snapped up and she looked at me in confusion, but only for a moment. After quickly writing me off, she turned her attention back to Savannah and continued her tirade.

"You are nothing but a skanky—"

"Trinity!" This time, I called her name even more forcefully. "Stop!"

Trinity slowly turned to look at me, her voice deadly quiet. "What?"

"You heard me," I said, stiffening my spine.

It only took a fraction of a second for Trinity's rage to turn on me. "You better take your bony—"

"Oh, save it, Trinity. I'm sick of your mouth," I said, feeling years of repressed emotion boiling to the surface.

"Devon's not yours and Savannah hasn't done anything to you. It's not her fault that you couldn't hold on to Devon."

All the color left Trinity's cheeks for a slow-motion second before it rushed back in vivid red blotches.

"I will crush you, Ridley! You were a nobody at this school before the squad and I can make sure that you are a nobody again. I'll burn you to the ground," she threatened, nearly shaking in her anger.

"Do it, Trinity. I don't care. It's not worth it anymore. I'm not like you," I said, feeling courage and momentum build. "I'm not like any of you. And I'm sick of pretending that I am. I already hate to look at myself in the mirror and I refuse to stand by and let you tear one more decent person to shreds. No more!"

"You know this is war, right Ridley? Are you sure you want to take me on?" Her voice was so low, I had to strain to hear her.

For one uncertain breath, the seriousness, the viciousness, in her eyes gave me pause. She was right: it was exactly like declaring war, but I'd come too far to stop now.

"Bring it," I finally said, equally quiet and serious.

"Fine," she said, taking a step back. "I'll bury you both. Together." Trinity gave first Savannah then me one more withering look before glancing back at Summer. "Come on, Summer," she said, turning on her heel and stomping back across the lawn toward the table of stricken onlookers that I used to call my friends.

At Trinity's sharp command, Summer jumped. She looked at me, indecision crossing her face for an instant before she shrugged and turned to follow Trinity. Silently, but very clearly, Summer had made her choice.

I watched them go, still a bit flabbergasted by what had happened, by what I'd done. When they were both seated once more at the table on the patio, I looked down at Savannah and said the only thing I could say. "I'm sorry."

She nodded, her eyes big and round. Inanely, I realized that, just as I'd suspected, Savannah's eyes are a soft, chocolatey brown.

Without another word, I turned and walked away. By sheer force of will, I didn't look back at Bo. A couple of times, as I made my way to the closest school doors, I thought I could actually feel his eyes on me, but I didn't give in to the urge to confirm it. Once I reached the building, I disappeared inside its walls, wishing that I could disappear altogether.

For the rest of the day, as I walked the halls and entered my classes, I saw people stop and stare and whisper. I knew what they were thinking, what they were talking about: my social suicide. That was all it meant to them. It was nothing more than the equivalent of opting out of a popular club. To me, however, my actions had much more significant consequences, ripples that I could see washing away bits and pieces of my future.

All day, I watched the clock anxiously. I wanted the day to be over, but I was also curious to see Bo in Chemistry, to see what his reaction would be to what happened.

When the bell rang to let out fifth period, I dashed out the door and down the hall to get to Mr. Dole's class. Despite all the other turmoil in my life, just the thought of seeing Bo made me achy all over and as jittery as a caffeine junkie. I thought it was funny that, of all the classes Bo and I could've shared, we were in Chemistry together. There was no doubt we had plenty of that.

When I reached the door to the Mr. Dole's classroom, I stopped to smooth my hair. I'd left it long and loose today, flowing down my back. Nervous and excited, I turned to walk through the door.

I couldn't help but feel crestfallen when I didn't see Bo's bag on his table. It would've been nice if he'd hurried as I had, anxious to see me, too. But then I reminded myself that it was still really early. Maybe his class had run over a minute or two or he'd been waylaid in the hall.

I took my seat and surreptitiously watched the door. Kids started dribbling in and, little by little, the seats started filling up, but still there was no sign of Bo. I kept my hopes up by making plausible excuses for his tardiness, but when Mr. Dole arrived and began the lesson, I had to admit with crushing disappointment that he wasn't coming. One of Mr. Dole's rules was that, once his lecture had begun, there were to be no interruptions. He closed his door and didn't open it again until the bell rang. Period.

Just as I'd completely given up hope, the door creaked and Bo slipped in, muttering an apology to Mr. Dole, who merely gave him a deep frown and kept right on teaching.

As Bo took his dangerous front row seat, he winked at me. Warmth flooded my body and I decided that my all-day agony was totally worth that one small gesture.

For the rest of the period, I couldn't take my eyes off him. Hungrily, I watched his every move, every gesture, as if they were what was keeping me alive, like the blood flowing through my veins. I cursed Mr. Dole's lesson plan, wishing that today was a lab day. I'd gladly have partnered with Bo to fire up the Bunsen burner, but instead, I had to be content with just watching him.

About five minutes before class was over, I heard a faint buzzing sound. Bo quickly reached into his pocket and glanced down at his phone, careful to keep it from Mr. Dole's eagle eye.

Sliding the phone back in his pocket, Bo gathered up his things and slipped out of his seat and out the door. Once again, Mr. Dole just frowned at him. I wondered vaguely if he was under Bo's spell, too. He sure wasn't acting like himself today.

I was a little deflated that I hadn't gotten to talk to Bo, so between that and the hoopla I expected from the other cheerleaders at practice, I was pretty cranky by the time I got to the field.

I half expected there to be a coup, one where Trinity usurped my position as Captain and then summarily dismissed me from the squad. But if that was to happen, it wasn't going to be today. Trinity didn't even show up for the camp, which didn't disappoint me one bit. I'd done enough emotional spewing for one day and I still had Drew to deal with.

Ugh, I thought, filling with dread at the reminder of what was yet to come.

When the camp was over and all the junior high cheerleaders had left along with most of our squad, I started packing up all the equipment and mentally preparing myself for what I had to say to Drew. The trouble was, I'd start thinking about Drew and, within a minute or two, I would find my thoughts had wandered back to Bo again.

"Are you alright, Ridley?"

It was Summer. She had her duffel slung over her shoulder and was apparently ready to go.

"Yeah. Why?"

I'm sure we were both thinking *Duh!,* but rather than saying anything, Summer just eyed me skeptically.

"You just don't seem like yourself today, that's all." That was a nice way to put it.

"Nope, I'm fine," I said, gluing a smile on my face.

"You're not, but it's alright if you don't want to talk about it."

"I'm fine. Really," I said reassuringly. I knew she wanted me to talk to her about Trinity, but if she didn't have the nerve to just come out and ask me, I wasn't going to volunteer anything. Besides, she'd picked sides and, whether she would admit it or not, we were at odds.

She started to walk off, but then she turned back. "You know you can talk to me, right?" When I nodded, she continued. "I mean, it's not like Trinity has to know *everything*."

Ha! I felt like laughing right in her face. Although she wasn't as bad as most of the other girls, she was certainly not a person to whom I'd tell anything important or confidential. In fact, I had no one in my life that I could talk to about things like that, serious things. I just held them inside until, like a cancer, they slowly ate away at me from the inside out.

"Well, there's nothing to tell, but thanks anyway."

"Do you want me to stay and help you clean up?" As she asked, she hoisted her duffel further up on her shoulder, as if a silent reminder that she was ready to go. Talk about your conflicting body language.

For the first time all day, I nearly laughed. "Thanks for the offer, but I'm almost done."

"Alright. Well, see you tomorrow," she promised, walking off the field toward the parking lot.

Five minutes later, I was still contemplating her behavior when Drew arrived. He leaned in to kiss me, but I put my hand on his chest to stay him.

"We need to talk," I announced.

I hated the look that came over Drew's face. It said that he knew what was coming and he didn't like it one bit. I must've been more transparent that I'd thought.

"Alright," he said slowly.

"Drew," I began, resuming my task of packing pompoms away. "I don't want you to think that this has anything to do with you or something you've done wrong, because it doesn't."

I put as much sincerity into my voice and my expression as I could manage. I had never wanted to hurt Drew.

He nodded, his face a tight, blank mask.

"Things are changing so fast this year, it's crazy. It's our senior year and things are probably only going to get *crazier*, not less crazy."

Drew's brows came together in a small frown of confusion. I was mucking this up and I knew it. I should've practiced what I was going to say, but I was too wrapped up in thinking about Bo to give it adequate attention.

I stopped what I was doing and stepped over to stand in front of him. "I don't think we should see each other anymore. Not like this anyway," I said, putting my hand on his arm. "You are a great guy and I don't want this to sound cliché, but I really hope we can still be friends. Besides, I'm sure you won't want to be associated with a social pariah for the rest of your senior year."

Drew hadn't said a word. He just stood there in silence, watching me. When he finally spoke, he surprised me.

"This is about that new guy, isn't it?" Anger was evident in every hard line of his face.

"What? No," I said halfheartedly. I was taken off guard and that was all the conviction I could muster.

"Don't lie to me, Ridley," Drew hissed through his gritted teeth, flinging my hand off his arm with a furious swipe.

"To be honest, Drew, I just don't feel the same way about you anymore. I'm sorry. It's not you, it's me," I proclaimed, regretting that last choice of words as soon as they were out of my mouth. They were sure to incite a reaction in almost anybody.

"It's you, huh?" He grabbed my upper arms in a steely grip. "Well that much I know. It's you screwing the new guy. That's what it is," he spat. "Look me in the eye and tell me you're not."

His fingers felt like they were digging all the way into my bones, he gripped me so tightly. "Drew, you're hurting me."

"You can't, can you?" As he spoke, he pulled me up onto my toes and into his chest so that my nose was nearly touching his. "Admit it," he shouted down at me.

"Drew, I told you—"

"Nothing but lies," he interrupted, giving me a little shake. "You're hot for the new guy, you just won't admit it. You're a whore just like Trinity."

A little thread of fear was working its way around my jack-hammering heart.

"Drew—"

"Admit it," he yelled again, shaking me harder.

Just as a real panic was about to set in, a voice sounded from the shadows.

"Let her go."

I exhaled in relief, instantly recognizing it. It was Bo. Drew and I both turned to look back at the bleachers.

Bo stepped out into the thin beam of light that shone across the grass from the field house and he stopped there. To me, he looked intimidating. He stood, half in shadow, with his arms crossed over his chest, eyeing Drew steadily, silently.

"Well, well, well. Look who it is," Drew sneered, pushing me away from him and turning his body to face Bo. "She's nothing but a lying whore. You sure you want to lose some teeth over a girl like that?"

"I won't be the one losing teeth," Bo said, his tone matter-of-fact.

Physically they looked pretty evenly matched. Nonetheless, I was nervous for both of them. I didn't want Drew to get hurt any more than he already was and I certainly didn't want to see anything happen to Bo. As far as I was concerned it was a lose–lose situation all the way around.

Although Drew and I were at least twenty feet from Bo, I still felt like the situation needed more of a buffer, so I stepped over in front of Drew to face him. I wasn't taking a stance in opposition to him, facing off *against* him *with* Bo, but that must've been how Drew perceived it.

"Bo, Drew was just leaving," I said, turning my head slightly to direct my words over my shoulder at Bo. My eyes never left Drew, and I addressed him more quietly. "This has gone far enough, Drew. We can talk more later, after you've calmed down."

Drew's hands shot out and grabbed me by the arms again. "What if I want to talk now?"

I don't know how he moved so quickly, but it seemed like the instant that Drew's fingers touched my arms, Bo was at my side. He was so close I could feel his body brushing mine from hip to shoulder. His chest and belly were pressed against me and his arm was stretched out beside my head. He was reaching past me, his fingers wound tightly around Drew's throat.

"Touch her again," Bo said softly, the warning clear in his tone.

I felt Drew's fingers loosen their hold as he released me. I was just about to move out of the way when I decided that maybe they were both safer with me between them. It was my indecision that caused what happened next.

I can only guess that when I started to move out of the way, Drew saw it as an opportunity to get in the first strike, a sucker punch. He brought his fist around in an upper cut aimed right at Bo's chin. Unfortunately, when I stepped back into position, his fist connected with my jaw on the way up instead.

Violently, my head snapped back on my neck. I saw a bright flash of light and heard a sickening crunch just before a pain more intense than anything I've ever felt sliced through my head. It lasted only for a fraction of a second before a black sea of nothingness drowned out sight, sound and, thankfully, feeling.

CHAPTER FOUR

Clarity and awareness came and went for what seemed like hours. I remember very little before coming semi-awake in a cool room that smelled like Bo. There was something wet against my lips and it made them feel warm and tingly. I licked them and whatever it was tasted salty with a hint of sweetness.

That taste and the smell of Bo were the only things that seemed even halfway clear. I heard voices, but they echoed as if I were listening to them from far away through a tunnel.

"She needs more," I heard Bo say to someone. "You're going to have to open her mouth."

"Her jaw's broken, Bo. What if—" a woman's voice was saying before Bo interrupted.

"It has to be done if I'm going to heal her. Just do it," he growled impatiently, cutting her off.

Next I felt the faint pressure of tender fingers at my cheek. It was like being touched when the numbing from the dentist is just beginning to wear off—barely perceptible. But then someone tried to force what felt like a finger between my teeth. Excruciating pain shot through my entire skull. A scream bubbled up in my throat, but the second my jaw strained the tiniest bit to let it out, the pain worsened, becoming so severe I lost that tenuous hold on the world again.

When next I woke, I couldn't decide if hours had elapsed since that horrible pain, or mere seconds. My body felt like lead and my head felt like cotton. With great effort I raised my hand to my face and touched my fingers gingerly to my cheek. I half expected to feel something swollen and totally misshapen, but I didn't.

I ran my hand all along my left cheek and jaw line then around my chin to the other side. It felt like my face, the same way it had felt all my life.

Slowly inhaling, I held my breath and pressed ever so slightly into the flesh where my jaw hinged. It was a little sore, but nothing like what I would've expected considering how badly it had hurt earlier.

Hazily, Bo's words came back to me as if reaching out to my consciousness through a dense fog.

It has to be done if I'm gonna heal her, he'd said. I had to have imagined that. I mean, obviously that couldn't have been what I'd heard. People couldn't just heal a broken jaw, which was what I'm pretty sure I had, thanks to Drew. I could still remember the white hot pain. I shuddered to think of it.

Letting my hand drop, I listened closely to what was going on around me. Muffled movements and faint whispers were coming from another room. I couldn't make out anything concrete and I still had no idea where I was.

I lay perfectly still, trying to remember what had happened, but the strain of thinking only served to make my head throb rebelliously.

I heard the creak of floorboards a few feet away. The hushed rustle of movement alerted me to the presence of someone in the room with me, but I wasn't ready to be awake yet, so I left my eyes closed and kept my breathing slow and steady, hoping I was convincing enough to fool the casual observer.

The footsteps didn't approach me, but whoever it was didn't move for a few seconds. They must've been checking on me, watching me from maybe a hall or a doorway.

Finally, the creak sounded again and I could hear soft footfalls fade as the person walked away. Seconds later, I heard a woman's voice coming from another room. It was the same voice I thought I'd heard earlier, talking to Bo.

"She's still out," she said quietly. "You need to feed before she wakes up. You'll have to take her home and you can't go like that."

I heard nothing for a moment, but then the dull scrape of what sounded like a chair scooting back sounded right before nearly silent tread approached the room I was in. I cracked my eyelids the tiniest bit, just enough so I could see through my eyelashes.

A dim light was shining through the doorway to my left. As I listened to the footsteps, I watched the doorway for someone to appear. I heard the boards creak as if someone had stopped just inside the room, but I saw no one.

That tangy, soapy scent that I associated with Bo became more pronounced, tickling my nose and bringing to mind an image of his endless dark eyes. I don't know where the smell was coming from, though, because I was still very much alone.

Deep and even, I kept breathing, watching covertly, until I heard the floorboards creak again, followed by the sound of footsteps fading back into the other room.

I listened and I waited. Just barely, I could hear the muted sounds of activity as well as a couple of short whispers. I strained to make out words or identify voices, but it was no use. They were just too quiet.

A sudden grinding sound caused me to jump, but when I heard ice cubes hitting the bottom of a glass, I calmed, recognizing the noise as an icemaker. The one at our house sounded just like that.

The refrigerator door opened and closed and then I heard some shuffling. Footsteps sounded on the floor, much more loudly this time, and then a shadow appeared in the dim shaft of light coming through the open door.

They knew I was awake.

"Ridley, my name is Denise Bowman. I'm Jonathan's mother," the kind feminine voice said from the doorway.

I turned my head as her shadow came further into the room. She reached beside my head to snap on a bedside lamp.

I squinted into the light and looked up at the tiny woman leaning over me. Though she was a very attractive woman, she didn't look very much like Bo. She was petite and had dark skin and blue eyes. The contrast with her midnight hair was striking. That was the only trait it appeared that they shared—their dark hair.

She smiled down at me and the corners of her eyes crinkled. It was a sweet, comforting gesture that put me at ease right away.

"Where's Bo?" The question came out as a hoarse croak.

"Don't try to talk too much yet. Here, have a sip of water," she said, holding a straw to my lips.

Tentatively, I pursed my lips and took a small sip. When nothing cried out in agony, I took a longer draw from it.

The cold liquid was like a soothing balm to my dry throat and burning tongue.

I cleared my throat. "What happened?"

I knew that I got punched, but little more than that was clear.

"Bo said you had a bit of a run-in with your boyfriend," she answered diplomatically.

"Ex boyfriend," I murmured.

"What?"

I asked instead, "How did I end up here?"

"Bo brought you here so he wouldn't have to take you home unconscious."

I nodded. That was probably smart. "What time is it?"

"Twenty after eleven," she said, glancing down at her watch.

Wow! I'd been out longer than I'd thought.

"I'm sorry to impose on you this way," I said, sitting up and dropping my legs over the side of the bed. I was only upright for a few seconds when the room began to tilt and sway. I teetered, leaning back on my elbow to keep from falling over. "Whoa!"

"You shouldn't move too fast. Apparently, you took a pretty good knock to the head."

I closed my eyes to give the room time to return to rights, but it was reluctant to do so. I felt a cold sweat break out on my forehead and my stomach sloshed with nausea.

"I think I'm going to be sick," I said weakly, saliva pouring into my mouth.

"Lay back down on your side. I'll be right back," she said, scurrying off.

I did as she instructed and the nausea and dizziness abated almost immediately. I heard Bo's mother opening and closing cabinet doors and then I heard water running.

While she was gone, I seized the opportunity to take in my surroundings.

I was in a small bedroom with one window, which was covered in thick, black curtains that matched the comforter on which I was lying. The walls were a medium gray and a plush black rug covered most of the shiny hardwood floors.

The colors alone made it clear that it was a guy's room, but as I looked more closely, I could see hints of Bo here and there. His black hoodie hung on the back of the door, a watch I'd seen him wear was thrown on top of the dresser, and his messenger bag lay in the floor by the nightstand.

It was incredibly comforting just being in his room, in his bed, much more so than I ever would've imagined. I melted into the mattress, turning my face into the pillow and inhaling deeply. I could smell him as if he was lying right next to me.

Bo's mother came back into the room carrying a bucket, a wet cloth, and an armful of assorted supplies. I had to smile. It was like the kit I kept under the sink for Mom.

She laid the wet rag on my forehead and asked, "Do you still feel sick?"

"No. I think I just got up too fast," I admitted. "I'm sorry to put you to all this trouble."

"You're no trouble at all. I'm only sorry we had to meet this way," she said.

I didn't know how to respond to that. Was that just a generic comment or did she know who I was? Had Bo mentioned me?

Warmth spread through me at the mere prospect of Bo telling his mother about me. I have no idea why that would please me so much, but it did.

Since she hadn't answered me the first time, I asked again, "Where is Bo, by the way?"

"He's running an errand for me. He'll be back shortly to take you home," she explained.

Thoughts of home made me remember my mangled face. I reached up to touch my cheek again, knowing it had to be at least three different colors.

"How bad is it?"

A strange look flitted over her face before it smoothed out. "What? How bad is what?"

"My face," I specified.

"Your face is fine. Why wouldn't it be?"

"Um, because Drew punched me. Hard. And I remember it hurting so badly that I thought my jaw was broken."

She was watching me closely. "Well, it looks fine to me. How does it feel?"

Gingerly, I worked the joint. It seemed stiff more than anything, but certainly not broken.

"A little stiff, but ok."

"Good. Maybe you won't even have a bruise."

"But how—" I began, but then remembered what I thought I'd heard Bo say. "Did Bo—"

I stopped myself.

Ms. Bowman's eyes were alert and a tiny frown creased her brow. "Did Bo what?" The way she prompted me seemed a bit anxious.

What exactly did I remember? Nothing that made sense, that's for sure. I could hardly admit to his mother that I thought I'd heard him say he'd heal me. She'd have me in the ER getting my brain scanned as soon as I could say spit.

I shook my head, hoping it might rid it of crazy thoughts and half-baked memories.

"Nothing. Sorry, everything's still a little hazy." I looked down, away from her perceptive eyes, and it was then that I noticed her clothes. "Are you a nurse?"

She seemed puzzled at first. "What?" But then she noticed me looking at her scrubs. "Oh, these? No, I'm not a nurse. I'm a lab tech and phlebotomist."

"Phlebotomist? Are those the ones that draw blood?"

"Yes, we're the ones that draw blood," she confirmed with a smile.

We stared at each other for a few moments, silence quickly closing in and becoming uncomfortable. I didn't know what else to say and apparently she didn't either.

"Well," she said, rising to her feet. "I'll let you rest until Bo gets back." She walked to the door and then turned back. "Is there anything I can get you right now?"

"No, thank you," I said, feeling like enough of a bother already. With a smile, Ms. Bowman disappeared into the hall.

"Ms. Bowman?" I stopped her. Though it was silly and ridiculous, there was one question I had to ask. When she poked her head back around the door jamb, I stammered awkwardly, "D-did Bo mention me?"

She smiled again, but this time there was a hint of sadness behind the curve of her lips. "Yes." Then, with no further explanation, she walked away.

Despite her strange reaction, my heart sang. I lay there for the next few minutes, happily drinking in Bo's scent and basking in the glow of this latest revelation.

My stomach twittered when I heard him come in. He asked, "Is she awake?"

I managed to sit up on the edge of his bed without getting sick, which I took as a good sign. I smoothed my hair as I waited for him to find his way to me.

Too quietly for me to hear, I heard him something else of his mother and then his heavy footsteps clonked toward the bedroom. With every thump, my heart beat a little bit faster. In a bizarre way, I could almost feel him getting closer.

When he appeared in the doorway, I couldn't stop the smile that spread across my face.

"Hey," I said simply, feeling like a nervous schoolgirl with a crush.

He leaned one shoulder against the door jamb. "Hey yourself," he said with a casual grin that made my belly flip over excitedly. "How do you feel?"

I shrugged. "Fine." Actually, now that he was here, I felt better than fine, but I wasn't about to tell him that.

Pushing himself upright, he crossed the room and sat down beside me on the bed. I turned to look at him. He was facing me and, therefore, facing the lamp. The dim glow of the bulb illuminated his features and I was struck by how perfectly handsome he was. Out of nowhere, desire curled inside me like a tightly-wound spring, making me breathless.

He reached up and stroked my cheek with his finger. Unlike what I'd come to expect from him, Bo's skin was extremely warm, almost hot. "Does it hurt?"

I shook my head.

He walked his fingertips all along my jaw and chin. I assumed he was inspecting me for injury, but I didn't really care. As long as he didn't stop touching me and looking at me like that, it didn't matter what he was doing.

"I thought he'd really hurt you," he confessed, his lips thinning angrily.

"I thought so, too."

"He's lucky I didn't—" He stopped himself on a growl.

I wanted to smile at his reaction, but I didn't. Instead I asked, "So, what happened?"

Bo shrugged. "You fell into my arms and I brought you here."

I rolled my eyes in exasperation.

"I kinda figured that out on my own. I meant what happened with Drew?"

"Well, after I convinced him not to put his hands on you—ever—he just stood there and watched me carry you off."

"Convinced?"

Bo nodded nonchalantly. I was afraid to ask about specifics; I was pretty sure I didn't want the details. I just hoped he didn't pulverize Drew. That would be adding another insult to his already injured pride, and I had enough to feel guilty about.

"Thanks for not taking me home." I looked away from his too-keen eyes when I said, "If my mom had been there, it would have been a disaster."

Most likely, she wouldn't even have been home, and even if she had been, she'd probably have been too drunk to notice or care what shape my face was in. The disaster would've been in Bo seeing that my mom is a lush.

"I'd say 'my pleasure,' but if I'm gonna carry you to my bed, I'd much rather you be conscious," he said with a wry quirk of his lips.

I felt the blood rush to my cheeks, not in embarrassment, but in pleasure. Just the thought of Bo carrying me to his bed and laying me down on the thick black comforter was enough to raise my blood pressure to stroke level.

I wondered if maybe he was thinking the same thing because, as I watched, the dark, dark brown of his eyes disappeared behind the widening blackness of his pupils.

With a quick shake of his head, Bo cleared his throat and looked away. "So I guess it's time I take you home, huh?"

I couldn't say no, no matter how much I wanted to. "I guess so."

Bo stood and held out his hand. "Come on," he said, tipping his head toward the door.

I slipped my hand into his. The room was so chilly, the warmth of his skin felt heavenly. I rose, letting him lead me out the door and down the hall.

We stopped just inside the doorway to a tiny yellow kitchen. "You met Mom, right?" His mother turned from the sink to smile at me.

"I introduced myself to her," she said, smiling. Then, to me, "Are you feeling better?"

"Yes, ma'am. Thank you."

"You're welcome. Come back any time," she offered kindly, turning back to the sink.

Bo tugged on my arm and we left through a door off the kitchen. It led to a back porch where a washer and dryer sat to one side and a huge trunk-style freezer sat to the other. The exit from that room led to the back yard, which was apparently where the driveway ended, as there was an old blue Volvo station wagon parked right in front of the door.

"Mom's car," he announced, as if by way of explanation. "She works nights."

He opened the passenger door and then closed it once I was safely inside. When he slid behind the wheel, I asked, "Does she have to work tonight?"

"Yeah."

"Is she going to be late?"

Bo shrugged. "Just a little, but she already called. It's no big deal."

Great! What a way to make a first impression on his mother.

The trip home went by way too quickly. Much to my surprise, Bo didn't live very far from me at all.

When he pulled into the driveway, Mom's car was already there, which was a shocker.

"Here we are," I said, turning to Bo. "Thanks again for…well, everything."

"So, do you mind my asking what happened with you and Connors?"

I smiled at the scathing way he said Drew's last name. "We broke up," I answered simply.

"Why?"

My smile died. The way he said it made it sound almost like a complaint, like something he couldn't understand.

I tried to sound casual. "Things change. Feelings change, that's all."

"Good. I didn't want it to have anything to do with me."

For some unfathomable reason, that hurt.

"I'm not good for you, Ridley. Not like I should be, not like you need me to be."

I was confused. He acted as if he really liked me, but now, here he was trying to convince me that he's not right for me again.

"Don't worry," I said, opening the car door. "It had nothing to do with you."

I got out of the car and closed the door on my lie. I caught myself before I stomped off petulantly. Instead, I took a deep breath and bent down to look at Bo through the open window.

"Thanks again," I repeated, trying to appear nonchalant when I felt anything but that. It was impossible to feel nonchalant about something that was crushing my chest.

When Bo said nothing, I walked quickly to the house, rushing to get inside before the tears that welled in my eyes fell and embarrassed me further.

As I was opening the front door, I heard Bo call from the driveway, "See you tomorrow."

I didn't get much sleep that night either.

****

The next morning, I woke up surprisingly alert and energetic. Not surprisingly, my first waking thought was of Bo. His scent, his eyes, his voice, even his name hummed through my veins. It was as if my body was as consumed with him as my mind seemed to be.

It has to be done if I'm gonna heal her.

Throwing off the covers, I ran into the bathroom, turned on the light and looked into the mirror. I almost wanted to see a rainbow of colors across my face, as if that would make the memory of those troubling words less bothersome. But, much to my consternation, there was no swelling, no discoloration, no evidence at all that I'd been brutally punched only twelve short hours before.

I opened my mouth wide and wiggled my jaw left to right, front to back. There was not even a twinge of pain.

"Huh," I said to my reflection. I know I didn't imagine the excruciating pain, nor did I imagine passing out and waking up in Bo's room.

It has to be done if I'm gonna heal her.

Shaking my head, I tucked the disquieting thoughts into a dark corner in the back of my mind, deciding instead to be grateful that I hadn't spent the night in surgery getting my jaw wired shut.

After getting ready in record time, I got in my car and headed for Starbuck's. I'd have plenty of time to make a coffee stop, especially since the shop was so close to the school.

The drive-thru was packed so I got out and went inside. When I stepped through the door, a gush of pleasure and relief washed over me. It was so intense and so unexpected, I literally had to stop to catch my breath.

I looked around at the many faces inside the tiny store. I recognized several people and, if the way they were looking at me was any indication, my outburst from the day before had only gotten juicier over night.

It wasn't until my eyes collided with Bo's unforgettably absorbing ones that I realized what I was so excited about, what my blood and my body had known even before my eyes could confirm it.

We stood facing each other, separated by tables and bodies, music and laughter, but we might've been the only two people in the world. My heart strained against my ribs as if someone had tied satin threads to it—threads that were tethered to Bo, threads that were insistently pulling me toward him.

I leaned back against the wall beside the door, pushing away from Bo as hard as I could, determined to resist. As I watched him, unable to tear my eyes away, one side of his mouth tipped up in a knowing grin and he took a step toward me.

Like a predator, he made his way through the crowd, stalking me with his eyes. With every step that brought him closer, my anticipation grew until it was almost unbearable, at fever pitch.

He didn't stop until he stood only inches from me, his body so close our chests would touch if I inhaled deeply enough. I couldn't take a deep breath, though. My lungs had seized and I couldn't breathe at all.

Bo bent his head and whispered at my ear, "Breathe."

And just like that, it seemed the spell was broken. On a *whoosh*, I let out the air I'd been holding and Bo leaned back to look at me.

"What are you doing to me?"

His brows pinched together, but he said nothing. I hadn't intended to say that out loud; it was more of an internal musing, one to which I didn't really expect an answer.

"Bo, are you ready?" It was a girl's voice that called from behind him.

I looked over Bo's shoulder and there stood Savannah. She grinned when she saw me peek up at her.

"Sorry to interrupt," she chirped happily. "I didn't see you there, Ridley."

"You're not interrupting," I assured her.

When I looked back to Bo, one brow was quirked. Ignoring that my stomach was aflutter and that my blood pounded in my ears, I slipped out from around Bo.

"He's all yours," I said, steeling myself and heading for the cashier.

Without so much as a glance behind me, I placed my order, paid and moved to the other end of the counter to await my coffee. I could feel Bo's eyes on me, but I refused to turn around.

I didn't have to look to know when he left. I felt it, like the draining away of something vital. I ached to turn and follow him, but I didn't. I waited for my coffee and then took it to my car where I waited for my pulse to return to normal.

When I finally managed to get my body under control, I drove to school and parked at the top of the lot. On the few occasions when I drove, I parked in that same spot. It was always available and it was always in the shade.

I walked slowly toward the building. I dreaded school more today than I had in…well, actually, more than I ever had. I knew it was just a matter of time until Trinity either exploded or executed some sort of vicious sneak attack. It hovered over me like a huge guillotine, its razor-sharp blade glinting in the morning sun. All Trinity had to do was pull the lever and *thwack!* I'd be headless.

Making my way quickly through the halls, trying my best to ignore all the stares, I saw a tight knot of people in the same general vicinity as my locker. My stomach curled in dismay.

I politely asked to be excused as I pushed my way through the masses to get to my locker. When I finally managed to wiggle my way through, I saw what was garnering all the attention, what they were all looking at.

Trinity had been hard at work during practice last night. She'd been defacing my locker. I knew without a doubt she was the responsible party and I'm sure everyone else knew that, too.

Taped to my locker were several photo-shopped pictures of me doing disgusting things with old men, other girls and farm animals. In between the pictures, written in black magic marker, were words like *traitor* and *whore* among many other, much more colorful slurs.

Unfortunately, though, that wasn't the worst of it. An overpowering stench was emanating from my locker. Upon closer inspection, I realized that there were feces smeared all over the pictures and a big hunk of it was stuck to the lock.

But there was something else. Beneath that smell was something that had an even more rancid odor than the crap all over the door. I feared that it was coming from inside.

I wondered if Trinity might have managed to get into my locker and put something nasty in there, something dead. It sure smelled that way, and it sure sounded like something she'd do. In addition to being curious just like everyone else, I was also a little concerned about my belongings. I hated to leave them in there with the funk, but there was no way I was touching my locker without a HazMat suit. If there was road kill 'possum in there, it would just have to wait.

Turning on my heel, I went straight to Home Room. I could do without books for one day. I'd just explain what happened to the teachers so they'd not penalize me for showing up without them and without my homework. I could take my duffel back to the car after first period so that I wouldn't have to lug it around with me all day.

No biggee, I told myself, but even so, I could feel tears of humiliation stinging my eyes. I'd known Trinity was vile, but I hadn't expected something like this. I had assumed it would be something much more…social, her revenge. And I still suspected that it would be. I could only assume that she was biding her time, which didn't bode well for me. That probably meant that it was going to be epic. I just wished she'd just get it over with so I could move on in peace. Waiting was the worst part.

I kept to myself through all my classes, but I made sure that, when I walked the halls, my chin was held high and my face as pleasantly blank as possible. I'd die before I let her or anyone else see that she'd rattled me.

Thankfully, I didn't see Trinity until lunch. When I walked out the cafeteria door, I saw that she had assumed my position between Drew and Summer. The door shut behind me with a loud click and all eyes turned toward me.

At my former table, several people shifted, scooting their chairs this way and that to make sure that there was not enough room for one more person to squeeze in between them. That person, of course, was me. Wordlessly, I was being put in my place, exiled.

I scanned each face one by one, challenging them. Many either dropped their eyes or glanced away when I looked their way. Only a few held my gaze, eyeing me defiantly.

When my eyes met Trinity's from across the patio, she glared at me in silent triumph. I hadn't really expected much more from such a group of blind followers, but the betrayal hurt nonetheless.

Having long since lost my appetite, I took my Coke to a huge maple tree and sat down in the shade at its base. I leaned back against it, facing away from Trinity and the others, trying to pretend that the rest of the world had disappeared.

I jumped when Bo spoke.

"Want some company?"

"Not really," I said without looking up. Even as the words left my lips, I craved his nearness like I craved fresh air.

"Too bad," he announced, sitting down beside me and leaning his back against the tree, too.

My plan was to ignore him, but that only lasted for about three minutes. My jealousy couldn't be contained any longer than that.

"Where's Savannah?"

"Enjoying the fruits of your labor."

Puzzled, I looked over at Bo. His head was turned and he was looking back at the picnic table he'd been sharing with Savannah. There was no mistaking her dark red hair glistening in the bright sunshine, but she wasn't alone. Devon sat across from her, laughing at something she was saying.

"How is that the fruit of *my* labor?"

"You stood up to Trinity," he said with a shrug, as if that explained it all.

"That has nothing to do with Devon, though."

"Maybe not directly," Bo answered meaningfully. "You're like an unsung hero around here."

"Yeah," I said, looking around at my own little spot in purgatory. "It sure looks like it."

"You can't see it now, but you will."

We spent the few remaining minutes of lunch in companionable silence. Afterwards, out of habit, I went to my locker. It wasn't until I was almost there that I remembered what Trinity had done to it. I nearly turned around, but I stopped myself. Going back the other way would take me longer to get to class than to just go the way I usually went, so I headed on.

My mouth dropped open when I rounded the corner and got a good look at my locker. It was perfectly clean. Well, *mostly* clean. Some of the words were still visible, but the pictures were gone and it had been scrubbed clean of poop, which was the biggest thing anyway.

I looked around, searching the faces for some idea of who'd cleaned it up. My eyes stopped on sparkling chocolate ones staring at me from the end of the hall. It was Savannah. She held my gaze for a few seconds and then winked at me and walked away.

I didn't need for her to tell me that this was her thanking me for standing up for her, and for the first time since it happened, I was actually glad that I did it.

Turning back to my locker, I reached for the lock, but it was gone. I could only assume that it had been too soiled to save.

"Looking for this?"

I jumped again at Bo's voice. He was standing behind me holding a shiny new combination lock.

"She had the janitor come and cut it off right after lunch so nothing would get stolen until you got here," Bo explained.

I felt more than a little ashamed at how jealous I'd been of Savannah. She was obviously a decent person, and Bo really seemed to like her. Devon, too.

"She didn't have to do this," I stated quietly, finding the painted toes peeking out of my shoes very interesting all of a sudden.

"She wanted to," he replied.

"When did she have time to clean it up?"

"She has third period study hall."

I felt near tears again and it didn't help when Bo tilted my face up to his. His eyes made me feel so amazing it almost hurt.

He'd been smiling, but slowly, his smile died as he stared into my eyes. For a moment, I saw exactly what I was feeling reflected in their lush depths—an attraction, a need, so great it was overpowering.

"Why can't I stay away from you?" With his whisper, he rubbed his thumb back and forth across my chin.

All I could think of was that I didn't want him to stay away, that I couldn't survive it if he did, and though some part of my brain registered that such a sentiment was utterly ridiculous, I knew it was true nonetheless.

"Why do you try?"

"Because it's the right thing to do."

"Do you always do the right thing?"

His lips twisted up into a wry grin. "Almost never."

He made me want to smile, so I did. "Then why start now?"

In a rich sound that seemed to steal all the air from the hallway, Bo laughed. But somewhere, behind the sparkle in his eyes, was a sadness that I was noticing more and more often.

Before I could delve into the intrigue of it, the bell rang, rudely interrupting our moment. With a sigh, Bo said, "See you in Chemistry."

I watched him go as if he was carrying a piece of me away with him.

CHAPTER FIVE

I watched the moonlit scenery fly by as the bus carried us home. For three days now, I'd managed to block out Trinity's wicked digs and nasty comments. Luckily, though they'd abandoned me and chosen to take Trinity's side, the others were a little less demonstrative in their shunning of me. Apart from the snickers behind my back, they more or less just ignored me.

Despite the fact that I'd known for a long time that I was surrounded by sharks, it still hurt to see them turn their backs on me so quickly, so easily. And it was all for the sake of popularity no less. It was a sickness, really, and they were fatally infected. I guess I should've been feeling sorry for them, but it was very hard to feel pity for them when they were all piled up in the back of the bus, laughing and making fun of me.

The fact that I was there at all was a monumental surprise to me. Not only was I still a member of the squad, I was also still its leader, at least for the time being anyway. Fortunately, my cheerleading fate had ceased to bother me anymore. It would be great to keep the status quo and get my scholarship to Stanford, but if I didn't, it wouldn't be the end of the world. My feelings for Bo had put that, along with many other things, in perspective.

In the last few days, my focus had shifted. My usually Stanford-focused tunnel vision was now a wide angle lens that captured all things Bo. When I wasn't with him, I thought of him. When I wasn't awake, I dreamed of him. When he was near, I could feel it, and when he wasn't, I ached for him to come back. It was like he'd invaded my entire being, right down to my red blood cells, which seemed to swell with a longing for him that I couldn't describe.

The closer we got to school, the more I could sense him. He'd be waiting for me when the bus pulled in. I was certain of it.

With a loud groan, the bus rolled to a stop in front of the school at the bottom of the parking lot. Being seated at the front (essentially exile in bus seat pecking order), I was the first one out the folding doors.

I wasted no time getting to my car at the top of the lot. I wanted to run, but somehow refrained from doing so. My pulse leapt when I saw Bo leaning up against the passenger side door of my car. It's where I'd found him the last two nights after practice, too.

"Hey," I said unimaginatively, wishing that my brain worked better when he was around. It went on hiatus and left my senses in control, which meant my vocabulary was roughly that of a toddler.

"How was the game?" He straightened and took my duffel from my shoulder.

"We won," I replied, having no interest in talking about the game.

"It was the cheering," he teased.

I rolled my eyes and laughed. "I'm sure that's exactly what it was."

"Do you have to go straight home?"

"No. Why?"

"Just curious," he said, enigmatically. "Can I drive?"

"Sure." I handed the keys to him and he unlocked the passenger side and held the door open for me.

Once I was inside, he closed the door and rounded in front of the hood. My eyes followed him as he walked. I loved to watch him move. It was like watching water ballet or space acrobatics. It seemed as though gravity didn't affect him like it did most people, like he was as light as the air through which he moved.

After pitching my duffel behind the seat, Bo climbed in and started the car, speeding away in the direction of his house.

Several minutes later, as I suspected, he pulled into his driveway and cut the engine. When he helped me out, he kept my hand tightly wrapped in his. Rather than leading me to the back door of the house, he surprised me by walking around the side to a set of concrete steps. He descended first, me following close behind.

At the bottom of the steps was an old red door with a small window at the top. I could only assume that it was the exterior entrance to a basement or cellar.

There was a padlock on the door that Bo unlocked using a small key on his keychain. When he pushed the door open, I expected to smell a gust of that musty odor that all basements seem to have, but I didn't. It just got a whiff of Bo's tangy scent.

It was pitch black inside the room. Bo reached back to take my hand and pull me inside, but before I'd taken even one step, Bo stopped me.

"What's wrong?"

"Shh," he whispered.

I listened, but didn't hear anything alarming. I don't know what kinds of ambient noises he was used to hearing around his house, but nothing sounded out of the ordinary to me.

With a note of seriousness in his tone that made chills race down my arms, Bo said, "Stay here. Don't say a word and don't make a sound."

He shifted back past me and through the door, taking the steps two at a time. Still, I listened. Still, I heard nothing.

Bo disappeared from view. Contrary to what he might've thought, I was not going to stay in a dark, unfamiliar hole under his house when he was nowhere to be found.

I crept to the top of the steps and poked my head up to look around. In the moonlight, I saw Bo standing a few feet away, facing a man. They were just staring at each other, neither making a sound, neither moving a muscle.

Finally, the other man shifted, taking one slow step toward Bo.

"I hear you've been looking for me."

"Don't know where you heard that. I don't even know you."

"But you knew John Gibbs," the man said.

Gibbs? Gibbs? Where had I heard that name?

The thought was interrupted when I heard a low growling. At first, I thought maybe Bo had a dog I didn't know about. I whipped my head around, half expecting a vicious Doberman to be right beside me. But there wasn't. As it grew louder, I realized that it was coming from Bo.

"That's what I thought," the man sneered. "I'm just here to tell you: you come after my friends, you come after me. And if you come after me," he said, taking another step toward Bo. "Well, let's just say you already lost your biggest advantage, because now I know who you are. Now, *I'll* be coming after *you*."

A light breeze chose that very moment to blow through the back yard, ruffling my hair. I caught myself before I reached up to push my bangs out of my eyes. I didn't want to move and risk exposure.

It didn't matter, though. Both Bo and the other man turned toward me and I quickly ducked out of sight. I don't know how they'd known I was there. I hadn't made a sound or moved an inch.

"See, it just takes one visit to learn all about somebody's weaknesses. You'd be wise not to forget that I know where to find you," the man said warningly. "And your friends."

"You shouldn't make threats you have no hope of living to carry out," Bo said evenly.

"Be careful, boy. You have no idea who you're messing with."

"I don't care who you are," Bo growled. "And I'm only gonna tell you this one time. Don't ever come near here again."

"I won't have to. Everyone leaves eventually."

I felt the whip of a gust of wind just before a loud crack split the night air. It sounded like a clap of thunder. I started to peek up and look around again, but just before Bo came into sight, I felt a sharp blow to the top of my head and the world went blissfully black.

****

Once again, I awoke to the scent of Bo in my nostrils. The tangy element—whatever delectable spice he smelled of—seemed stronger than usual and, despite the strange circumstances, it still made my insides melt.

I inhaled deeply, relishing the aroma. I tried to open my eyelids, but they were stubbornly ignoring my commands.

"Bo," I called hoarsely.

My tongue felt sticky with something sweetly salty. I licked my tingling lips. Even the delicious residue made my mouth water.

"I'm here," he said.

The sound of his voice was like a purr, rasping along my nerve ends like the brush of velvet against my skin.

"Be still." The "s" made an odd hissing sound and I thought Bo's voice sounded scratchy, like his throat was dry.

I remembered that I'd been looking for Bo when something had hit me in the head. As if on cue, my skull throbbed painfully. I reached up to touch my scalp, not sure what to expect, but a hand grabbed mine to still it before it got very far.

"Don't try to move," Bo advised in a low voice.

"Bo," I groaned, a sound born both of pain and of need.

I ached, but not from a truly physical pain. It was with a strange yearning that I couldn't describe, like I wanted to take Bo into my body, drink him in like a fine wine. It seemed that my blood was on fire, crying out for him and him alone.

I felt his hand sweep my forehead and I thought I detected a slight tremor in his touch. I wondered vaguely if he felt it too, that desperate need.

His movement caused the air to stir around my face. I felt an unusual wetness all over my skin, on my ears and my neck. I tried to open my eyes again and this time I succeeded, but I still couldn't see anything. We were in the dark. I couldn't even see where Bo was in relation to me; I could only feel that he was near.

"Where are we?"

"In the basement," Bo ground out, it seemed through gritted teeth.

"What happened?"

"A tree fell across the yard, across the steps and hit you."

"Am I alright?" A silly question, I know, since I was alive and talking, but somehow, I thought the answer might not be that simple.

"You'll be fine," he answered gruffly.

"Why are we in the dark?"

"The, uh, the tree knocked out the lights down here."

"So, who was that guy?"

"I don't know. I think he had me confused with someone else." Bo's tone was withdrawn and abrupt.

"Oh," I said, feeling absurdly suspicious, but if he didn't want to talk about it, I wouldn't press. "Maybe we should go upstairs. I feel wet. I think I might be bleeding."

Other than an aching head, I didn't feel like I'd been wounded, fatally or otherwise. Surely if I was hurt badly, I'd know it. I probably needed to check anyway. That was the smart thing to do.

"Here," he said, sliding an arm beneath my shoulders. "You shouldn't walk. I'll have to carry you."

The fact that he didn't seem too pleased about that hurt my feelings, which then irritated me. Both feelings were eclipsed, however, by the heavenly feel of his chest pressed against my side when he picked me up.

When I was firmly in his arms, he gasped. It hadn't occurred to me until that very moment that he might be hurt, too.

"Are you alright? You don't have to carry me," I said earnestly, all the while my body was rebelling at the idea of being out of his arms—ever.

"I'll be fine," he assured me, though I could tell that his teeth were still gritted.

He carried me remarkably easily up the concrete steps and around to the back door. Once inside the dark house, Bo walked through to the bathroom and deposited me gently on the toilet. He didn't turn on the light.

"I'll let you get cleaned up. The sight of your blood…" he trailed off in a very telling manner.

"Oh, I'm sorry. You're one of those people that can't stand the sight of blood?" I hadn't even thought of that, but it would explain his behavior and his sharpness.

"Something like that," he said uncomfortably. "Holler if you need anything. There are wash cloths under the sink." With that, he closed the door and I was alone in the dark.

Luckily, it seemed like a tiny bathroom, which made sense in such a small house. When I reached out, I could feel the sink to my left and walls to my right and in front of me.

I stood and walked my hand around beside the door jamb until I felt a light switch. I flipped it and turned around to face the mirrored medicine cabinet that hung over the sink.

As soon as I saw my reflection, my heart tripped into a faster cadence. I looked like Carrie in the scene from that movie where they dump the bucket of pig's blood on her. My hair and clothes were saturated with blood, and my face and neck were streaked with thick rivulets of it.

Reaching up, I felt through my hair for some kind of wound. One spot on my scalp felt a little sore, bruised almost, but I felt no gashes or punctures. I'd always heard that the scalp bled a lot; maybe I'd been scraped by the tree and it had broken the skin enough to bleed, but not do any real damage.

I closed my eyes and leaned on the sink, encouraging myself to calm down. It's incredibly alarming, the sight of your reflection covered in blood. Even if the injury isn't serious, it's still a scary thing to behold.

Reaching beneath the sink, I took out a rag. I hated to ruin one of Bo's wash cloths, but I had to get myself cleaned up so I could get past Bo and get home. My parents would freak if they saw me like this. Mom would probably even be home and sober since Dad's flight got in before lunch.

I wet the cloth and wiped at my face and neck then rinsed and repeated dozens of times until I'd gotten most of the blood off and had disguised it as much as possible on my uniform top. Luckily our school colors were black, white and maroon and most of the blood had gotten on my shoulders where the colors were darkest.

When I was once again presentable, I made my way through the house toward the only other light I saw shining. It was the kitchen light and Bo was standing at the sink. I would've been able to find him anyway, just following my nose. I could smell his scent like a heavenly musk trail through the house.

Bo was facing the hallway. He must've heard me coming.

"Are you alright?" As he asked, he walked over to where I'd stopped just inside the doorway. The closer he got, the harder my pulse drummed in my ears.

Coming to a stop in front of me, he rubbed my arms comfortingly.

"I'm fine. I can't really figure out where all that blood came from."

"Scalp wounds bleed a lot," he confirmed matter-of-factly.

I couldn't help but grin. "That's what I've always heard, too."

Bo had a smudge of blood across his cheek. I reached up to wipe it away.

"What is it?"

"You must've gotten some blood on you when you carried me up the stairs." I looked at his clothes. There was not a single drop of blood on them.

"I changed," he offered, as if reading my mind.

I nodded, just then noticing the clock that hung on the wall behind Bo's head.

"Ohmigod! Is that clock right?"

Bo turned to look at the clock, too. "Yep."

It read 2:40.

"I've got to go. My parents are gonna freak!" Once again, I'd been unconscious longer than I'd thought. No wonder there was so much blood on me.

"I'll drive you,' Bo said, walking with me to the door.

"You don't have to do that. I'm fine. Really," I promised. Not that I didn't want to spend a few more minutes with Bo, but I'd feel terrible that he'd have to walk all the way back home, especially at 3:00 in the morning.

Bo stopped just outside the door, turning to look back at me. "I'm sure you are, but I'm not willing to take the chance."

My stomach fluttered and I had to work to suppress the grin that was pulling at my lips. Bo took my hand and tugged.

"Come on."

At my car, Bo let go of my hand long enough to get me inside and shut the door. Once he was seated behind the wheel and had pulled out into the street, however, he casually reached over and wrapped his fingers around mine again.

Surprisingly, instead of the coolness I'd come to expect from him, his skin was really, really warm where he held my hand over the gear shift, just like the last time I'd awakened at his house.

My house came into view all too soon. Even though I'd spent most of the night unconscious—again—I still didn't want my time with Bo to end.

Both my parents' vehicles were in the driveway and Bo wasted no time with a lengthy goodbye.

"I'll get out of here so you can get inside. I hope you're not in too much trouble," he said genuinely.

"It'll be fine."

The way he was staring into my eyes, I thought he was going to kiss me, but instead, Bo brought my fingers to his lips and kissed them.

He asked softly, "Call you tomorrow?"

I nodded and then he was gone, getting quietly out of the car and disappearing into the night.

I sat in the passenger side for a few minutes, thinking of Bo, basking in the lingering scent of him. If Target had a Bo-scented car freshener, I'd buy one. Or ten.

The thought was so silly I had to laugh as I got out of the car to go inside.

I stood at the front door, listening for sounds from inside. Even through the thick wood of the door, I could hear some light snoring. Dad.

The door was unlocked so I cracked it just enough to squeeze through and then shut it silently behind me. The house smelled of barbecue sauce and old wine.

I crept to the door of the living room and peeked inside. Mom was crashed with her feet in Dad's lap and he was sound asleep with his head leaned back against the couch cushions. His mouth was hanging open and he was snoring, just as I'd suspected.

As I crept to my room, I was surprised I could hear Dad's snoring outside; it didn't seem that loud at all.

The first thing I did in my room was to go and raise my window, though I left the screen down this time. I could hear the frogs and crickets outside, as well as the breeze ruffling the leaves and bending the tree branches. I inhaled deeply. The cool night air teased my nostrils, carrying the scent of rain. Somewhere in the distance, I could hear the patter of a light drizzle.

I was turning away to change into my pajamas when a familiar thrill skittered down my spine, racing through my blood. A faint hint of citrus tinged the air for just a moment before it was gone.

I looked out the window, past the grainy grid of the screen, peering into the night. Other than the gentle shift of foliage, there was no movement, no evidence that someone was out there, that I wasn't alone in the night.

Shrugging it off as my overactive imagination, I grabbed my pajamas and headed for the bathroom to clean up and wash my hair.

****

The next morning I woke early. The birds outside my window were cheeping more vivaciously than ever and I could hear Mom banging around in the kitchen like there were no walls between us.

I lay there, feeling the blood pulse beneath my skin, enjoying the remaining scent of Bo in my hair where it was spread across my pillow.

Mom said something to Dad about waking me up for breakfast, so I went ahead and rolled out of bed and headed to the bathroom.

When I stumbled into the kitchen a few minutes later, Mom was scooting pancakes off the griddle and onto three plates.

"Rise and shine, sleepyhead," she chirped cheerfully.

I eyed her skeptically. At times, I don't think I gave her enough credit; she was quite the actress. Behind her overly bright smile and strategic makeup, I could see the tremble of rising discomfort in her bloodshot eyes. Her need for a drink was almost a tangible thing. Dad seemed not to notice, but even if he did, he would do his best to pretend otherwise, which is probably exactly what he was doing.

With a sigh, I fell in to the recently-established grand tradition of the Heller household and pasted on a fake smile of my own, jumping head first into the façade.

"Smells good," I said, taking a seat at the perfectly set table. I took a big gulp of orange juice and thought surely it was the best I'd ever had, the sweetly tart liquid coating my tongue and sliding down my throat like fruity silk.

Mom served me and Dad then took her seat at the table. Dad said the blessing and we dug in. The only thing that ruined the Cleaver-like meal was the depressing squawk of the reporter that was dishing out news from the television on the counter.

I was surprised that I hadn't already heard the report. I'd fallen asleep again last night without the aid of the television. Maybe I was cured.

"…indication that the violence raging through Southmoore has made its way south to Harker.

In the early hours, Harker police discovered the body of Southmoore resident Trent Edward Long just inside the city limits on East Highway 5. Long had been a long-time associate of the recently deceased John Gibbs and had, at one time, been included in a suspect pool for the Southmoore Slayings. More information..."

I looked up to see the face of the victim about whom they were speaking and my throat seized around the lump of pancakes I was trying to swallow.

Though it was taken several years ago at a party somewhere, I had no trouble recognizing his face. I'd seen him last night. Even in the low light of the moon, I had been able to make out the features of the guy who'd basically threatened Bo. Now, I was looking at his smiling face on the television. He was dead, and I'd probably been one of the last people to see him alive. Me and Bo.

My appetite disappeared as I thought back to where I'd heard the Gibbs name. Not only had the guy, Trent Long, mentioned him last night, but his name had been referenced on the news as last year's Southmoore Slayer suspect. He'd also been accused of killing a man named Travis Bowman. Bowman.

Something unsettling occurred to me and my stomach clenched tightly. My entire being rebelled against the very idea that Bo might be involved with those men and their nefarious, nocturnal dealings. But...

Silently, I prayed. *Please God, please don't let him be involved,* I chanted over and over and over in my head.

"Aren't you going to finish your breakfast, Ridley? Pancakes are your favorite," Mom said.

Pancakes had never been my favorite and probably never would be. They'd been Izzy's favorite breakfast food. If Mom had ever bothered to commit my favorites to memory, I had no doubt that the knowledge had been steadily drowned out by gallons of vodka. Now, all that remained were random memories of Izzy and little else.

"I-I'm just not very hungry," I said, trying to sound casual when I felt anything but.

"Did the bus stop on the way back from the game to get you something to eat last night? I noticed you didn't get home until late," Dad observed.

"No, but I went out with some friends afterward."

He nodded. He had no idea exactly when I'd gotten home; they'd been fast asleep on the couch. But even if he had, I should've known neither he nor Mom would've caused a stink over it. That would be too emotionally real and draining for a family of pretenders.

"I think I'm going to go take a shower. Mom, can you just save the rest of my pancakes?" I asked more to be polite than anything. I'd choke them down later if need be, but not because I liked them.

"Sure, honey," she said, smiling sweetly.

A shower had me feeling a little better. My skin felt more alive than ever, like I was wearing it differently, my shampoo smelled more floral than usual and the water hit the shower walls like a violent waterfall of sound.

Afterward, I lounged in my room most of the day, checking my phone every few minutes to make sure it was turned on and still charged, which it was. It never rang, though. I couldn't remember the last time it had gone so long in absolute silence, especially on a Saturday. It was just another indication of how much had changed in recent days.

A *Matrix* marathon started at 2:00. I made it through the first two alright, but about a quarter of the way through the third one, my attention started to drift back to other matters. I wasn't sure if it was because it was by far the weakest of the three movies or because I'd just reached my threshold of time having passed without obsessing over Bo. Either way, by 9:00, I'd already dialed Bo twice, and both times I ended up listening to his voice mail. At 9:20, after giving my parents the vague excuse of needing to run to a friend's house for just a minute, I was in my car heading toward his house.

As I pulled into his driveway, I looked up at the dark windows and wondered if I was making a mistake. What if his mom was sleeping? What if he was with someone else? What if he was some kind of homicidal monster and I was walking into a trap?

The end of the driveway showed me that the car wasn't there. Either Bo was out in it or his mom was gone.

Turning off the engine, I sat in the car considering whether or not to start it back up and leave rather than going to the door. Something in me wouldn't let me leave, though. It seemed that I had to see Bo, not only for peace of mind, but to silence the constant clamor of him in my head, in my heart, in every single cell of my body. It was as if something inside me searched relentlessly for him in the air around me, seeking. Always seeking.

When I finally felt courageous enough to approach the door, I knocked lightly, hesitant to disturb his mother if she was in there, but I got no answer. The house was silent and still.

I had opened the car door and was about to slide in behind the wheel when a muffled sound reached my ears. I remembered the basement, the room Bo had taken me to. I imagined that it was likely some kind of hangout for him, one worth checking out if I had any intention of finding him.

Quietly, I walked around to the steps. I peered down the dark well. At the bottom was the old red door. I could see pale streaks of light shining out from around the curtain that covered the small window towards the top.

Though I felt compelled to find Bo, for a minute, I reconsidered. Approaching the door felt wrong somehow, like I was stalking him or spying on him, overstepping bounds that we hadn't yet had a chance to set.

A voice in my head reminded me that if Bo had wanted to talk to me, he would've either called or answered his phone when I'd called. But he hadn't.

Then, as if helping me to make up my mind, Bo's tangy, soapy citrus scent wafted up the steps, creeping out from beneath the door to lure me in. I felt the invisible strings of it tugging at me, tugging at my guts.

Another muffled thump had me descending the steps. I raised my hand to knock on the door when movement caught my eye.

The curtain that covered the little window had been pushed to the side a tiny bit, leaving a small triangular opening through which I could see.

Inside, Bo was on his knees in the center of the concrete floor, kneeling on a black towel. He was shirtless and covered in blood spatter. Under the slimy red sheen, I could see a sickly greenish black color seeping across his chest, radiating from the left side outward. It was darkest over his heart and it pulsed as if gangrenous death was being pumped throughout his body with every slow squeeze of the muscle. That, however, was not the most alarming part. The thing that caught and held my attention was his face.

The blackness hadn't reached that high yet and his face wasn't covered in blood like the rest of him. I could see his skin perfectly. It was almost entirely translucent. I could make out the intricate webbing of his blood vessels as clearly as if they were drawn on the surface with an ink pen. But apart from the roadmap of his veins, there were other lines, deep cracks in the skin itself, like the damaged plaster of an ancient sculpture.

In the center of his face, I saw that his normally hypnotic eyes had been affected as well. Gone was that rich almost-black color, washed away by a milky pale green that nearly matched the whites of his eyes. Something in them looked completely wild, feral even, and they started a shudder in me that rippled throughout my entire body. Though I was afraid, I continued to watch Bo, unable to tear my eyes away from the window.

Bo moved, arching his back and letting his head fall back on his shoulders. He let out an agonizing howl that had the tendons in his neck straining beneath his bizarre skin. With a moan that bordered on a cry, he raised his right hand to his mouth. Bearing four elongated teeth, two on the top and two on the bottom, Bo sank his teeth into what looked like a bag of blood he'd been holding.

I watched in nauseous horror as he made sucking, chewing motions and devoured the contents of the bag, blood dripping off his chin and falling onto the towel. He closed his eyes. Pleasure was written all over his face, belied only by the trace frown that pinched his brows together, as if he was resented the euphoria, wanted to resist it.

My breath was coming in shallow pants and I felt a fearful sweat break out on my forehead. My heartbeat throbbed in my ears and pounded behind my eyes. I wanted to look away, but it was like watching a train wreck—I couldn't *not* watch. I was frozen, rooted to the spot where I peeped through the curtains.

Just when I thought for sure I was going to throw up, Bo quieted and his eyes snapped open. He turned his head a few degrees and looked right at me. I'm certain the surprise in his eyes mirrored the shock in my own, right before sheer panic set in.

Frozen no more, I turned and bolted up the steps. Behind me, I heard the sounds of the basement door opening and Bo bounding up the stairs behind me, but I didn't look back. I ran for all I was worth.

It seemed like it took me ten minutes to get to my car, though it couldn't have been more than a few seconds. My mad dash wasn't fast enough, though. When I opened the car door, Bo was standing in front of the hood, chest heaving, staring at me.

"Ridley, let me explain."

His voice was gravelly, like his throat was dry. I thought of the previous night and I shivered.

"Stay away from me," I shouted, slamming the door shut and starting the car.

When I flipped on my headlights, it only further illuminated the slick fluid covering Bo's body. With trembling hands, I jammed the shifter into reverse and sped backward down his driveway and out into the street.

On the way home, my mind raced incoherently. By the time I arrived at my house, instead of being less freaked out, I'd worked myself up into a bigger tizzy. I was convinced that Bo was some kind of evil, blood-sucking mass murderer that was on a killing spree and would now be coming after me.

The strange thing is that, all the while I was concocting terrible back stories for Bo, my heart yearned for him, my body ached for him. I didn't understand how my emotions and my body could be so disastrously disconnected from my head, from logic and rational thought.

Shouting a quick "I'm back" to Mom and Dad, I bypassed the living room and went straight to the bathroom. The mirror showed me that I'd cried on the way home. I hadn't been aware of any tears falling, but my swollen eyes and red face promised me they had.

I splashed cold water over my eyes and cheeks, wishing it was cold enough to numb the growing devastation I felt.

When I walked into my bedroom and shut the door behind me, the first thing I noticed was that it smelled of Bo. I was instantaneously filled with trepidation. I reached back for the knob, starting to twist it and run. My body was wired and readied for escape when a voice broke the stillness. Despite my inner turmoil, it flowed over my frazzled nerves like raw silk.

"Ridley, please let me explain."

Even in the darkness, I could plainly see him standing outside my open bedroom window, looking nothing like the person, the *thing,* I'd seen only minutes prior. Though he made no move toward me, I was still afraid of him. The screen was in place, but I knew it would provide very little protection if he decided to come in after me.

"If you don't leave this very second, I swear I'll go screaming out that door and call the police," I said warningly. The slight waver of my voice gave me away, however, a blatant indication that my bravado was superficial at best.

"Just give me—"

"I mean it, Bo," I declared, my voice rising as I pushed the words through my tight lips.

"Don't you—"

"I'm going," I said, turning to open the door.

"Wait, Ridley."

"I don't want to hear anything you have to say."

His next words caused my hand to still on the knob and my heart to constrict painfully inside my chest.

"I'm dying, Ridley."

CHAPTER SIX

"What?"

I could eek out no more than a whisper. My throat and my lungs failed me. I thought, I *prayed,* that my ears had failed me, too. Deceived me. Although at the moment I was terrified and confused by what I'd seen, it hadn't seemed to affect the way I felt about Bo deep down. Apparently, my heart hadn't gotten the memo.

"I'm dying," he repeated softly, sadly.

A crushing tide of devastation swept in to wash away the fear and disappointment I'd been feeling. Its violent current nearly erased all traces of the creature I'd seen only moments before, leaving only traces of a strange sickness that threatened the life of someone I didn't want to live without.

Slowly, I turned to face him. On the one hand, I was hesitant to believe him, especially after having seen him drinking blood.

"You could be lying," I pointed out.

"But I'm not."

"But I wouldn't know."

"Yes, you would."

On the other hand, I wanted desperately for it to be true, if for no other reason than that it meant he wasn't a monster. It just wouldn't be right, wouldn't be *normal,* to fall in love with a monster.

But if he wasn't a monster, then that meant he was dying. As the room slanted this way and that, tilting all around me, I realized that it would be far better to fall in love with a monster than to lose Bo altogether.

Walking to the bed, I perched on the edge, staring down at my hands, wondering what I should do now, what I should say. Bo took care of that dilemma when he pushed on the screen until it popped out and then crawled carefully through my window.

He stopped just inside it and leaned up against the frame, sure to maintain a safe distance from me, one that wouldn't make me feel threatened. Whether he knew it or not, his thoughtful consideration of my feelings put me at ease more than anything he could ever have said.

"You're sick?"

I asked the question as gently as I could, as if speaking the words quietly would make them less true, less concrete.

"Can we turn on some music so that your parents won't hear us talking?"

"Oh," I said, getting up to dock my iPhone. "Good idea."

I selected a random play list of soft music so that it would provide background noise, but not be annoying to us or to my parents. That would defeat the purpose entirely.

The first song to play was an old 80's ballad that sang of dying in someone's arms. I wanted to cringe. Bo and I looked at each other, he on one side of the room, me on the other. I thought about changing it, but I didn't want to be too obvious, so I just restarted the conversation.

"Are you really dying?"

I pushed decorum and tact aside in favor of getting answers, answers I needed more than I needed food or water.

Bo nodded. I felt the air close in around me like thick soup—too thick to breathe.

"What is it? I mean, what's wrong?"

"Over the last few years, do you remember hearing about some of the victims in Southmoore that they thought were being attacked by animals, but then discovered it was a person doing it? The Southmoore Slayer?"

A leaden ball of dread began to swell in the pit of my stomach. "Yeah."

"Well, that's what happened to me."

"You were attacked?"

"Yes."

"When? Do you know who did it?"

"It's been three years now," Bo said.

"What happened?"

Moving from his position against the window, Bo walked to my desk and picked up a clear glass heart-shaped paperweight. He toyed with it, rolling it from one palm to the other and back again.

"My father and I were hunting at the edge of Arlisle Preserve. We'd just gone into the woods and it was still dark outside. I heard some noises and thought it might be a deer moving around." He paused. "But it wasn't."

"What was it?"

"Who," he corrected.

"Who was it then?"

Bo looked at me intently for several seconds before turning his attention back to the heart. He answered me. "I don't know, but I'm getting closer to finding out."

I thought of the previous night, when Trent Long had come to visit. "Does it have anything to do with Trent Long?"

Bo's head snapped up. "How did you know about him?"

"I saw him at your house then I saw his picture on the news. He's dead," I said swallowing. "Did you have something to do with that?"

"Ridley, you have to understand—"

"Ohmigod, you did!" I couldn't help but take a step back, away from him, away from the truth, but the wall was behind me. There was nowhere to go.

"I think he killed my father," Bo said, breaking into my rising panic.

"What?"

"Whoever attacked us killed my father and only managed to...*infect* me."

"Infect you? Is it-is it contagious?"

"Not in the way you're thinking."

I shook my head, trying to focus on one thing at a time. "But you killed somebody, Bo," I cried.

"He wasn't human, Ridley. None of them are."

Mouth agape, I stared at Bo in stunned confusion. "What are you saying?"

"They were—" Bo stopped suddenly, sighing. Palming the glass heart in one hand, he ran the other through his hair in frustrated indecision.

"They?" This was getting worse by the second. My mind scrambled for something safe and sane to latch onto, but it found nothing.

"Ridley, all I've done is rid the world of killers, cold-blooded killers. They were all- they were—"

He stopped again, as if still considering whether or not he wanted to tell me. I wondered, doubted, that I really wanted to know what he was going to say, but he'd already begun. I couldn't let him change his mind now.

"Were what?"

"Ridley, they were vampires." He paused. "Just like me."

"They were *what?*"

My voice sounded shrill in the confines of my room.

"Vampires," he repeated quietly.

"You think- you think you're a vampire?"

Bo nodded.

"Bo, I hate to break it to you, but there are no such things as vampires."

"That's what I used to think, too."

My mouth opened and closed like a fish's. I had no idea what to say to that, but I thought it was probably a good time for him to leave.

"Maybe you should go," I suggested as calmly as I could. I certainly didn't want to make a crazy person angry.

"You don't believe me," he said, more a statement of fact than an accusation.

Duh was the first thing that came to mind, but I swallowed it. "Did you honestly expect me to believe something like that?"

He shrugged. "I don't know. I've never told anyone before."

All things considered, I thought it was pretty remarkable that he managed to make me feel guilty. But he did exactly that.

I relaxed a bit against the wall. My head was pounding, my pulse throbbing dully behind my eyes. I pinched the bridge of my nose and sighed.

Maybe I should try a different tack, let him say what he needed to say and then pray that he left. I'd always heard that you shouldn't try to talk an unbalanced person into reality. I'd heard that you should just go along with their delusions.

"Is that why you were so bloody tonight? You were-were…"

Bo nodded. "There was someone I had to take care of."

"Because this person was a vampire."

Bo nodded again.

"And you think you're a vampire."

Again, a nod.

"Alright, so you say you are, in fact, a vampire. Let's just go with that for a minute. If I'm not mistaken, vampires are dead. Yet you told me not five minutes ago that you're dying. How do you explain that?"

"Well, first of all vampires aren't technically dead right from the start. We can 'die'," he said, using air quotes. "But we can only die the same way once. The venom, it mutates our cells, our DNA, causing us to regenerate very quickly. When we do, we're sort of immune to whatever harmed or killed us. We can no longer be killed that way, not again."

"So these people that you killed, you think they'll…come back?"

"Oh, no. They're very much dead."

"Wait a minute," I said, shaking my head. "Then how did you kill Trent Long? I'm confused. "

"The only way you can actually, *truly* kill a vampire. I destroyed his heart."

"Well, if that's the case then what do you mean when you say you're dying?"

Bo returned his attention to the heart in his hand. He leaned back against the desk and held it up to the moonlight pouring through the window, peering through the thick bubbles of heart-shaped glass. He didn't speak until he lowered it.

"I know I'm dying because I'm killing myself."

My heart lurched in my chest. I wasn't expecting that.

"What? Why?"

"The very last blood that pours from a vampire's heart contains memories of his life, his knowledge, his experiences. But it's toxic. Very toxic. These men that I hunt, one of them will lead me to the person behind my father's murder, but to learn that, I have to drain them before I kill them."

Out of all that, out of all the questions that his explanation generated, the only thing I could think of was that he was killing himself. For a moment, I was drawn into his world of make believe.

"So you're killing yourself to learn who killed your father?"

"Yes."

"Your life is worth so little to you that you'd just throw it away for revenge?" That hurt more than I was ready to acknowledge.

Bo looked up at me, his eyes meeting mine in the low light of the room. As they did the first time I saw him, they burned into me, searing me all the way to my soul.

"I had nothing to live for until I met you."

Despite what he was telling me, despite the fact that he was crazy or sick or deranged or something, my heart swelled inside my chest. It was as if he held *my heart* in his hand rather than the glass paperweight. It was no longer mine to control. And it felt just as fragile.

That's when it hit me. What if he's telling the truth? The way he looked in the basement, he barely looked human at all. What if vampires really are real?

"But you said the only way to kill a vampire is to destroy his heart."

"Correct."

"So you should be fine then, right? I mean, you should…come back," I said, searching for the right phrase.

"The poison attacks the organs, Ridley. Including the heart." His expression was grave, hopeless.

"Is that why you looked the way you did earlier?"

Bo nodded, dropping his head in either shame or embarrassment. I wasn't sure which. "It's worse for a day or two after I drink the…the poison."

"Well, can't you just stop?" Finally, I felt brave enough to step toward him. "Can't you just let it go, let them go, before it's too late? Can't you just… live?"

Bo shook his head sadly, lowering his gaze once more to the heart he held in his hand.

"It's not that easy."

"Why? Why can't it be exactly that easy?"

"I've taken in too much of their blood. I can tell that it's killing me. The human blood that I drink, from the blood bank, is barely keeping me alive now and I don't know how much longer that will last," he confessed. "I'm having to drink more and more, but still this form wears down that much more quickly."

"This form? What do you mean?"

"We—vampires—regenerate so quickly, our cells multiply and divide so fast, that they have a translucent appearance once we've metabolized our food. Kind of like we're in a constant state of flux, like we're growing too fast for light or human eyes to track," he explained. "But the blood that I drink is used up fighting off the effects of the poison most of the time, so I can't maintain a human appearance for as long as others."

A sinking feeling began in the pit of my stomach and seeped into my arms and legs, making them feel like lead, like dead weight. "What do you look like when it wears off, when the poison's gone and the blood's gone?" Even after the question was out, I wasn't sure I wanted to know the answer.

Bo's lips curled up into a bitter, mirthless twist. "Invisible. I look like nothing."

I knew that answer alone would spawn hundreds of questions, but right now my focus was on his demise and just how imminent it was.

"So, what will happen when you," I paused, swallowing the enormous lump in my throat. "When you die?"

Bo looked out the window. "I don't know. The only information I've been able to find out about it is that draining a vampire will kill you, poison you. That's it." He shrugged. "Nothing else ever mattered until now. The only thing I cared about was finding out who killed my father."

"How long do you have until…"

"I don't know that either, but I'd say not very long."

I felt the sting of tears and, though I blinked them back, there was no stopping the drops of heartbreak as they welled in my eyes.

The words to the song that had begun to play stabbed at my soul. The sad voice of a woman singing of doomed love resonated within me. Though they had little time, she had a love for him so strong that wild horses couldn't drag her away.

"There has to be something that we can do," I said, trying to still my trembling chin.

A look of sheer agony crossed Bo's face as he laid the glass heart back on the desk and crossed the room to me. Slowly, gently, he pulled me into his arms. He was giving me the chance to pull away, to turn away, and my heart wrenched all the more at his tenderness.

"This is why I should've stayed away from you," he whispered against my hair.

"Don't even say that. I wouldn't have traded this time—however much we have—for anything," I said, leaning back to meet his eyes. "Not for anything."

Bo's eyes searched my face for a few seconds before he lowered his lips to mine. He kissed me with such sweetness, such hopeless softness, that my throat constricted even further. When a light saltiness reached my tongue, I knew that my tears had finally overwhelmed my eyes and spilled down my cheeks, mingling with our kiss.

Bo dragged his lips away and leaned his forehead against mine, his eyes still closed.

"I wish I could just walk away from you. Just walk away and leave you alone, to live your life," he breathed.

"You can't save me from pain, Bo," I cried.

"I can when I'm the one who brought pain into your life."

"You think you're the only pain I've known? I know all about pain and loss," I said, pulling back once more to look into his eyes. "My sister died in a car accident three years ago and *I* was with her. *I* survived when I shouldn't have and everyone in my life wishes it had been the other way around. I might as well have lost my entire family in that accident, so I know all about loss." I reached up and touched his face, which was burning hot. "But even after that, after surviving all that, I don't think I could survive losing you, Bo. Not you. Not you," I sighed, leaning my head against his chest.

I felt his arms come around me again, hugging me close to his feverish body.

"You're burning up," I murmured. "Is that part of it?"

"Sort of. My temperature will run hot while I metabolize the blood I just drank. When my body starts to cool, I know I need to feed soon."

That explained a lot about his widely varied body temperature. Until recently, I must've always seen him when he was nearing a feeding.

"So I guess you feed before school and it wears off throughout the day?"

"Yeah. A couple of times I've had to run home in the middle of the day. It just depends on what's going on."

"What do you mean?"

"Well, if I exert a lot or get overly excited, I burn more energy."

Bo was rubbing his hand slowly up and down my arm and, even in these terrible circumstances, I felt a tiny flame of desire flicker to life deep in my belly.

"So when you say excited, what kinds of things do you mean?"

I heard Bo's breath hitch in his chest. When he finally let it out, it hissed through his pursed lips.

"Let's not talk about that right now. You're liable to get a first hand look at what happens."

Bo pushed me back to arm's length and took a step away from me. When I looked into his eyes, I knew why. He was feeling the same kindling of passion that I was and he was struggling to resist it.

We were saved from further temptation when my father called my name from the living room.

I yelled in answer, mainly to keep him from coming in search of me.

"Coming!" When Bo cringed, I cast him a sheepish look. "Sorry."

He grinned and my heart skipped a couple of beats.

"No problem. I should've known, being a cheerleader, that you'd have some serious lungs on you," he teased. "I guess that's my cue to leave, huh?"

Before I could answer, he turned and walked back to the window.

"Will I see you tomorrow?" I was anxious, almost fearful, to let him out of my sight, afraid that I wouldn't see him again.

Bo stopped at the window, still facing away from me. "Are you sure this is what you want?"

Every fiber of my being cried out in answer, even before I could get the word off my lips. "Yes."

Bo looked back at me and smiled, a breathtaking lift of his lips that said he was pleased with my answer. I couldn't help but smile in return. "Then yes, you'll see me tomorrow. I'll call you, ok?"

"Ok," I said, walking to the window.

"Ridley!" Dad shouted again.

I turned my head toward the door this time, so that I wouldn't blast Bo.

"Coming!"

When I turned back to the window, Bo was gone.

CHAPTER SEVEN

The next morning, I woke with the most confused feelings I'd ever had. I was elated that Bo and I had talked. It seemed he was feeling the same thing for me that I was for him, whatever that "thing" was. But on the other hand, I was beyond distraught that he was dying and there was nothing I could do to stop it. I wanted to laugh and cry at the same time. I ended up doing neither. Instead, I got up and showered to get ready for church.

Just over an hour later, as I walked down the aisle, I realized that it was the first time since Izzy's death that I'd actually wanted to be there. I finally felt like I needed God, like I wanted Him in my life. I'd purposely avoided Him since the accident three years ago. I hadn't wanted to have anything to do with God in a long, long time.

I guess it was both sad and disgusting that I would wait until I needed something to go to Him, but at least I was going. I'd been to church enough to know that *going* was the main thing. Most people put it off, but when they finally make up their mind to go, most of them do it when they're at the end of their rope. Unfortunately, that's the nature of humanity.

All through the service, I prayed intermittently, listening with half an ear to the sermon about redemption and eternal life. At the end, when the pastor performed his standard altar call, I shuffled down the pew and walked quickly up the aisle to kneel at the base of the pulpit.

With every ounce of my soul, I reached out and I begged for divine intervention for Bo. I knew that nothing was impossible for God and that if He willed it, Bo would live. I didn't know how, but I knew it could happen, and at this point, I was willing to try virtually anything.

On the way home, I noticed that, also for the first time since Izzy's death, I didn't feel like a pretender. I watched Mom and Dad interact in the front seat. I listened to them tiptoe around any subject with the slightest bit of significance. It was like seeing two actors film a made-for-TV movie about the humdrum life of a humdrum southern family. There was no depth, no genuineness, no truth. There was only the façade, the superficial veneer I'd come to know so well.

Back at the house, I was surprised when Dad came knocking on my bedroom door right after we got home, telling me that I had a visitor. Not having heard an engine, I assumed it was Bo. My heart beat in an excited tap dance at the mere prospect of seeing him.

The sun was shining brightly, but it was a cool day, another indication that fall had arrived. I quickly changed into jeans and a long sleeve t-shirt that said *Sweet Baby Ray's* across the front, pushed my feet into my Sketchers and hurried out the door.

My smile faltered a bit when I saw Drew standing in the foyer instead of Bo.

"Oh, Drew. Hi," I said, trying to recover.

"Expecting someone else?"

His tone was sharp and he was eyeing me suspiciously. I doubted that anyone else would've been able to detect the venom in his tone, but trust me, it was there.

"No, I'm just surprised. That's all," I said, coming to a stop several feet from him. "What are you doing here?"

"You said we'd talk later," he said, shrugging. "Is this 'later' enough?"

"Yeah," I replied, shaking my head. "Of course."

"Let's take a ride," he suggested.

A tiny twinge of apprehension shot down my spine, but I reminded myself that this was Drew. We'd dated for over a year and I knew him well. I had nothing to fear.

I thought of my phone and how Bo was supposed to be calling me today, but I knew that I shouldn't go back to my room for it. If Bo called while I was with Drew, it was sure to make matters worse. Much worse. So, in the interest of preserving relations with Drew, I left it.

"Alright," I finally said, preceding Drew to the door. Before I opened it, I stopped and called out to my parents. "I'm taking a ride with Drew. I'll be back in a little while."

I heard a mumbled acknowledgment coming from somewhere in the vicinity of the kitchen. That was about the most response I could expect, so I left.

At the car, it didn't escape my notice that, unlike Bo, Drew didn't bother opening the door for me. I climbed in the passenger side and he slid in behind the wheel. Wordlessly, he started the engine, pulled out of the driveway and then we sped off down the street.

After we'd traveled several miles, I had to break the increasingly uncomfortable silence.

"Where are we going?"

"Just riding," he responded.

The narrow back road we were on was a winding two-lane that led to Arlisle Preserve and, beyond that, to Southmoore.

"So, what did you do last night?" I tried to put my focus elsewhere. I hated this road because it's the one Izzy wrecked on.

"Went to Josh's to work on the Mustang." His answer, like his attitude, was short and clipped.

I nodded. "Is it close to being finished?"

Drew sighed loudly. "Ridley, I don't want to talk about a stupid car."

"Then talk about something else."

"Fine," he snapped, shifting up into third to take a curve entirely too fast.

"Drew, slow down."

"Don't tell me how to drive, Ridley. You gave up that privilege."

"Drew—"

"Don't 'Drew' me," he warned, accelerating through yet another curve. "The only thing I want to hear from you is the truth."

"I told you the truth, Drew."

"No, you didn't. I want to hear you admit that this is about that freak, Bowman," he spat.

"Drew, Bo has—"

"Don't lie to me, Ridley," he shouted, the tires squealing as he rounded a hair pin curve without even so much as tapping the brakes.

I gripped the edges of my seat tightly. "I'm not lying, Drew. Please slow down," I begged.

"You've got a thing for the new guy and I want to hear you admit it," Drew said, his voice booming inside the confines of the car.

As he took another corner at a dangerous speed, the back tires slipped off the road and we skidded in the gravel. The car fishtailed alarmingly and I felt my heart flopping fearfully in my throat.

My head was plastered to the head rest as I pushed my feet into the floorboard.

"Alright, Drew. I admit it. I have feelings for Bo," I confessed.

"I knew it," Drew hissed.

"But it had nothing to do with us. My feelings for Bo came after," I continued. "I swear."

And that was true. While I might have been intrigued by Bo, a bit taken with him, my feelings for him had been child's play compared to what they are now.

Drew said nothing. I looked over at him to gauge his reaction, but I couldn't read his expression. I was not inclined to believe that my confession had helped, however, when I saw the tight set of his lips.

"I never meant to hurt you, Drew," I declared, putting as much truth and feeling into the statement as I possibly could. "I—"

My words were cut off when I saw the deer from the corner of my eye. A horrible and unwelcome sense of déjà vu swept over me. I'd been through this before and I knew I only had a fraction of a second to react before it jumped in front of us.

"Drew!"

My cry didn't help. As if in slow motion, the deer leapt from the trees up onto the road. I heard Drew's sharp inhalation right before he jerked the steering wheel with both hands to avoid the deer.

We began to spin and I squeezed my eyes shut and held onto the seat so tightly my fingers ached.

I felt it when the two wheels on the driver's side left the pavement. It was as if the entire world tilted toward me for an instant before we started rolling. I braced myself as much as I could and held my breath.

As if the sounds played in my head from a distant recording, I heard the crunch of metal and the breaking of glass right before I felt a sharp pinch in my stomach just as the car came to a halt on its side in the woods. The reason I knew we were in the woods is that, when I opened my eyes, part of a tree branch was sticking through the windshield.

Shaken and confused, I looked around.

The car had come to rest on the passenger side. Drew was unconscious and dangling from his seatbelt, his arms lolling lifelessly toward me. If I unfastened his seatbelt, he would no doubt fall right on top of me.

"Drew," I called. No response.

"Drew," I said, more loudly this time. Still no response.

I tried to move, but something was holding me in my seat. The seatbelt strap was on the left side of my chest rather than my right, so I reached down to unbuckle it. When I did, I stared in confusion at the tree branch that was coming through the windshield. It seemed to disappear right into my body, into my left side.

At first I didn't understand how that was possible. I thought maybe the branch had broken off and it was just pressed against my body, looking as if it disappeared inside me. I thought surely if I was impaled, it would hurt. Right? I'd probably be unconscious, too. Right?

When I tried to move out from around the branch, pain lanced through my back and side. Thinking I'd move the branch instead, I pulled at it in one sharp tug. Blood oozed out from around it.

Following the sight of that branch shifting inside my stomach, a surge of adrenaline flooded my body and burned away the fog that had settled over me. As the haze lifted, there was a moment—a single moment of perfect clarity—when I realized that the branch was indeed deeply imbedded in my abdomen and that if I didn't find a way to get us some help, I was in serious, *serious* trouble.

I fought against the hysteria that welled up inside me, knowing it was imperative that I keep my wits about me. We could die if I didn't. I knew from experience. Sort of.

I closed my eyes and took a deep, cleansing breath, deep enough to make my side start to hurt again. I cringed in pain. When I reopened my eyes, it was to see a pale face hovering over the hood of the car. In it was a hauntingly familiar pair of eyes, eyes I'd seen in a similar circumstance three years ago. Only today, I recognized them. They were Bo's.

A flash of relief was followed by even more confusion. I thought to myself that it couldn't have been Bo's eyes I'd seen that night so long ago. It just couldn't have been.

"Stay still," he cautioned.

I nodded, fending off a surreal sense of disorientation that was threatening to swallow me up.

Bo crept carefully up to the car and looked in to assess me. His face was a tight mask, but I thought I probably knew why. The sight and smell of my blood was likely very hard for him to tolerate.

"How did you find me?"

"Google maps." Obviously, he felt the need to lighten the mood. Why, I don't know.

Turning his attention to Drew, Bo reached through the broken windshield and checked his pulse.

"Is he alive?"

"Yeah," Bo confirmed. "Just at a glance, I don't think his injuries are that severe. Probably hit his head after the airbag went off, when you rolled. Yours must've been punctured by the tree," he concluded.

Backing away from the car, Bo disappeared for a few seconds. I heard the rustle of leaves and gravel as he moved around. When he reappeared, his expression was grave.

"Ridley, I'm going to get you out, but you're gonna to have to trust me, ok?"

I nodded.

"The branch is still attached to the tree. I have to break it off so I can pull it out of you, ok?"

Again, I nodded.

"It's gonna hurt," he warned.

I looked out at the piece of wood protruding from my left side and I felt my heartbeat speed up in fear and dread.

"Ridley, look at me." When I looked up into the eyes that plagued me day and night, I felt a strange sense of calm permeate me, body and mind. "You're going to be fine. I promise."

I nodded again, believing his words despite what my eyes saw as a life-threatening injury and an impossible situation.

Once more, Bo disappeared. I heard some crackling and then a loud snap followed by a jarring to my side that felt like it was pulling my guts out. My head swam dizzily, the pain was so incredible. I bit my lip to keep from crying out.

When Bo popped up in front of the windshield again, the air he stirred cooled the clammy sheen that was covering my face.

Bo's brow was furrowed in obvious worry. He reached in and cupped my cheek.

"Hang in there. It's almost over," he said softly.

He dropped his hand and I saw him wrap his fingers around the branch up close to where it entered my body. I took a deep breath, trying to steel myself against what was coming. Bo looked at me and I nodded, giving him a silent go-ahead.

"I'm so sorry," he whispered, closing his eyes.

Then, with a quick and violent jerk, Bo yanked the huge stick from my side. It hurt, but no worse than it had when he'd broken the branch from the other end. I looked down to make sure it was gone and what I saw made my stomach churn nauseously.

Dark red blood was gushing from the hole in my side. I felt the warm wetness of it all down my hip and stomach and between my legs where it pooled. Strictly from the amount of blood I was losing, I knew the tree had pierced something important, either an artery or my spleen. Not surprisingly, at that moment I was not very successful at retrieving information from my anatomy class.

I looked up at Bo and he was staring at the blood, his face looking paler, his skin thinner than usual. Right before my eyes, it seemed to become more and more translucent. I wanted to touch it, but I was finding it increasingly difficult just to focus on his face, much less touch it. It was already blurring before my eyes. My head was growing lighter by the second, as if someone was lowering a dimmer switch on my consciousness and I was slowly fading into darkness.

"Bo," I whispered, short of breath, too.

Bo's abnormally pale green eyes flickered up to mine and through my wavy vision, I could see the instant that he returned to me from whatever hungered state he'd been in, like he was seeing me for the first time. As I watched, I saw the color seep back into his irises, assuring me he was Bo once again.

"Hold on," he said, reaching in to release my seatbelt and snatch me from the car.

Even if I hadn't been hovering between consciousness and oblivion, I doubt I would've been able to keep up with where we were going. Bo carried me deep into the woods, whipping through the trees and across the uneven terrain at a speed I knew wasn't humanly possible.

"Hospital," I managed breathlessly. I knew I needed serious medical attention.

Finally Bo stopped and lowered me gently to the ground. His face doubled in front of my eyes and I blinked to bring him back into focus.

"Ridley, you need to drink from me. If you don't, you'll die before I can get you help," he said, sounding like he was a million miles away.

"Then we can be together," I whispered.

I felt my lips pull up into a weak smile at the thought of being with Bo somewhere, *anywhere,* for eternity.

"Ridley," he barked. "Stop it! You're not dying. You're not leaving me."

I blinked my heavy lids, trying to keep them open long enough to look into Bo's one last time.

"It's alright," I said.

"No, it's not. Open your mouth," he ordered, sinking his teeth into his bare forearm.

With every passing second, I was exponentially more exhausted. I didn't think I could open my mouth like he wanted me to. I tried, but my jaw just wouldn't work.

"Ridley!"

I felt rough fingers at my cheeks, pinching them together to force my lips open.

A drop of tepid liquid hit my tongue and the taste of it, both salty and sweet, was the most amazing thing I could ever remember tasting, though it did seem vaguely familiar. I smacked my dry lips together and managed to open my mouth the tiniest bit, feeling a ravenous thirst for more of the thick fluid.

Several drops hit my tongue and I closed my mouth to swallow. I felt something cool press against my lips and I opened my eyes a crack. Bo was holding his forearm over my mouth, a panicked expression on his handsome face.

"Drink," he said simply.

I opened my lips and wrapped them around his skin and sucked, drawing a pool of his blood onto my tongue. It made my mouth feel warm and tingly, and my throat as well, as it traveled down.

I'm not sure how long he fed me that way. I'm pretty sure that I passed out at least twice, maybe more. Little snatches of time were lost to me, but the one thing that never changed, never left me, was Bo. I could hear his shallow breathing. I could taste him on my tongue. I could feel him inside my veins, as if I'd taken in some living part of him that was now a part of me.

Little by little, I felt energy, feeling, *life,* return to my body, but as it did, an overwhelming need to sleep began to drag at my eyelids. I fought it, wanting to stay with Bo, to spend every available second with him, staring into his eyes.

I knew when I'd lost the battle. Like drawing the curtains across a window, my lids fell and blocked Bo from my view. Just before I drifted off, I heard him whisper, "Rest." And then there was nothing.

****

Some time later, a cold hand to my face and Bo's voice woke me. I opened my eyes and looked around. Though my eyes told me I was alone, my body told me Bo was near.

"Bo?"

"I'm here," he said, taking my hand in his.

The sun was setting and the forest floor was dappled with the golden light of a dying day. To my right, where Bo's voice and touch was coming from, I saw the tall, gilded trees shimmer, like I was looking at them through the distorting waves of heat you see coming off of hot pavement.

I sat up and looked more closely. Raising my other hand, I reached toward it. I jerked a little when I made contact with something solid and cool, but then I realized it was skin I felt. I rubbed my hand over it, feeling the crinkly tickle of hair against my palm.

As I sculpted the curves and dips, I realized that I was touching Bo's chest. His naked chest. I paused and laid my spread fingers flat over his left pectoral. I could feel the excited patter of his heart.

"Ridley," he groaned, part in warning, part in pleasure.

The sound of my name on his lips, with that hint of need in it so clear and plain, sent a surge of desire rippling through my core.

Slowly, I let my palm trail across his chest and down his belly. I jumped when his icy hand grabbed my wrist.

"Stop," he ground out. His voice was notably strained.

"Sorry," I muttered, pulling my hand away. The only thing I was honestly sorry about, though, was that I had to stop. "Where is your shirt?"

"You're wearing it."

I looked down and, sure enough, Bo had slipped his rugby shirt on over my own. When I inhaled, my nostrils were filled with his scent and I thought I might never give his shirt back.

"Oh." I looked back up and "through" Bo and I could see that a pile of clothes lay just behind him in the leaves. "Whose are those?"

"Mine," he answered.

"You're not wearing any clothes?" A flush of heat stung my cheeks. Although I was a little embarrassed, the red stain had much more to do with the other things I was feeling.

"How would it look when the ambulance gets here if they see jeans and a rugby shirt walking around without a person inside them?"

I considered that scenario for just a moment. "Good point." When it sank in, what he'd said, I asked, "Ambulance?"

"Yeah. I went to check on Connors and found his cell phone at the edge of the trees. I guess it got thrown when you flipped. I called 911."

"When will they be here? What should I tell them?"

"Crap," he said under his breath. "I'd say they'll be here in the next five or ten minutes."

It took me a few seconds to put it together, but I assume that he had glanced down at his watch before realizing that he'd taken it off with the rest of his clothes. That's why the "crap" comment. The whole situation was almost comical. Almost.

I asked a second time. "What should I tell them?"

"Just tell them what happened and that you crawled out of the car and found the cell phone and then called for help."

He made a noise, as if he'd started to say something, but changed his mind.

I'd discovered I didn't like him keeping things from me. Bo's secrets tended to be a pretty big deal, so I prompted, "What?"

"Well, they'll probably want to check you out."

"Yeah. So?"

"Well, it might be a good idea if you got rid of that bloody shirt with a hole in it and just wore mine."

"Oh. Good idea," I said. At least someone was thinking. I was still having trouble getting rid of the image of a naked Bo only a few inches away.

"Would you mind if I checked your side?"

I didn't have to see his face to know that's what he'd been hesitant to ask. He was so careful with me, so considerate of me. I just smiled and shook my head.

"Let me help you up," Bo said, tugging on my hand.

I stood and pulled Bo's shirt over my head. "Here. Hold this," I said, holding his shirt out in his general direction. He took it and the shirt just hung there as if suspended in mid air. I tucked the vision away for later, when I'd likely pull it out and remember, with awe and wonder, what crazy things I'd seen in my life since I'd met Bo.

I took a deep breath and sucked in my stomach before reaching for the hem of my tattered t-shirt and peeling it up to my shoulders. I was careful not to get more blood all over me, though it wasn't too difficult since most of the blood had already dried.

As I pulled the shirt over my head and shook my hair loose, I became aware of heat traveling up my stomach and across my breasts. Even though I couldn't see them, I could actually feel Bo's eyes on me, like he was touching everything I was exposing. It was incredibly unnerving, but one of the most erotic things I've ever experienced.

Letting my shirt dangle from my fingertips, I raised my arms over my head and turned slightly to the side so Bo could look at my belly.

My abdominals clenched when I felt his fingertips brush lightly over the bloody skin where a hole had been not so long ago.

"Give me your shirt," Bo said, his voice hoarse and low, not much more than a deep rumble in the quiet forest.

I handed him my shirt and I watched as he used one of the clean spots on it to rub as much of the residual blood from me as he could. He was so close I could feel his cool breath on my skin and a rash of chills broke out across my stomach and chest.

I closed my eyes and let the stimulation of my senses flood my mind. I could hear Bo's shallow breathing. I could feel the gentle rasp of cotton on my skin. I could smell Bo's tangy scent enveloping me. My body tingled and throbbed with every beat of my heart.

Though I couldn't see him, in my mind's eye, I could plainly see Bo's head at my navel, as if it played like a movie against the backs of my lids. It wasn't hard to let my imagination rewrite the scene in a much different way.

I saw Bo's arms wrap around me and I felt his lips on my skin. I felt his thick hair running through my fingers and his rough palms against my bare breasts.

Warmth poured through my veins as I lost myself to the fantasy. When Bo spoke, his voice startled me.

"Ridley, if we're gonna make it out of here, you're gonna have to stop thinking about stuff like that."

I felt heat rush into my cheeks. How could he know what I was thinking?

"Stuff like what?"

"Stuff like what you were thinking. This is hard enough for me as it is, without that," he said.

"How could you possibly know what I was thinking?"

"I can smell it on you. It saturates your blood with hormones and heats it up," he explained. "And it's driving me crazy."

If possible, even more heat scorched my cheeks. I'm sure they were probably beet red.

"I- I—" I stuttered, not knowing what to say.

I saw his shimmer as he stood. He was so close I knew that I could nip his chin with my teeth without moving more than an inch.

"And knowing that my blood is pumping through your body, that a part of me is inside you," he paused, his sigh a shaky puff of air that tickled my face. "It's killing me."

His words poured through my veins like lava, making my knees weak and my skin flush.

"Bo," I groaned.

I felt it when he stepped back.

Bo thrust his shirt at me. "Here, put this on and get to the road. They're coming."

In the quiet, I could hear the wail of sirens from far away. As I pulled Bo's shirt on, I heard him turn and walk through the woods and then I saw his pile of clothes rise into the air, as if by magic.

"I'll see you later," he called softly and then he was gone.

When I could hear Bo no longer, I turned and made my way toward Drew's car. I had no trouble finding it; I could smell it. He'd always kept a cherry scented air freshener hanging from the rearview mirror and I followed the aroma through the forest like a trail of bread crumbs.

I jogged easily through the woods, feeling more energetic than ever. Once I got to within a few hundred yards of the car, I could see it—clearly, as if I was standing near it in the bright light of day, even though dusk had almost given way to night.

The ambulance pulled up a couple of minutes after I arrived at the car and, as Bo suspected, they immediately wanted to give me a thorough once-over. Luckily, because I was walking around and making sense and I didn't appear to be bleeding, they didn't dig too deeply (like underneath my clothes). One of the cops who accompanied the EMTs did, however, dig into my story as he drove me back to my house.

When a cop dropped me off at the house, I got the fifth degree from Mom and Dad, which surprised me. I think it brought back terrible memories for them. I'm sure they were terrified of losing another child in a car accident, even if that child was like a phantom houseguest to them most of the time.

When they finally fulfilled their parental obligations, they let me go to my room. I pushed the door shut behind me and leaned back against it, closing my eyes and breathing a sigh of relief. My room was my sanctuary.

The air smelled stagnant and made me feel claustrophobic, so I walked to my window to raise it. Before I reached it, I heard the screech of wood scraping against a metal track as my window rose.

My feet faltered and I slowed, creeping closer to the window. Just as I stopped in front of it, the intoxicating scent of Bo assailed me and I felt that bone-deep yearning that so often overcame me when he was near.

"Bo?"

"I'm here," he said from somewhere outside my window.

"Did you just—"

I trailed off. Of course he did. How else would my window get raised?

"What?"

"Nothing," I said.

I saw the screen pop out and then heard the shuffling sounds of him crawling through the window. I wondered about how he'd gotten the window up through the screen, but the thought was lost as soon as Bo started walking toward me. I couldn't see him, but my nerves stirred with every step he took in my direction. It made the hairs on my arms stand at attention.

"I wanted to make sure you were alright," he said, coming to stand in front of me. He was so close, I could feel the coolness of his body radiating toward me, like standing in front of an open refrigerator door.

"I'm fine." And that was entirely true now that he was here. "I see that you didn't go home," I said, referring to his transparency.

"I wanted to keep any eye on you until you got home safely." Gently, he rubbed the backs of his fingers over my side, where I'd been impaled. Even through his shirt, my skin felt chilled. "How does it feel?"

"Fine, like it always has. It doesn't even hurt," I assured him. I left out any mention of how his touch was affecting the rest of me.

Bo lifted up the edge of his shirt and slid his fingertips along my skin.

"Yow! Your hands are like ice," I yelped.

Bo jerked his hand back as if I'd slapped him. "Sorry," he mumbled.

I felt him step back from me, and I instantly regretted my reaction. I stepped toward him to close the gap between us. I wrapped my arms around his neck and pressed my body to his, goose bumps breaking out all over my skin. I steeled myself against the cold, determined not to shiver.

"Bo, you're freezing. How long can you stay like this? Without food?"

"A while."

I could hear the weakness in his voice, feel the little tremor that vibrated through his body.

A solution occurred to me, one that brought a hint of fear and dread, but one that I felt compelled to offer.

"Could you, um, drink from me?"

Again, Bo jerked back as if I'd hurt him. "No!"

His reaction made me feel dirty or unsavory, like the thought of drinking my blood was somehow repugnant to him.

"Why?" I couldn't keep the hurt from my voice.

"I will never do that," he spat.

"But why? You need blood. I can give you that, just like you gave me yours."

"I don't drink from humans. Only killers and monsters do that."

I felt ashamed for even having suggested it, though my motives had been pure.

I didn't understand his reaction. He was a vampire. Vampires drink blood. He needed blood. I had blood. What was I missing?

"You've never taken blood from a human?"

"I drink blood donated to the blood bank," he replied, not really answering my question at all.

"Have you always done that? I mean, you've never had it from a real live person?"

Bo's hesitation answered my question before he even opened his mouth.

"Ah," I said, comprehension dawning and bringing with it more hurt. "You just don't want my blood."

Bo's voice was tender and sincere when he responded. "If I drank from humans, you would be the only person I'd want to drink from."

"Then why don't you?"

"I just," he paused, sighing. I heard a rasping sound and I knew he was running his fingers through his hair. "I did, once. But I promised myself I'd never do it again. And I haven't. It's like poison of a different kind, poison for your soul."

I tried not to be frustrated by his not-an-answer answers. "I'm assuming you don't want to talk about it."

"It's not my favorite topic, no."

"Then maybe you should go," I suggested. It sounded pouty and I hated that, so I added, "You need to feed and I'm pretty beat."

Bo was quiet for what seemed like an eternity before he responded. "Alright."

I heard his practically silent footsteps as he made his way to the window.

"Will you be alright?"

"I'll be fine. I just wanted to check on you," he said.

I heard the sounds of him exiting through the window just before his voice traveled back to me.

"Sweet dreams, Ridley," he whispered and then, once again, I was alone.

CHAPTER EIGHT

Monday dawned clear and cool. When I got to school, the halls were abuzz with tales of Drew's recovery from our car accident. He was quite the miraculous survivor, if the chatter of the girls was any indication. Apparently he was made of steel, superhuman and quite invincible.

I just shook my head and pushed through the throng, making my way to my locker. A few rows down from mine, I saw Savannah standing with Devon at his locker. He looked up and I smiled. He looked happier than I'd seen him in a long time. I watched as Savannah stretched up on her tiptoes to whisper something in his ear and then she turned to walk away—and made her way to me.

"So," she said, coming to a chipper halt to my right and leaning up against the locker beside mine. "I totally owe you."

Puzzled, I glanced over into her cocoa eyes and asked, "Owe me for what?"

"For getting that skanky strumpet off my back," she clarified, wrinkling her pert nose.

I couldn't help but smile. Savannah was a very unique personality, and very animated as well. "Strumpet?"

"Yeah. I read trashy romance novels. They've scrambled my brain and ruined my vocabulary."

"Strumpet," I repeated, resisting the urge to laugh.

"Yeah, it's like slut or whore. Tramp."

"No, I know what it means, I just haven't heard anyone use that word in, oh I don't know…*ever*," I teased.

She shrugged, unperturbed. "What can I say? I'm a trendsetter."

This time I actually did laugh.

"What's so funny?"

Bo's velvety voice caused my blood to jump excitedly inside my veins. I'd been so focused on Savannah, I hadn't felt him coming.

He spoke right beside my ear and a shower of goose flesh rained down my neck and chest, causing my nipples to tighten. I could feel a burning heat emanating from Bo's body where he stood at my back. I wanted to melt right into him. It was all I could do not to close my eyes and sigh at the pleasure running through me.

"My stunning grasp of the English language," Savannah supplied in answer to Bo's question.

I could almost have forgotten she was there. I could almost have forgotten the rest of the world at that moment.

"Ah," was his only response.

Savannah threw me a cheeky smile. "Although I've thoroughly enjoyed our stroll through the thesaurus, what I really came to talk to you about is a double date."

"A what?"

"A double date," she repeated.

"With who?"

"Me and Devon."

"That sounds like a great idea," Bo answered. "We can talk some more about it at lunch."

"Fabulous," she beamed, turning to flounce off down the hall.

I turned around, so close to Bo our thighs touched. "A great idea, huh?"

"She's gone, isn't she?" His eyes twinkled in mischief and his deep grin brought out twin dimples on either side of his mouth. I'd never noticed them before, but I thought they were the sexiest thing I'd ever seen on a man.

"Why did you want to get rid of her?" My belly was squirming with butterflies.

"I thought I'd steal you from Home Room and—"

Bo trailed off, distracted. A fraction of a second later, I smelled something. I had no idea what it was, or even how to describe it really, other than it smelled wonderful.

"What's that smell?" I drew a huge breath into my lungs, relishing the aroma it carried. I could almost taste the scent it was so heavy in the air.

I felt Bo's body tense. "You can smell that?" His eyes were narrowed suspiciously on me.

"Of course I can."

He frowned, but then his eyes moved off to lock onto something behind me. I looked over my shoulder to see what had caught his attention.

A hush fell over the crowd in the hall and they began to part, mashing themselves up against the rows of lockers on either side of the corridor. That's when I saw him.

He stood alone at the end of the hall, towering at least a head over everyone else. No one moved or said a word. No one even breathed. It was like the world stopped spinning for a split second, time itself standing still to admire this one person.

With intense blue eyes and wavy blonde hair that brushed his forehead and his collar, he could've been a surfer but for his pale skin. His eyes met mine and the left side of his mouth pulled up into a cocky smirk. For a second, I thought I was going to actually swoon. Swoon! Who even does that anymore?

"Ridley," Bo said from behind me, his voice low and deadly. "Go to class. I'll meet you back here after Home Room."

I wanted to argue, but I knew by Bo's tone that it wouldn't be wise. Just before I turned to do as Bo suggested, I saw the stranger's attention flicker to my left. Struggling to tear my eyes away from him, I physically turned my head just in time to see Trinity round the corner and come onto the hall.

Like everyone else, she stopped and stared, instantly entranced by the new guy. Altering her course the tiniest bit, she drifted unerringly to him, almost as if he was reeling her in.

When she stopped in front of him, the top of her head barely reaching the middle of his chest, she recovered more quickly than the rest of us had. As I watched, she turned on her charm full blast, eliciting a deep chuckle from the newcomer. I shivered when the sound rang through the hall. It was like the auditory equivalent of heroine.

Bo stepped up to my side and I swung my gaze to him. He was tight-lipped and frowning, but there was something in his eyes, something I hadn't seen there before.

"Do you know him?"

His response was terse, anxiety evident in his tone. "No, but I know he's one of us."

"One of us as in…" I trailed off, looking at him meaningfully.

Bo nodded, one short, curt bob of his dark head.

"What's he doing here?"

"I don't know, but I intend to find out."

The bell chose that moment to ring. Bo and I stood together, watching Trinity point to something on a paper that the guy was holding and then gesture down the hall. I can only assume he was asking for directions and that she, exemplary citizen that she is, was giving them.

Not one to embrace minimalism, Trinity no doubt offered to show him the way, because they walked off together. When they were out of sight, I felt the air come back into the hall, everyone around me snapping out of their stupor and scrambling to get to class.

Bo started to walk off, but then, as if in afterthought, he turned back to me. "I'll see you in a few minutes," he said, brushing his lips over mine.

He looked at me absently for a few seconds before I saw him mentally return to me with a faint shake of his head. It was evident by the clearing of his expression that he was no longer with Trinity and the stranger down the hall; he was with me in the here and now.

"Promise me you'll stay away from him," Bo insisted.

"Of course."

The concern on his face had me agreeing immediately, but it also worried me. It couldn't be a good thing when someone elicited this kind of reaction from Bo.

"See you soon."

He turned and walked away and I watched him until he was out of sight. Plagued with an odd sense of foreboding, I turned and made my way down the hall in the opposite direction, toward Home Room.

By the time I was seated in class, the whole incident in the hall seemed strangely distant and confusing. I couldn't remember what had been so fascinating about the new guy. In fact, I was a little embarrassed that I'd gawked like an idiot, and right in front of Bo no less. I didn't know what was wrong with me, but I had no intention of letting it happen again.

Contrary to what he'd said, I didn't see Bo after Home Room. In fact, I didn't see him at all until lunch. I did, however, see the new guy quite a bit. Every time I turned around, he was with Trinity somewhere. He was even sitting with her at lunch, holding the entire table captive by his peculiarly compelling presence.

I was sitting under the tree I'd claimed as my new lunchtime hangout when Bo found me. He saw that I was studying the newcomer and he leaned up against the tree behind me to watch, too.

"His name is Lars Swenson."

"How do you know?"

"Student Services."

"Is he from around here?"

"No. He's supposedly an exchange student from Switzerland."

"Do you think Trinity knows him?"

"No. I think she's just fallen under his charm like everyone else," he said pointedly.

I craned my neck to look back and up at him. "I'm not under his charm."

I felt a little insulted that he'd lump me in with all the nitwits that were hanging on his every word.

Bo's eyes darted down to me and he quirked one brow suggestively. "Maybe not *now.*"

I chose to ignore that comment, mainly because I had no defense. It was true—I had been nit-witting over the guy this morning, just like everyone else. "Why doesn't he affect you like that?"

"Probably because we're the same."

"You're nothing like him," I declared in Bo's defense. Though I knew nothing about the stranger (other than he had piercing blue eyes and a mouthwatering smell), instinctively, I had no doubt that he was trouble, trouble of a magnitude that I'd never seen. He made me feel twitchy inside, and not in a good way.

"No, I think he's probably very, very old," Bo said, his voice dropping down low.

"What does that mean?"

"That he's also very, very powerful."

"What's he doing *here*?"

Just then, Lars lifted his head from where he'd had it bent listening to Trinity and his eyes locked with Bo's across the lawn. Though his expression never changed, menace rolled off him in thick, black waves.

"I think he's come for me," Bo muttered, apparently unconcerned.

"What?" I was immediately alarmed. I wasn't sure what that even meant, but it sounded terrible. It sounded deadly. "Why?"

"I don't know yet, but I'm sure it won't be long until I find out," Bo said, never taking his eyes off the stranger.

I looked back and forth between them, wondering what kind of silent battle was being waged and why no one else seemed to notice. When my gaze flicked back to Lars, I saw a cold grin drift across his lips right before he glanced at me and then turned his attention back to Trinity. In a way, I had the feeling that we'd somehow been marked, but marked for what I didn't know.

"Bo!"

Bo and I both turned to look toward the picnic tables, where Savannah sat with Devon. She was motioning us to come over.

I felt Bo's fingers brush the back of my head. I turned to look at him over my shoulder. He squatted down, twirling a lock of my hair around his finger, seemingly fascinated by it.

"I guess it's time we go make some plans for a double date, huh?"

Bo's lips were curved in a casual smile, but when his eyes met mine, I saw a hint of something worrisome in their depths, something he was trying to bury beneath his carefree expression.

I reached up to grab his hand where he fiddled with my hair. It was cool, where only a few short hours before I'd been able to feel intense heat.

"Tell me everything is going to be fine," I requested, knowing that it was impossible for him to guarantee such a thing, especially considering that he was dying.

"I'll make it as fine as I can," he replied.

"You're cold, Bo. Didn't you get…something to eat before school?"

"Yeah."

I wondered if worry or fear would burn through the blood he drank more quickly, like he said excitement would. I wanted to ask, but I didn't think I needed to. Something in his eyes told me that it did, and that he was much more concerned than he was willing to admit. He obviously didn't want me to know just how bad it was, so for his benefit, I stood to my feet and plastered a bright smile on my face.

"Then let's go make a date."

****

The weird parts of my day had apparently only just begun. Since I'd so publicly challenged Trinity, she hadn't really made as much of a stink as I'd suspected she would. The locker thing was a mild stunt, something that only brushed the surface of Trinity's deep and disturbing repertoire of vengeful schemes. Each day, especially when it came to cheerleading, I wondered when she'd make her move and how bad it was going to be.

Today, however, she threw me for a loop. She arrived at practice late, which wasn't unusual for Trinity, but she was all smiles, something that I hadn't seen much of since the incident.

I ignored her for the most part, the same as I'd done since I'd stood up to her. No sense waking up that sleeping dog any sooner than was absolutely necessary. The strange thing was that she responded to me cheerfully when I asked her to change position or straighten her arm or…well anything really. Her smile was wide and seemed genuine, but it was her eyes that concerned me. There was a gleam in them, a malevolent twinkle that made me extremely uncomfortable. It seemed as though she was laughing at me, like she'd made the final plans for her revenge and she was overflowing with the juiciness of it.

The thing I worried about most was whether or not her plotting, her ultimate revenge, now involved Lars.

Bo wasn't at my car when practice was over, which disappointed me more than I cared to admit. I scolded myself for wanting to spend every waking minute with him, for expecting him to feel the same way, but it had virtually no effect. I still felt deflated and depressed by the time I got home.

Those feelings were quickly forgotten, however, when I pulled into the driveway and parked behind Mom's car. I glanced at the dashboard clock. It was 5:45. Mom was never home before 10:00 unless Dad was there. Never. She always had some serious drinking to do after work and that took time.

The gloom of a dark, ominous cloud pressed down on my shoulders like a physical weight, making my feet feel like they were shod in concrete shoes. With each step, it seemed an effort to drag them forward, on toward the front door.

Carefully, cautiously, I raised my key to the lock, but the door flew open before I could even push it into the slot. Mom stood there, all smiles and sparklingly clear eyes.

"I'm so glad you're home!" Both her face and her voice were animated and strangely excited. She stepped forward to throw her arms around my neck in a hug that would've staggered a grown man.

"Mom, what's wrong?"

"Wrong?" She pulled back to look at me. "Nothing's wrong, Ridley. Why would you ask such a question?"

I wasn't quite sure how to answer that. I thought about saying something like *Because you're usually at O'Mally's getting three sheets to the wind by now,* but that probably would have been neither advisable nor appropriate.

"No reason," I answered, deciding on a strategy of evasion. Pretense and light deceit had worked well in our house for years. Why stop now?

I smiled, moving past her into the foyer.

"The chicken smells great," I commented, breathing in the savory smell of meat.

"I haven't even started cooking yet. How can you smell it?" She asked this as she took the duffel strap off my shoulder. "Here, let me take this to your room while you go wash up." She walked my bag down the hall, calling over her shoulder, "You can help me with dinner."

I just stood there, mouth agape, watching the person who looked like my mother walk my bag back to my room.

When she reemerged, she looped her arm through mine and pulled me toward the kitchen, like two best friends at summer camp.

"I'm fixing chicken spaghetti, garlic bread with parmesan cheese, salad, and key lime pie for dessert. How does that sound?"

She deposited me in front of the sink while she went to the refrigerator for supplies.

"All that just for two?" I lathered my hands beneath the warm water.

"We might have company," she announced.

"Who?"

"Your friend from school."

"Which one?" She didn't have to know that the list was much, much shorter than it used to be.

"Lars."

I could barely think over the shrill scream of Def Con Five sirens going off inside my head. Hands dripping and eyes narrowed suspiciously, I turned toward Mom. "Lars? How do you know about Lars?"

"You don't have to play dumb, Ridley. I know all about him. He stopped by while you were at practice and you know what?" She turned around to look at me. "I really like him."

I felt the blood drain from my face. Lars had been in my house, alone with my mother.

"What were you doing here, Mom? Don't you usually work late?" That's what she called getting her drunk on—"working late."

Mom wrinkled her brow. "Hmm," she said, slightly dazed. "I can't remember why I came home early, but I did." She shook her head. "It doesn't matter. What matters is that I really like him."

"You really like him," I repeated, racking my brain for the best course of action. Something was very wrong with my mother and it evidently had something to do with Lars.

"I do," she reiterated. "That should please you, right? I mean, what girl doesn't want her parents to like her boyfriend."

"Boyfriend?"

"Well, whatever you call them these days, but you know what I mean."

"So," I began, trying to adopt a matter-of-fact tone and demeanor. "What all did you and Lars talk about?"

My mother actually sighed as a dreamy look came over her face. "All sorts of things, but mostly you."

"What about me?"

"Oh, I don't know. He wanted to know all about his new sweetheart," she said, winking at me.

"And you told him everything he wanted to know, I guess."

Mom rolled her eyes. "Don't worry. I didn't bring out the naked baby pictures. Your pride is safe with me."

That was the least of my concerns, but it was fine if she thought that's what this was all about.

"Thanks," I muttered. "So what all did you tell him?"

A far away look came over Mom's face and I could see her struggling to think back to the conversation. When it apparently didn't come to her, she waved her hand nonchalantly and said, "Just stuff."

Mom handed me the chicken.

"Here, put this on the stove," she directed.

I did as she asked, emptying out the raw ground chicken into a pan and turning the heat on beneath it.

When I walked back to the island, she was cutting vegetables for the salad. I watched her for a minute, no idea what to do or say or how much of a problem this was, though I suspected it was a huge one. Mom used the back of her hand to push her bangs out of her eyes and I saw a red spot on the cuff of her long-sleeved blouse.

"What's that?" I was pointing to her wrist as I asked.

Mom turned her arm over and looked at it, shrugging. "Just a spot," she answered, as if it didn't even register in her mind.

As most people tend to do when they don't have all the information, I took what details I had and filled in the gaps between them, painting my own picture of what had happened today, and it wasn't good.

Pointing to the mountain of carrots and peppers on the cutting board, I addressed Mom. "Since we're going to have a ton of food, would you mind if I invited another friend? He knows Lars, too," I added, the beginnings of a plan taking shape in my head.

Mom smiled brilliantly. "That would be wonderful."

Wonderful? Lars must've done a number on my mother. She probably hadn't thought of anyone or anything as wonderful in three years.

"Cool. If you'll keep an eye on the chicken, I'll go call."

Hurrying from the kitchen, I took my cell phone to my room and picked Bo's number from my contacts list. It rang and rang and rang, but he didn't answer. When his voice mail came on, I left him a simple, innocuous message and hung up, hoping he'd call back quickly.

When he hadn't called back in about three minutes, I changed into a t-shirt and yoga pants, shoved my cell in the waistband and headed back to the kitchen.

Mom was actually humming when I sat back down at the island. It was like stumbling into a bad episode of *The Twilight Zone*.

She maintained her upbeat, Stepford Wife-like smile all through supper preparation. I'd wondered if it would falter when we sat down and it became clear to her that no one else was joining us, but it didn't. All through the meal, she chattered on like this was a normal occurrence for us. Meanwhile, I used most of my energy trying to keep my eyes off the blood on her shirt.

Almost two excruciating hours later, the dishes were done, leftovers were in the fridge and Mom was sitting down to read, something she hadn't done since I was a little girl. I excused myself to my room, stumbling over my thanks for Mom's culinary efforts. It just seemed weird to be talking to her about dinner, like normal people.

I called Bo again as soon as I got into my room, but still I got no answer. I was starting to worry, wondering if he'd had a run-in with Lars or…something else, something worse. There was evidently a whole world out there that I knew nothing about, a world filled with dangers that seemed suitable only for Hollywood's big screen.

Opening my window, I took a deep breath and sat down in my desk chair, toying with the idea of driving to Bo's house. I was staring blankly at the glass heart paperweight he'd seemed so fascinated with when Bo's heavenly scent drifted past my nose. It was like I blinked and suddenly he was there, standing in my room behind me.

Though I should be getting used to it, it still startled me, looking up and seeing him just standing there, and even though my heart stuttered a beat or two, relief flooded me. I was so glad he was safe. I wasn't ready to give him up yet, and I seriously doubted I ever would be.

He'd been smiling when I turned, but now his face sobered. "What's wrong?"

"Bo, what happens when someone gets turned? How does it work?"

Bo didn't move a muscle. I think, for a moment, he didn't even breathe. His beautiful eyes just drilled holes into mine.

"A vampire with mature fangs has to bite you and release enough venom in you to infect your blood."

"Then what?"

"The venom starts destroying your red blood cells and you become severely anemic."

"And then?" I couldn't help my sharp tone. It was like pulling teeth, trying to get straightforward answers from him.

"Your body starts changing and you have to feed. What is it that you want to know, Ridley? Specifically?"

"Does it change your personality?"

"Not really. It just sort of…enhances it. Why?"

"Lars visited my mother today," I murmured, my heart heavy with worry, this time about my mother.

Before I could even blink, Bo was hauling me up from the chair, his hands gripping my upper arms tightly. "What? What happened?"

"Not so hard, Bo," I cautioned, prying his steely fingers loose. He relaxed his hold and rubbed my arms soothingly. "I don't know exactly, but she's acting like a…a…a *sane* person."

"In what way?" His eyes roamed my face.

"She was here when I got home, we cooked dinner together and then we actually ate together."

"So, what's the problem?"

In a perfect world, Bo would never have had to know that my mother has a serious drinking problem, but since we don't live in a perfect world, I knew I'd have to tell him eventually. I had just hoped I would be able to pick and choose the time a little better.

"My mom's an alcoholic. She's rarely ever here before 10:00 and, even then, she's always wasted. I can't remember the last time we ate dinner together when Dad was gone."

"Is it possible that she's just trying to straighten up, turn her life around?" Bo asked the question gently, stooping a little to look into my downcast eyes.

"It's not that, Bo. Trust me, she's acting really, really strange. And," I paused, swallowing the emotion that bubbled up in my throat. "I saw blood on her blouse. She had no idea where it came from and couldn't have cared less. That's not like her either."

Bo's brows drew together in another frown. "Where was the blood?"

"It was just one drop, right at her wrist."

"Did you see any marks? Bite marks, holes, scratches, a rash?"

"No, but the sleeves were long. I couldn't really see her wrist at all."

"What did she say Lars wanted?"

"She couldn't really tell me specifics. It's like she only remembered him, not what they talked about. She didn't even know why she came home in the first place."

Bo exhaled, the air hissing through his teeth in a way that made me apprehensive. He stepped back, rubbing the nape of his neck.

"What? What are you thinking?"

He hesitated briefly before he spoke. I wondered if he was considering not telling me.

"I haven't been this way for very long. What little I know, I've learned either from draining other vampires or from Lucius, but it sounds like he might be trying to establish a bond."

I wanted to ask about Lucius, who he was, but other questions were more pressing.

"A bond? What's that?"

"When a vampire feeds on a human, if he lets that human drink from him, apparently it bonds them together in such a way that he has some amount of mind control."

I smothered my gasp with my hand.

"Do you think that's what Lars did to my mother?"

"It's possible," he admitted, his unsettled expression anything but encouraging.

"So what does that mean? What now? What happens to Mom?"

Bo shrugged, a gesture he used frequently, but one that irritated me this time for some reason.

"Depends."

"On what?"

"What he wants with her."

"What could he possibly want with my mother?"

Bo paused, casting an inscrutable look in my direction.

"There's only one thing that I can think of."

"What's that?"

"You."

The blood drained from my head so quickly, I had to sit back down in the desk chair before I fell down.

"But what could he possibly want with me?" That just didn't sound right. I didn't know him, I posed no threat to him, I—

I stopped when I realized why he might want to get to me.

"Unless he wants to use me to get to something else, some*one* else." Bo said nothing to this, confirming my suspicion. "He wants me to get to you."

Bo's expression was full of guilt and regret. "That's what I'm afraid of," he confessed. He rubbed a weary hand over his face. "I should've stayed away." Obviously frustrated, he turned away from me.

I stood and crossed to him. I touched his shoulder, letting my hand rest there until he turned back to face me.

"No, you shouldn't have. Avoidance is never the answer. Yes, life is all about pain and trouble and frustration and anger, but it's also about love and friendship and good days and sunshine. You can't have one without the other. If you avoid pain, you avoid living. My family has walked that road for years and, trust me, it's no way to exist."

He looked miserable. "You've had enough pain in your life without me adding to it."

It was my turn to shrug. What he said was true, to a certain extent. "But you've also brought me more happiness than I've seen in a long time." More like ever, though he didn't need to know that. But then, as I looked into his face, I realized that maybe he did. "Actually," I said, casting my eyes down, shy and a little embarrassed all of a sudden. "I'm happier than I've ever been. And it's because of you, Bo."

I was afraid to meet his gaze, heat staining my cheeks after having poured my heart out. He drew me into his arms and I went willingly, glad to bury my burning face in his shoulder.

"It doesn't matter. I don't think I could've stayed away from you for even one more day anyway," he admitted quietly.

One more day?

"What do you mean?"

I felt him stiffen at my question, so I pulled back to look up into his face, to gauge his odd reaction.

I repeated, "What do you mean?"

Bo just watched me, searching my face for something. I waited for him to explain, but he didn't. A sinking, breathless feeling began to gnaw at my insides.

One image flashed through my mind over and over again, like an eerie strobe. It was the sight of Bo's compelling eyes hovering outside the windshield of a car. Only it wasn't Drew's windshield that I was remembering; it was Izzy's.

Air slowly filled my lungs in a long gasp of comprehension. I held it there until it burned inside my chest like a raging inferno.

"You were there," I whispered. "Three years ago, you were there."

CHAPTER NINE

Several emotions flickered across Bo's face, but neither confusion nor denial ranked among them.

"Bo?"

He sighed, and it was a weary sound that carried a heavy weight. "Even though it was so long ago, it seems like it happened only yesterday."

Bo walked to the window and stared out into the dark. I could tell he wasn't seeing the night, at least not this night. His eyes had a distant look about them, the look of someone peering into the past.

"I hadn't been turned very long and, fortunately, I slept through most of it. I'd been in the woods for days when I woke up. And there was this thirst—a thirst I couldn't explain, a thirst that no food or water would quench. That's the day I met Lucius.

"He'd been feeding me. He's an elder, but he lives a...different kind of life. He explained what I was, what I needed. It was like waking up to a different world. My dad was dead. The prime suspect in his murder had been released on a technicality. I was turning into some kind of creature from the movies.

"For weeks after that, I searched the woods day and night, waiting, hoping to find the person responsible. I needed blood, but I refused to drink from humans. I realized that I could survive on animal blood, just barely, but enough to find Dad's killer.

"I was going into the woods one night, stalking a deer, when I heard the squeal of the brakes. I ran back to the road and got there just before the car started rolling. Just in time to see your face through the windshield. For a second, I couldn't move. I can't describe what it felt like, but I can still feel it when I remember that night."

He paused, lost in the feelings that he couldn't articulate.

"The sounds of metal and glass on asphalt were so loud. I wanted to turn and run, knew that I should, but when the car hit the tree and stopped, I knew I had to get to you, to make sure you were alright."

Though he was finally telling me how he felt—something I'd wondered about and agonized over for quite some time now—it was another thought that took center stage in my mind. He'd come after me. *Me.*

"I had to know that you were alright," he groaned.

"Me?"

Bo nodded.

A tiny red spot of anger penetrated the gray cloud of confusion that had settled over me. It swelled and surged until it had enveloped me in a blinding crimson haze of fury.

"You let my sister die to save *me?"*

Bo said nothing.

I was beside myself, unable to contain the pain and the rage swirling inside me. I wanted to lash out. Drawing my arm back, I brought my hand around as hard as I could, my palm connecting with Bo's face in an ear-splitting crack. "How could you? How could you do that? How could you let her die?"

"I didn't, Ridley. She was already gone," Bo explained softly, sadly.

"No she wasn't, she—"

"Yes, she was, Ridley. I knew when I saw her that she wouldn't make it. Even if I could've gotten my blood into her, it wouldn't have mattered. Her injuries were too severe. There was no way she could've survived that. There was just no way."

It took a few seconds for his words to penetrate my addled brain. Looking at him, Bo appeared calm and sincere, yet devastated, too. But, strangely, he also looked somehow deserving, like he was willing to take the blame for something that wasn't even his fault just so I could have someone to blame, someone to be angry with.

As quickly as it had come, my anger died, leaving behind only an intense sadness. I knew what he was saying was true. Izzy's head had been crushed against the tree. Everyone knew that she was ninety percent gone as soon as it happened. But that didn't make it hurt any less.

Putting a hand to my chest, as if to stop the ache that throbbed there, I apologized. "I'm sorry, Bo. I'm so sorry."

"Don't be," he said, so forgiving and understanding it made me feel even worse.

Though I could easily get caught up in the guilt and misery of mindlessly lashing out at Bo, I couldn't focus on that right now. I had to know the rest of the story.

"So then what happened?"

Bo sighed. "I pulled you out and carried you to the grass. I could hear your heart beating, but there was so much blood," Bo said, his face contorting in remembered pain. He closed his eyes against it. "And you smelled so amazing."

"Did you- did you…" I trailed off, unable to finish the question.

Bo hung his head. His nod was barely perceptible, but I saw it nonetheless.

"I couldn't control myself. It was like being taken over by some kind of demon that didn't think or care. It just felt. And tasted. I couldn't stop myself, no matter how wrong it was," he said.

I didn't know what to say to that. I stood quietly by, watching Bo relive those moments that I couldn't remember, the agony of it, the disgust of it. The pleasure of it.

"How am I still alive?"

"I heard your heartbeat slow and then I remembered your face from behind that windshield. You were so scared," he recalled. "But you were so beautiful." His lips curved into a bitter smile. "I just couldn't take your life. I just couldn't do it, so I made myself stop drinking. I realized that I wanted to help you. I wanted to feed you—my consciousness, my energy. I wanted to feed you life. *My life.* So, I tore open my wrist and I fed you."

I was silent for a long time, digesting what he'd said, working his words into what I knew of the accident and my recovery.

"You saved my life," I stated, as much for my benefit as his. As if he hadn't given me enough, Bo had given me back my life. He'd saved me.

"I almost took it," he said miserably.

"But you didn't."

"But I wanted to."

"But you didn't."

"As you were waking up, I promised you, promised myself, that I'd never drink blood from another human. And I haven't. I live on blood from the bank and nothing else."

Listening to him, something he'd said before, when I'd asked about my mother, popped into my head.

"You said you couldn't stay away from me."

Bo nodded.

"And I feel like I can't breathe when you're not around," I stated absently.

As I rolled the two puzzle pieces around inside my head, I stopped and looked up at Bo when, with an ominous click, they came together in my brain, showing me a picture that terrified me.

"It's you," I breathed in horror. "It's that bond. You're doing this to me through that bond." I began backing away from Bo, betrayal and anguish rising up inside me. "You're doing this to me on purpose!"

"Ridley, I'm not."

"Yes, you are. You're making me feel this way."

"No, I'm not."

"Yes you are." It was easy to convince myself that the way I felt about him—the desperation that I felt to be with him, the need I felt to have him near—was manipulated, manufactured. It was easier to believe that than to believe that feeling like I couldn't live without him was real.

"Why, Ridley? Why would I do that? To what end?"

"You're using me. You- you're—" I stammered, not having a good answer.

"No, I'm not!" Bo reached for me, grabbing my shoulders. "It doesn't work that way. But even if it did, I would never, *never* do that to you. What you feel is real.

Even if I wanted to, my blood is not powerful enough to control you."

"But Mom was acting all smitten with Lars. He was doing that to her, just like you're doing this to me," I accused bitterly.

Bo squeezed, his fingers biting into my arms. I flinched and he immediately released me, dropping his hands to his sides where they curled into tight fists.

"No, I'm not. You saw the way people reacted to Lars. It's because he's so powerful, his blood is so potent. His presence is like a drug," he said.

I had to admit that Lars did have a very profound affect on people, one even I'd reacted to a little. That also probably explained why Bo hadn't thought much of my temporary thrall. He'd known what it was.

"I'm not that strong yet. Even with our bond, I couldn't make you do anything that you didn't want to."

On the heels of that thought was one that was even worse, or at least it seemed that way to me.

"Is that why you have feelings for me? Because you drank my blood?" It was bad enough to think that *my* feelings weren't real; it was nearly intolerable to think that Bo's weren't. It was devastating to think that his attraction was all about my blood, not my heart, not *me,* that it was chemically-induced.

"Of course not," he declared vehemently. "Naturally, I crave it. More than I can even describe, but it's not *you.* The way I feel about you has absolutely nothing to do with your blood. Yes, I felt drawn to find you, probably because of the bond, but that link doesn't make you fall in love. If anything, it clouds my feelings for you."

Though not intentionally, he'd made an admission of sorts, one that was not lost on me.

"Are you saying that you're in love with me?"

"My god, yes!" He flung his arms wide in exasperation.

Against my will, my heart swelled. I watched him, and his reaction seemed authentic, his frustration genuine. Could he be telling the truth? All our time together had felt real, on both sides, and I wanted so badly to believe that it was.

"What did you think this was all about?"

"How am I supposed to know? I can't read minds you know," I said, a little frustrated myself.

"Sometimes I wish you could," he claimed, running his fingers through his hair. The gesture left several pieces sticking straight up, begging for me to smooth them. But I resisted, needing to maintain distance from him so I could figure out what to do now.

"So what do we do about Lars?"

Bo's brows snapped together. "I think I might need to pay Lucius a visit."

Bo had said Lucius was an elder, someone who'd answered many of his questions and explained things to him. Though I wished it otherwise, Bo hadn't managed to convince me that all this—our relationship, his feelings, my feelings—wasn't fabricated and it didn't set well with me. I wondered if maybe Lucius could answer some questions for me as well.

"Could I go with you? I mean, this is my mother we're talking about." I tacked that last on there to sway Bo in case he was considering saying no.

He shrugged. "I don't see why not."

His consent seemed casual enough and I really needed some objective answers, information that it sounded like this Lucius would be able to provide.

"When can we go?"

"How about tomorrow after school?"

"I've got practice. Can we do it Wednesday? It's our off day this week."

"Wednesday's fine, but we probably shouldn't put it off any longer than that," he warned.

"Alright. Wednesday it is."

****

The next day I felt out of sorts. For virtually the first time since I'd met him, I looked forward to time away from Bo. My heart and my body ached when he left the night before, and it was all I could do not to ask him to stay, but I just couldn't seem to shake those creeping doubts that had cropped up as a result of our conversation.

I had a headache from the frown that I knew I was wearing. Not being around Bo, not giving in to my feelings for him and my desire to be near him, was wearing on me. I was determined, however, to resist as much as possible until I'd had a chance to interrogate Lucius.

When lunch rolled around, I was glad when Savannah corralled me to her table. At least she would alleviate the uncomfortable tension that I felt existed between me and Bo.

Turns out, she managed much more than that. Savannah was quite entertaining. It wasn't hard to see why Devon and Bo liked her so much.

"...but that hair! There was probably a disturbance in The Force when she got out of bed this morning," Savannah was saying. "I wanted to poke out my own eyes when I passed her in the hall."

Devon chuckled, eyeing Savannah with nothing short of adoration. "You know what I love about you?"

"Um, everything?" She looked comically hopeful.

Devon chuckled again. "I meant aside from your abundant humility."

"My outrageous fashion sense?"

"Fashion sense?" Devon looked pointedly at Savannah's black fedora. "Not quite. I was referring to your complete lack of theatricality."

She managed to look offended. "I don't have a dramatic bone in my body."

"Let's see," Devon said, narrowing his eyes and tapping his chin with his finger. "Just last night, wasn't there some mention of a worldwide boycott followed by a withering death if Starbuck's discontinues the Cinnamon Dulce?"

"Hey," she said, her eyes round. "It could happen."

"Yeah, right. No drama here," Devon teased, rolling his eyes. They both laughed.

I was smiling as I watched the interaction, envying their easy affection and uncomplicated relationship. I sneaked a peek at Bo; he was watching me watch them. There was a sadness just beneath the surface of his pleasant expression. It drifted across his face like a ghost moving through the vacant rooms of an empty house.

For a moment, when our eyes met and held, it seemed as though he could feel the anguish that was plaguing me, that he too felt the unsettling shadow that hovered over us, over our relationship.

Reaching up, he brushed his thumb over my brow bone, as if to wipe away the frown I knew still lingered there, and, for a moment, it almost felt as if he had. All too soon, however, Trinity's boisterous laughter cut into our moment and I looked up to see her fawning all over Lars.

He didn't look particularly thrilled with her at that instant, but Trinity was oblivious. She was on cloud nine, a thousand light years from reality. I wondered if she was overdosing on the "drug" of Lars's presence.

But what a way to go, I thought, looking back at Bo. He was my drug.

He'd turned to watch them as well. Although his expression had gone sour as he brooded, it only served to make him even more painfully handsome, just in a dark and dangerous way.

I sighed quietly, careful not to draw his attention. It seemed our relationship was destined to include pain of one form or another.

That afternoon, I noticed that Trinity was not in the Government class that we shared. I had no trouble picturing her ditching class to spend the rest of the day on an elicit tryst with Lars. I'd love to do nothing more than enjoy such a day with Bo.

As much as I disliked her ways, I couldn't bring myself to feel ambivalent about Trinity walking into situation rife with danger. She had no idea who or what she was dealing with, what she was unwittingly involving herself in. I didn't take it lightly, and I felt bad for not at least trying to warn her off sooner.

Resigning myself to the distastefulness of such a conversation, I decided that the next time I saw Trinity, I would talk to her.

Of course, I had no idea what I'd say. I couldn't very well explain that she was unintentionally consorting with a vampire. Yet I had to say something that was compelling enough to get her to stay away from him.

I assumed I'd have more time to think about it, assumed that Trinity would skip practice like she'd skipped the latter half of classes, so I was surprised when I saw her making her way to the drill field. Brushing off the dread that was weighing me down, I took a deep breath and rushed out to meet her, hoping to have a word out of earshot of the pack of gossip-hungry cheerleaders that stood by the bleachers.

"Hey," I said casually when I fell into step beside her. "Can we stop and talk for a second?"

Not only did Trinity not even bother looking at me, she didn't stop walking either. She just kept right on going. "I have no interest in listening to your lame apologies."

"It's about Lars," I announced, hoping that would get her attention.

And it did.

"What about Lars?" She stopped and turned to look at me.

It was then that I noticed how terrible she looked. Trinity was a petite girl with natural blonde hair and uncommonly olive skin. She looked perpetually tanned and was the envy of virtually every female in a fifty mile radius. Today, however, her skin looked sallow and her face looked gaunt. Her eyes, which normally glistened with a vivid (if not vicious) sparkle, were dull and lifeless. To me, she actually looked like a drug addict, one who was in desperate need of a fix.

"Trinity, I don't think he's the kind of guy you need to get mixed up with."

She snorted. "Of course you'd say that, Ridley. Jealous much?"

"Trinity, I'm not jealous. I'm just…concerned. That's all."

"Yeah, right. Because you spend *so* much time being concerned about me." With a roll of her bloodshot eyes, she started to walk off.

"I think he's dangerous," I blurted.

Rather than making some snide comment or blowing me off like I was being ridiculous, Trinity just looked at me, a tiny frown creasing her ashen brow.

I could see the wheels turning, which made me wonder what she'd seen or noticed or perceived that was giving her pause. It must've been something significant because it was unlike Trinity to hold her tongue.

"Dangerous how?"

"Just dangerous. Period. He's not who you think he is."

Her frown deepened and I could see a flicker of apprehension darken her blue eyes. Just when I thought I was about to make some progress, an intoxicating smell teased my nose. At first it sort of scrambled my senses, just as it had the last time I smelled it. I looked over Trinity's shoulder and I saw Lars walking toward the bleachers.

I might've been lost to the aroma, like before, had it not been for Trinity's expression. It sobered me. Her face relaxed immediately, a barely-concealed look of ecstasy settling over it, like she'd just been dosed with some incredible narcotic. I felt alarmed by her reaction; it was like she'd been brain-washed.

"You smell that, Trinity? That's not normal," I said quietly, knowing Lars could probably hear me perfectly.

Trinity sniffed a couple of times, her happily dazed look never faltering. "I don't smell anything but the stench of your jealousy, Ridley," she replied pleasantly, almost dreamily. "You just can't stand the fact that I found someone like Lars, someone so…so…" She trailed off absently, smiling contentedly.

She didn't know he was behind her, didn't know that it wasn't a coincidence that she had suddenly forgotten all her misgivings. But I knew. I knew that his close proximity was likely what triggered the change in her. As long as he stayed close, she stayed under his spell. I wondered if they'd had each other's blood yet. Maybe that's why it took Mom's thrall a little longer to wear off; she'd had his blood.

Lars called to Trinity and, with a delighted squeal that brought her eyes back to life, she turned and ran toward him. He pulled her up against his huge frame and kissed her.

I knew without looking that every eye was trained on them. The kiss was so steamy it was embarrassing to watch. It didn't belong in public. It belonged in a boudoir on black satin sheets with no one else around. Just as I was about to turn away, not interested in seeing Lars swallow Trinity whole, his eyes popped open and he met my gaze from across the way.

Although warmth did leap to life in my belly, my head was far too aware of what was going on for me to be swayed by his tactics. In a defiant gesture, I hiked my chin up a notch, a silent challenge for him to give me his best shot. I was no easy target.

Abruptly, tossing one last scathing look over my shoulder, I turned on my heel and walked to the gaggle of gawking cheerleaders, snapping commands as I went, spurring them into action.

Slowly, reluctantly, their attention turned back to the task at hand, a difficult half-time routine we'd been practicing for our next game, the Friday after next. When they were all tending to their role in the choreography, I glanced back over my shoulder. As I suspected, Lars and Trinity were gone.

****

The next morning, I lay in bed looking at the ceiling. The first lights of dawn had painted an intricate, shifting pattern on the smooth surface. My heart was still heavy, but maybe not quite as heavy as it had been.

Last night, Mom was more herself. By that, I mean she came stumbling in at 11:45 wasted. I personally believed she was the only person in the history of time who actually drove better while intoxicated. She'd never so much as been in a scrape or gotten a speeding ticket while she was loaded. Sobriety, on the other hand, was a whole different story.

Thankfully, she hadn't needed much in the way of care. It was one of her fairly self-sufficient and pleasant binges. She chattered on about work-related things, citing people and places I knew nothing about. But she laughed a lot, which was infinitely preferable to the times she came home a crying, drunken mess.

The most important thing I noticed was that she didn't mention Lars one time. It was as if she didn't even remember meeting him. In fact, she'd acted confused when I asked her about him. I could only assume that the blood, or whatever he did to her, had worn off and she was once again my mother. Flawed though she was, I was glad to have her back.

Spending the evening without so much as talking to Bo turned out to be extremely unpleasant, but when I compared it to Trinity and her drug-addicted behaviors, I thought my feelings were surprisingly normal for someone who was in deep like, or whatever I was in.

I was hesitant to call it love yet, especially since Bo's most recent confession. I wanted to know that, when love finally found me, it would be real. I also wanted to know that it happened for all the right reasons. So as long as there was one tiny seed of doubt in my mind about me and Bo, I was going to put off naming my feelings for him for as long as I possibly could.

It seemed that Bo was somehow able to sense my inner struggle. Without me even having to ask, he had graciously given me some space. I gave him huge credit for that, and, though we'd been apart only hours (that felt like weeks), that time had been very revealing.

There was no denying my intense yearning for Bo's company. There was a physical need, yes, but there was an emotional longing that far outweighed it, by several tons in fact. I'd dissected and closely examined each and every one of my feelings for Bo and it didn't take me long to realize that I crave his presence and all that comes with it—his smile, his laugh, his confidence, his closeness, his voice, his smell, his touch, the safety that I feel when he's around.

But I also came to the important conclusion that I was still me whether Bo was around or not. I was happy when he was close and miserable when he wasn't, and there was no doubt that his influence had made me a better person in many ways. But either way—with or without him—I was still me, unlike Trinity who seemed like a totally different person altogether since Lars had come into the picture.

Sliding out from beneath the covers, I decided to go ahead and take a shower, give myself plenty of time to prepare for the day ahead. I was going on a field trip to see Lucius tonight and somehow—instinctively I guess—I knew it would be a very significant visit.

The day ticked by uneventfully. I passed Trinity on a few occasions and each time, she cast me an odd look that appeared to be a mixture of hatred and curiosity. Beneath her tan, she was even paler than she'd been the day before and I wondered if I'd been too late in my warning.

I was leaving my locker, heading through the empty hall toward the cafeteria, when Trinity sprang around the corner and surprised me.

"Trinity," I gasped, throwing a startled hand up to my throat where my heart was lodged. "You scared me."

Trinity didn't say a word at first; she just stepped slowly forward until she was almost in my face. When she didn't stop, but continued to approach me, I began taking a step backward for every step she took toward me.

She inhaled deeply, closing her eyes as if in ecstasy. "He's right. I can smell your blood," she said. When she opened her eyes to look at me, I saw that Trinity was still in there; she'd just been liberated from the constraints of humanity. "Right through your skin."

"What?" Even as I stumbled back, away from her, I played dumb. "What are you talking about, Trinity?"

Her lips curled up into a malevolent sneer. "Oh, I think you know exactly what I'm talking about, Ridley."

"No, I don't. I think—"

"In that case, would you like me to show you?" Her eyes were wide and innocent for a moment, but then her devilish smile slid back into place. "I'd really like to show you, Rid."

"Trinity, you don't have to do this."

For the first time, fear of Trinity—real fear—lanced through me. I could only hope that she didn't pick up on the nervous tremor in my voice.

"Oh, but I do," she said quietly, still stalking me.

"No, you don't. You don't have to live this way. You can survive without hurting people."

Her bark of laughter sent a cascade of chills raining down my back. "And why would I want to do that?"

Looking into her eyes, it occurred to me that I'd never fully realized the sickness, the blackness that resided inside Trinity. This would be a dream come true for her. And Lars must've known that. He could probably sense evil, smell it like some kind of hell hound.

"Because it's the right thing to do."

"But it's not the *fun* thing to do, is it?"

"Trinity, if you hurt me, they'll hunt you down and throw you in jail," I warned, grasping at straws. Truthfully, if anyone could get away with murder, it would probably be Trinity. She's about as diabolical as high school kids come.

She knew that, too. "They'd have to catch me first," she said, confirming my suspicion.

"Well, the police might not, but Bo would find you."

I saw the flicker of fear, the flash of uncertainty dash across Trinity's face. It was only there for a heartbeat before it vanished, but I saw it and now I knew. She had enough sense to be afraid of Bo.

As quickly as it had come, the fear was gone, replaced by more bravado. "And Lars would find him."

Now was not the time to back down; I had to go for the kill, pull out all the stops.

"Seriously, Trinity? After all of a few dates, you think Lars is going to fight for you? To risk his life for you?"

There it was again. Just a trace of the insecurity I knew Trinity harbored deep down. She kept it hidden, well-concealed from the masses, but it was still in there, lurking just beneath whatever god-like power she felt coursing through her body. Though it was tiny, it was still enough for me to work with.

"That's what I thought," I said, squaring my shoulders. "Just remember that, Trinity, when you think about doing something stupid. We'll be watching."

I chose that moment to make my exit. Well, more like my escape. Although I thought the confrontation had ended in my favor, I wasn't willing to risk pushing my luck any further.

Besides, now I knew that not only does Trinity know about Lars and Bo, she'd apparently become one of them.

After that, I was antsy to get to lunch, to tell Bo about my discovery. Unfortunately, by the time I got outside, Savannah had already lured him to the picnic table and they were embroiled in a discussion with Devon about the superior acoustic stylings of Slash's Gibson over Eric Clapton's Fender.

Strangely, it was a conversation that penetrated my otherwise-consumed brain fairly rapidly. For one thing, I actually knew who they were talking about because I loved classic rock. Secondly, I was pleasantly surprised that three people—at this school, in my now very small circle of friends, that weren't burn-outs—liked that kind of music, too. In a bizarre but good way, it was as if our four lives were fated to become intertwined.

Bo waited for me after Chemistry and walked me to my car. We were both silent during the walk. It wasn't really an uncomfortable silence. It was one that seemed to be filled with all sorts of things that needed to be said, things that loomed on the horizon. I didn't really want to talk about most of it now, however, preferring to wait until after our visit to Lucius. With that in mind, I introduced a fairly innocuous subject that I actually did find interesting.

"So you like classic rock, huh?"

The way Bo's face relaxed made me realize that he was feeling the same tension that I was.

"I love all kinds of music, but that's what I listen to most."

"You know, it's weird, but I realized today that I don't know very much about you."

"I was attempting to remedy that the night I took you to my basement," he said with a wry grin.

Bo skipped ahead and then turned to walk backwards, facing me.

"Oh." I bit my lip in frustration. I felt like the end of that conversation had come way too soon.

Bo stopped, forcing me to stop as well. His expression turned serious.

"Do you still want to know me?"

Looking into his eyes, I knew what he was asking. It was much more than Bo asking if I wanted the answer to trivial questions about him. He was asking if I still wanted him in my life.

There was only one answer I could give, at least if I was being honest.

"Yes."

For all the questions and doubts that I had, none of them had affected the way I felt about Bo. Beneath all the muddy waters that contained the particulars, my heart still cried out for him.

The tension he'd been carrying around his mouth melted away and he smiled. It was a genuine curve of his lips that engaged those dimples at the corners of his mouth. I hadn't realized until that moment what a rare treat they were and how much I missed them.

"Then come with me to my lair," he said in his best Transylvanian accent.

A shiver coursed through me when I silently finished that comment with *I want to suck your blood.*

Bo took the keys from me and drove us to his house in my car. He parked at the back of the house and we got out. We walked to the top of the basement steps, and as I looked around, I couldn't help but hope that, this time, no vicious rival vampires showed up.

Always in tune with me, Bo turned as he unlocked the door. "I bet you're having flashbacks of vampires chucking trees at your head, aren't you?"

My mouth dropped open, not because he'd picked up on my train of thought so perfectly, but because he'd left out that little tidbit of information somewhere along the way.

"He threw that tree at me?"

Bo cringed, nodding. "I told you, these are not nice people."

"How are you so different?"

As soon as the question was out, I regretted it, and Bo's expression just made me feel that much worse about asking.

"I didn't meant it like—"

"I know you didn't," he interrupted. "And I don't have an answer for you." As I watched, the happy, relaxed lines of his face vanished into thin air. My heart sank; it was my fault that they were gone. "In fact, I'm not convinced that I'm that much better than they are."

He pushed the old red door open and flipped on the light switch. Holding the door wide, Bo stepped to the side so I could precede him.

The first thing I noticed was the intensity of that tangy smell that I associated with Bo. It seemed concentrated in this spot, like the further I walked into the room, the stronger it got.

I stopped and looked around. The floor of the room was concrete, painted a dark gray like the walls. A daybed was pushed up against one wall. It was covered with a black spread and a mountain of pillows in varying shades of gray. Beside it, in the corner, was a small table, and on its surface a half-burned incense stick and a lighter.

Across from the daybed was a shelf that held a stereo and various pictures and mementos, along with rows and rows of CDs. I trailed my fingers along them, reading the names as I went. Bo was right; he listened to a little bit of everything.

There was truly classic rock from like Led Zeppelin to The Rolling Stones. He also had 80's rock, everything from Motley Cru to Def Leppard. There was some 90's music sprinkled in—Nirvana, Dave Matthews Band, and Santana. He even had a Backstreet Boys CD. When I saw that one, I had to smile.

On top of that, he had a few country bands, some blues titles I vaguely recognized and a few more current groups, the music I heard on the radio all the time. He had a very eclectic palate.

Bo closed the door and walked to the stereo to turn it on. When he hit play, I was curious to hear what he'd been listening to most recently. I recognized the beginning guitar riff of *Sweet Child O' Mine* instantly.

He turned to lean back against the wall, crossing his feet at the ankles and his arms over his chest. He seemed content to quietly watch me as I looked around.

I pointed to a picture of an older man, a face that was featured in all of the pictures scattered around. "Is this your dad?"

Bo nodded.

I figured as much. In some pictures, he was by himself. In some pictures he was with Bo's mother. But in every picture, he was there, like the image of a ghost that refused to fade with time. I thought of Izzy's room. I knew all about those kinds of hauntings.

My heart ached for Bo's loss. It wasn't a shrine really, but I could see that Bo probably got a lot of his motivation from the articles in this room. His relationship with his dad was written all over the place.

There was a baseball mitt, a football, some tennis balls with faces drawn on them, a floppy fishing hat and fishing pole. There were some model cars and a model airplane, projects I guessed Bo completed with his father. The whole room was like the sad history of a life cut short and the evidence of a son who couldn't let go.

The one thing that I found odd was that Bo was not featured in any of the pictures with his family. I wanted to ask him about it, but I'd already done enough to taint his good mood. I could wait until another time to find my answers.

I slid my eyes over to Bo. He was watching me closely, an inscrutable look on his face. I glanced away quickly. I felt as if I was intruding on a very intimate family gathering.

"He would've liked you." When Bo finally spoke, the thick walls absorbed the words as soon as they left his lips. Behind the music, the room was an eerie kind of quiet, almost tomblike.

"What was he like?"

Bo leaned his head back against the wall, his eyes on the low ceiling, a sad smile curving his lips.

"He was great. He taught me everything," he said. "He always said he wanted to prepare me to do anything I wanted to do, to 'take the world by storm', he'd say." He laughed, a bitter bark of a sound, and then his eyelids drifted shut. "He didn't deserve the death they gave him."

"What happened to him?"

"As far as I can remember, there were two guys at his throat. They attacked him so viciously, they almost decapitated him. He was nearly drained of blood. The coroner's report said he was dead within seconds."

"And you had to watch?"

Bo's eyes opened to meet mine. They were fathomless pools of agony. "They were stronger than you can imagine. Even after years of playing sports, of football and weightlifting, they held me easily. There were two more guys holding me and a girl was watching. She said she wanted me to watch, that she wanted my heart pumping for her. Pumping hard."

I covered my mouth with my fingers. I wasn't sure whether I wanted to cry or be sick. Probably both.

"Then what happened?" It was so gruesome, I could hardly stand it, but I had to know what happened to Bo and to his father, what had caused this need for revenge that was costing him his life.

"When they were finished with Dad, they held me while she bit me. She went wild when she tasted my blood, said that it was sweet, that she could taste the power in it.

"The other two started complaining about wanting to feed, but she wouldn't let them. My guess is that she decided to keep me for herself, but the two guys holding me didn't like the new plan. One of them attacked her, just let go of my arm and pounced on her.

"The other one held on, but he was distracted by the fight. I guess my adrenaline was jacked up, so I was finally able to get away from him. I went to check on Dad," Bo said, closing his eyes again, this time in remembered pain. "But he was already gone."

Bo shook his head. "Anyway, I looked back and they were tearing each other apart, blood and spit flying everywhere. I took off, ran as fast as I could to an old cabin in the woods, one I'd seen several times when we'd been hunting. I remember banging on the door, but no one answered. I knew I needed to get away, but I didn't have the energy to go any further. I remember falling against the door and sliding down to the ground. I guess I passed out there. That's all I remember until I woke up like…this."

"Bo," I breathed, my heart breaking for him.

"When she bit me, she must've injected me. I found out later that she did it on purpose. She wanted to keep me as some sort of weird drinking buddy, almost like a mate."

"How do you know that?"

Bo paused, giving me the strangest look before he answered. "I saw it in her memories when I drained her."

I tried to remain calm, not to get all judgmental about Bo talking so casually about murder. All I had to do was remind myself what they'd done to his father and it didn't seem quite so bad anymore. I'm sure, for Bo, it was more than adequate justification for killing them.

"Who was she?"

"Her name was Jolene Turner."

I remembered the name. I'd heard the news report about her death a couple weeks ago.

"That was you?"

Bo nodded solemnly.

"They thought it was the...the…" I couldn't finish the sentence. I couldn't get the name *Southmoore Slayer* past my numb lips.

CHAPTER TEN

A number I'd heard in the news report kept running through my head like a ticker tape. *Twenty-seven. Twenty-seven. Twenty-seven.*

"No," Bo said, casting his eyes down.

"No what?" My breath was coming in short, quick pants.

"No, I didn't kill all of them."

I closed my eyes and a sigh of relief blew through my lips. "Thank God," I whispered. "How—"

I stopped myself from asking how many Bo had killed. Information like that would only make things harder, and I didn't need things to get any harder.

"Never mind," I said. "So, you still haven't been able to find the one who killed your father, right?"

"No."

"And you won't stop until you do?" I couldn't keep the bitter edge from my voice.

"There's no point. I'm dying. Nothing can change that. If I give up now, it will all be for nothing," he said, pushing himself off the wall and stepping toward me. "My death and the life I'll never have with you will have been for nothing."

My chest squeezed painfully. I couldn't bear to think about it, much less talk about Bo dying.

As I looked into his eyes, I could see that demons were eating away at him on the inside, and I doubted things were going to get any better. He'd started down a path that he couldn't come back from. He'd chosen a fate that he was locked into—no way out, no going back. And now, like it or not, I was traveling that road with him. My fate was going to be just as ugly, at least for my heart. I could see that our epic love story was going to end badly. And there was nothing I could do about it.

In an effort to avoid bursting into tears like an emotionally unstable psychopath, I looked back to the framed pictures dotting the shelf to my right. I saw the smiling, happy faces of Bo's parents.

"What does your mom think about all this?"

Bo shrugged. "She's devastated, of course. But even though she's not at all pleased with my choice, she understands it. She's tried to help me as much as she can. She gets me bagged blood to help me keep my strength. She's been taking samples of my blood to the lab, trying to find a cure, or at least a way to slow the effects of the poison. She's been great."

A cure? My eyes darted back to him. I latched on to the mere suggestion of hope with both hands and I held on tight. "Has she found anything?"

Bo shook his head in defeat. "No. And I don't think she will. Not in time anyway."

"Is that why she seemed kind of…sad to meet me?"

Bo's grin had a hint of irony behind it. "Yeah. In school, I guess I was a pretty typical guy. You know, string of semi-serious girlfriends, lots of texts from lots of different people in between, all that. She was always after me to settle on one."

He chuckled at some memory. "She used to complain and say I left a trail of broken hearts that she had to clean up. They'd all call and cry on her shoulder."

When Bo looked at me, his expression changed. The look on my face must've plainly indicated my displeasure. I wasn't liking the Bo I was hearing about, the one I hadn't met, and I doubted very much that I would've wanted to know him.

"In that way, what's happened to me hasn't been all bad. I met you," he said, tucking my hair behind my ear. "Being…this has changed me in ways that I can't describe, but not all of them are bad."

Needing to hear something positive, I asked, "Like what? What good has come of it?"

"You," he said, as if that was enough.

"What else?"

"Besides you?"

I nodded.

"I'm stronger than I've ever been. I don't need much sleep. I heal almost instantly. I can hear and smell and see things a thousand times more clearly and farther away. I can run fast, jump high, move more quickly than human eyes can see. I can be invisible if I need to be," he said, adding that last with a sardonic smirk.

"Huh," I said, at a loss as to how to respond to that. Tossing my hair over my shoulder dramatically, I said, "Well, little did you know, but I can do all of those things, too."

Bo's grin widened and he reached out and set his hands at my waist.

"Is that right?"

"Oh, yeah. You didn't know I have super powers?"

"Oh, trust me. I knew you had some kind of power."

"You don't know the half of it."

"I'll bet."

"What about aging. Do you age?"

"Not really. You?"

I pursed my lips. "Occasionally."

Getting into the spirit, he countered, "Can you grow limbs?"

"No, but my sister's pet lizard could drop his tail off and grow a new one."

He smiled at that. "Touché."

"See, you're not so special."

"Well, do *you* have venom that can kill a bear and turn a human into a vampire?"

I wrinkled my nose. "Surely you're not counting that as a positive."

"Only if one of us is getting mauled by a bear."

"So what about all that stuff you see in the movies, like garlic and sunlight and crosses? Is any of that true?"

"Only the part about a stake through the heart. *Anything* through the heart would kill me, just like it would a human."

His venture into the subject of his "abilities" had me thinking. "So, if you bit me, would I turn into what you are?"

"Depends."

"On what?"

"Well, I'm old enough now to where I have pretty good control over my fangs and how much, if any, venom I excrete with a bite."

"These others, the ones you've been…taking care of, have they turned humans?"

A guarded look came over Bo's face, like a thick curtain dropping down into place behind his eyes.

"Some, yes."

"But why? Why would they want to do that?"

"That's another question I'm trying to get an answer to."

"Would you ever consider turning someone?"

"Never," Bo declared with a resolute shake of his head.

Even though it wouldn't happen, couldn't happen—and if it could, I wasn't even sure I'd want it—I was curious about one thing.

"So if you weren't dying and I wanted you to turn me, you still wouldn't?"

"No."

"Why?"

Bo stepped back and pushed his hands into the pockets of his jeans. "The venom, it does something to you. It makes you crave things, think things, things that aren't good, aren't right."

"But you're fine."

"I'm living with the pain and the constant reminder of what someone like me did to my father. If it weren't for that—for that consuming vision of them tearing his throat out—I don't know what I would focus all this energy, all this hunger and thirst on." He paused, looking away from me, toward the dying light that was streaming through the door. "But I'm afraid it wouldn't be good. And I could never subject another person to that. It would be like issuing a death sentence to possibly hundreds of people, potential victims."

"You're sure the only reason you're strong enough to resist it is because of your dad?"

He bit his lip in thought then looked back at me. "Probably not entirely. I'd say it has a lot to do with the amount of vampire blood I take in and what it's doing to my body. I'm degrading, more and more every day. I think it's affecting my thirst."

I didn't want to go down that depressing road again, so I completely changed the subject.

"When can we leave to go to see Lucius?"

Bo glanced back at the door, as if when he'd been staring out it only moments before, he hadn't really *seen* anything.

"Any time now. Do you want to go now?"

"Maybe we should, so we don't get back too late."

Bo shut off the stereo and headed toward the door. I walked out and started up the steps while he cut off the lights and relocked the door.

"Do you mind if we take your car? I usually run, but that's not really an option for you," he said with a quirk of his lips.

"How far is it?"

"About thirty miles or so."

"Just thirty?"

"Yep. Just a hop, skip and a jump," he teased, his grin maturing into a smile that made my knees weak.

When Bo reached the top of the steps, I asked, "How do you know that's not one of my super powers?"

Bo looked deep into my eyes. "Because I know what your super power is."

"What?"

"It's to drive me crazy." The soft way he said it made my stomach flip over.

I laughed nervously. "Ya think?"

"I know," he said, winking at me and taking my hand. "Come on."

Once we were in the car and on the road, my apprehension started to kick in.

"So, this Lucius, how will he feel about a strange human paying him a visit?"

"He'll be fine. He's…old school in many ways."

"What's that supposed to mean?"

"He was born in the days when women were still treated like fragile princesses and people still had manners."

"Ah, the stone ages," I quipped.

"Close," Bo replied.

"How old is he, really?"

"Just over four hundred years I think."

"Four hundred years? Lucius is four hundred years old?"

Bo nodded. "He's one of the oldest ones left."

"Why is that?"

"He's managed to stay hidden from the younger ones, the ones that kill and turn without thought for human life. Like the ones that killed my father."

"Why would he be hiding from other vampires?"

"According to Lucius, hundreds of years ago, vampires were mostly found in Europe and they lived in peace, adhering to a very strict code of conduct. They rarely turned anybody and they sort of had a policy about killing humans.

"But then, some time ago, apparently one of the elders broke the rules and turned a few humans just for fun, a few 'bad seeds'. None of the newer ones respected the code. They were like animals. They craved the thrill of the kill, the power of being higher on the food chain. When the other elders realized that they couldn't control the new turns, they set out to terminate them.

"They started a war that ended up killing most of the vampire population. The younger ones killed many of the elders, and evidently still hunt them today. Because of that, the elders scattered to the four winds. That's when Lucius came here. He says that this country was his salvation, and that it's been a peaceful refuge until recently."

"Does he know who's doing it now? Turning people, I mean?"

Bo shook his head. "No, but with every one that I drain, I'm one step closer to finding out. I'm pretty sure there's one person who's responsible, one who's been spearheading all the activity around here."

"Why do you say that?"

"Because I can see hazy images of all these vamps feeding from another vampire, a stronger one, but it's like their memory is so saturated in pleasure and endorphins, I can't get a clear picture or even a name of the one they're feeding from."

"Why would vampires feed from each other?"

"I think the vampire that's turning them is feeding them some of his blood right at the beginning and establishing some kind of control over them. The thing is, it takes very powerful blood to control another vampire. Maybe even an elder's blood. I'm not sure."

In my head, I went back over everything that Bo had just explained. I found that several things were bothersome.

"So, did you ever…you know?"

"What?" Bo's eyes left the darkening road ahead of us to find mine.

"Feed from another vampire?"

"Only to kill them."

"They didn't try to make you drink any blood when they turned you?"

"They might have tried if I hadn't gotten away when I did."

"What would've happened if they had?"

Bo shrugged. "It's hard to tell. I don't know how much power, how much influence the controlling vampire actually has. I mean, for all I know, these people could've been sick freaks long before they turned. It does make you wonder, though."

I fell quiet after that, digesting all that Bo had revealed. It was so surreal, so scary this other world out there; I wasn't at all sure I was ready to be a part of it.

My last question to Bo, before we reached our destination, was hypothetical, or at least I hoped it was.

"If your blood was powerful enough to give you some control over me, what would you do with it?"

The look Bo cast me was one of mild horror. I'm sure he was thinking *What a question!*

When I merely raised my eyebrows expectantly, Bo sighed deeply and fell silent to give the matter some thought.

Finally he spoke, answering my query. "I'd try to make you forget about me."

I didn't know what to expect in his answer, but that wasn't it. "You would do that?"

We looked at each other intently, far too long for one of us to have been driving. He seemed to have an instinct for the road, though, that allowed him to stay on the asphalt no matter in what direction his eyes were turned.

"I'd like to think I would, but honestly, I don't know if I'm strong enough, selfless enough. But yeah, I'd like to think I could do it."

Once again, a thoughtful silence descended over the interior of the car. Bo appeared to be as lost in thought as I was, so when he pulled off the road and parked along the edge of some trees, I was surprised.

"Where are we?"

"As far as we can go by car," he answered, getting out to come around and let me out.

Bo offered me his hand, but he didn't let go of it. He shut the door behind me and tugged my hand, pulling me close to him as we set out into the forest.

"So how far does Lucius live from here?"

"About three miles."

Inwardly, I cringed. I was in good shape, but a three mile hike through the woods was not my idea of a fun night.

As we trekked along the well-disguised path, Bo led me over fallen trees and through a shallow creek, around water holes and in and out of pine stands. It seemed we'd been walking forever when Bo stopped.

His head whipped around and his eyes darted to and fro, trying to locate something. His expression was one of fierce alertness. The tiny hairs on my arms rose to attention.

I whispered, "What is it? What's wrong?"

Without looking at me, Bo raised a finger to his lips. I held my tongue, swallowing my next worried question. Something about Bo's body language had made me immediately apprehensive. It was more than his caution; it was as if an ominous warning was rolling off of him and crashing over me in cold, menacing waves.

Though there was no denying that my senses had been more acute since drinking Bo's blood—something I didn't even want to think about, much less question—I still wasn't able to discern what had him so tense, and that just made me all the more concerned.

But then, milliseconds after I detected a pleasant brown-sugar smell on the light breeze, I heard the whoosh of an object flying through the air right before something slammed into me, sending me careening through the woods like a human projectile.

CHAPTER ELEVEN

It took me a few fuzzy seconds to realize I'd been hit by a person. It felt as if I'd been hit by a cement truck going a hundred miles an hour, or so my wavering mind believed. My consciousness faltered like a flickering light bulb and I struggled desperately to stay awake, determined to hold on to the world.

I lay on the ground with half my face buried in a bed of dry leaves. I was trembling from head to toe, but otherwise completely immobile. I strained to focus my eyes on the figures I saw looming in the distance.

I was facing the direction from which I'd come and I could see Bo a couple hundred feet away. He stood in a shaft of moonlight as it filtered through the trees. It dappled the ground all around him and sprinkled his rigid body with silvery spots. Even in the pale light, I could see the tension in him.

Bo's face was contorted in fury and his eyes were an unnatural, ghostly green that looked almost white in the low light. His lips were curled back from his teeth in a gruesome, fang-laden snarl and, even from where I was, I could see that his pale skin was cracked like an old canvas painting.

Multiple low growls rang sinisterly through the still of the night. I couldn't tell which noises were coming from Bo and which ones were coming from the two men that were circling him like vicious predators. Their backs were to me, so I could only see that one was taller and thicker than the other. I imagined, however, that their faces were distorted in much the same way as Bo's. It didn't take a genius to figure out that they were vampires, and they were on a mission—a deadly mission.

Bo backed up a step from the two and dropped slowly into a crouch. I saw him grab something from the ground at his right hip. His fingers curled around the dark object and he stilled. He was poised to strike, battle ready.

In a flash of movement so quick I could barely follow it, the taller vampire charged Bo, hurling himself through the air toward him. Bo straightened, catching the vampire in flight and, turning, used the vampire's momentum to throw him to the ground.

Bo landed on top of him and raised his arm above his head. He paused for one long heartbeat, his moonlit form like a mercury-dipped statue. I saw what he held in his hand. It was a piece of wood as thick as a baseball bat with ends just as blunt.

My vision pulsed with every heavy throb of my heart. It stopped beating for one instant when an animal-like roar split the air. A shiver raced down my back as Bo brought his arm down in one lightning-fast motion.

I heard the sickening crunch of bone followed by the hiss of spraying blood as a chest exploded. I couldn't keep my eyes open, but against the backs of my eyelids, my mind painted a clear image of the scene. I could plainly envision the broad head of the makeshift stake crushing the sternum of that vampire and obliterating his heart.

When I was finally able to open my eyes again, it was as if I'd fallen asleep and awakened hours later to a totally different scene. And Bo was not making out as well in this one. He was being held aloft by the shorter of the vampires, his feet dangling several inches off the ground. I could see the chalky fingers that were wrapped around his throat.

In one sharp movement, Bo jabbed his fist into the other vampire's elbow. I heard the splinter of bone as the arm buckled. The milky fingers lost their grip and Bo fell to the ground.

The other vampire backhanded Bo, a violent strike, but one that barely moved Bo's head. Bo's lips lifted in a scary smile before he slammed his flat palm against the vampire's chest.

The vampire stumbled back, but righted himself quickly and charged Bo in a tackling motion that put his shoulder right into Bo's stomach. I heard a grunt as the vampire drove Bo back against a tree, pinning him against it with a branch-shaking thud.

Straightening, the vampire lifted his arm and punched at Bo's face. Bo shifted his head to one side and the fist missed his face by a scant inch. The vampire's knuckles made contact with the tree and it crumbled under the impact, bark and shredded wood flying out in an explosion of debris.

Bo grabbed the vampire by the shoulders, holding him still for a head butt. When their skulls collided, it sounded like a clap of thunder. The vampire growled, not even dazed, and drove his curled fingers deep into Bo's side.

The fight went on, first one then the other gaining the upper hand. I watched every movement with bated breath, every answering strike with a hammering heart, praying that Bo would emerge victorious.

Slowly, as the two vampires danced violently through the woods, I felt life return to my stubborn limbs with a near-painful tingle. I willed my arms and legs to move, the need to get to Bo, to aid him somehow, an almost tangible force.

As the battle wore on, I saw that each of the vampires was operating with fewer and fewer intact limbs. Gaping gashes and broken bones were highlighted with every movement. Though some of the wounds were already beginning to heal, I didn't know how much more damage either of them could sustain and remain upright and battle worthy.

Even though I was only human, I knew that my intervention—that adding my strength (however meager) to Bo's—could mean the difference between his life and his death. That's what drove me to my hands and knees and then, eventually, to my feet, where I leaned unsteadily against a nearby tree.

I'd managed to stumble a few yards forward when I saw Bo, in a burst of energy, lunge forward and trip the other vampire then pin him to the ground.

Bo swung his fists a few times at the guy, and, though I couldn't see the man lying on the ground, I could hear the dull thwack of flesh being pummeled.

Relief washed over me. It appeared that it would soon be over, that Bo was going to win and that he would live at least a little while longer. Unfortunately, my relief was premature.

Something bright flashed through the woods. It was like a match head flaming to life and then being dropped immediately into a cup of water. The light was there and then it was gone.

The streak swept Bo off the other vampire and carried him deep into the woods, far past the point where I could still see him.

A breathless panic constricted my chest and I searched the dark forest and moonlit ground for signs of Bo. There were none.

Far-off sounds tickled my ears and I cocked my head to the side, trying to triangulate the location of the ruckus, a ruckus that I could only assume was Bo and the phantom creature. Pinpointing their position to my left, I pushed myself away from the tree on which I'd been leaning and forced my legs to propel me over the uneven ground toward the commotion.

It seemed I limped and exerted for miles before I could actually make out shapes among the motionless trees. And when I did, my heart stopped.

Bo was nailed to a huge boulder, spread eagle fashion, by thick wooden stakes that were protruding from his shoulders and thighs. A shimmering apparition of a man stood over him, as if waiting for the perfect moment to deal death to Bo.

There was blood everywhere and Bo's head lolled lifelessly to one side. My heart stopped and I watched his chest for movement, to see if he was breathing. He was so absolutely still that my knees nearly buckled in relief when he finally rolled his head upright and spoke to the man.

Blood spewed from his lips with every syllable.

"This isn't over," he said. "If you kill me, someone else will come along, someone stronger than me, someone who can take you down. And they will. They'll rip out your black heart out and salt the earth with your blood and then they'll tear you apart and bury the pieces."

An eerie chuckle rippled through the trees like the dark echo of an empty soul. The hairs on the back of my neck prickled uncomfortably.

"You don't even know who you are, why you must die, and yet you would send others to fall for your cause. Are you sure it is only my heart that is black?"

Bo jerked as if the man's words physically pierced him, but he said nothing.

The man continued. "If others come, they will meet the same fate as you—death. Eternal death. The death of the soul that nothing can regenerate. You will never know of the power that I wield, power that can remove your life force from your body and extinguish it from the universe. The memory of your existence will be no more. It will be as if you never were."

My mind reeled as I listened, my heart thudding wildly, painfully, inside my chest. Was what he threatened even possible? And if it was, what kind of entity could accomplish such a feat? There was only one thing, one manifestation of the purest evil, that came creeping to mind and it made my blood run cold.

Bo wrestled against his restraints, but he barely managed to move at all. Judging by the cracks in the rock to which Bo was affixed, the stakes must've been deeply embedded, an accomplishment that must have taken incredible strength.

"Stop your struggling. You brought this on yourself. Now it's time to reap the whirlwind."

With that menacing warning, the ethereal man raised his hands, fingers splayed and curved in a claw-like manner, toward Bo. At his gesture, the trees around me began to creak as the wind whipped through the branches. It stirred the leaves on the forest floor and sent them spinning through the air. A low hum began to sound, as if the ground was coming alive beneath us. Louder and louder it got until it was a dull roar in my ears.

Above the ambient noise, I could hear Bo panting, his breath coming in shallow bursts like he was in pain. His moan caused my guts to twist in agony. In my mind, I was scrambling to find a way to help him, to put an end to whatever atrocious things this man was planning to do to Bo.

As if he could no longer contain it, a reluctant scream burst through Bo's gritted teeth. The sound ripped through me like a scalpel, tearing my heart open in one quick swipe.

With no thought as to what I was going to do, or to the consequences of my actions, I stepped forward, making my way to the man who hovered ominously over Bo.

When I was no more than three or four feet from him, he turned toward me and I gasped—in recognition.

I was standing face to face with Lars—only not. He looked ghostly and chilling, more frightening that anything I'd ever seen, even in the best of scary movies.

His entire body seemed to be in constant motion, but motion that remained within the confines of his shape. It was as if he was changing, growing with every second, shifting and moving right before my eyes.

His blondish hair was adrift about his head, wiggling in a peculiar golden halo, squirming even. And his face, it was paler than Bo's, and beneath its surface, I could see movement there as well. It was like seeing hundreds of faces fighting for control, for dominance. It was as if his inner demons were visible to the naked eye, like they could be seen writhing and fighting for escape.

"The beautiful Ridley. I see you've had the blood of your mate."

Confused, my eyes flickered to Bo. My bravado faltered when I saw the stunned expression he was wearing. I didn't understand it.

"Let him go, Lars."

"If it's all the same to you, I think I'll keep him. After all, I've only just begun," he declared with a smile that could freeze water.

"He hasn't done anything to you."

"On the contrary, little flower, he has perpetrated quite the offense. And, sweet as it is for you to come to his rescue, young Bo here knew what he was getting into, knew the risk he was taking. I'd wager that he even expected death to come calling for him some day soon, isn't that right Bo?"

Lars didn't turn to look at Bo, but I couldn't help stealing one more glance in his direction. He had closed his eyes again. Whether in exhaustion or defeat, I couldn't know, but it didn't matter to me. Either way, I had to save him.

"Now, if you'll excuse me," he said, turning back to Bo in one fluid motion. He gave me no more thought than he would an irritating fly.

Lars moved closer to Bo, pausing for only a moment to look down at him and say, "I would say I'd be seeing you around, but…I won't."

Arching his back and throwing his head back, Lars let out a deep growl, one that curdled my blood and quieted every noise in the forest. The silence that followed was deafening, a loud roar of nothingness in my head as I watched his hostile takeover of Bo's body.

The erratic movement inside the shape that constituted Lars increased for several tense seconds, wriggling desperately, frantically within the bounds of his frame, until I began to see a rhythm emerge.

It was as if a million tiny points of light slowed and began to shift in a choreographed dance that held me captive. And then I saw something reaching for Bo, like the essence of Lars was stretching forth to claim him.

Thousands of wispy white fingers floated out from Lars like tendrils of smoke gravitating toward Bo. They settled on every surface of Bo's body, tethering him to Lars with thin, milky threads.

Pinpricks of blood sprang up at the tip of each tendril and Bo's body began to convulse, spasms squeezing his muscles from head to toe. His legs and shoulders strained against the stakes that bound him to the boulder, blood weeping from each wound and trickling down the face of the rock.

Within seconds, Bo's entire body was covered in blood and, though he was silent, his face was contorted in pain. It wasn't until I saw the telltale greenish black gangrenous color creeping up his neck toward his chin that I felt something foreign stir within me.

In that moment, something changed inside me. I doubt I'll ever be able to adequately describe it. But I'll never forget it. It was terror mingled with determination, desperation mixed with rage. It was an earth-moving force that welled up in my body, threatening to break it apart.

Building and building, a pressure started in my chest and radiated down into my stomach where it churned angrily. Bo's pain bubbled and gurgled in my veins, like my own blood was in agony, trapped inside my body.

Building and building, my lungs burned with the scream that crouched there, one that I held in and fed from like a fire feeding from oxygen. It fueled me somehow, pulsing and thriving inside me, pushing me to act.

Building and building, fury swelled behind my lids like a red tidal wave, washing away all reason and logic. I felt as if my skin could no longer contain the tsunami.

Like a broken vase, I was busting open and wrath was gushing out through the cracks. In every fiber of my being, I felt it, all the way to fingertips that vibrated like they were about to explode.

And then I did.

Every nerve in my body was suddenly on fire, and every surface cried out in pain. If a thousand knives were slicing me open all at once, it couldn't have hurt any worse. My very skin was splitting. I could feel it.

My eyes met Bo's and I couldn't look away. His were wide with awe and something else that I couldn't identify. But it didn't matter. Nothing did, nothing but Bo's safety.

My gaze and my focus shifted to Lars and I let go. Like exhaling a pent-up breath, I released what I was feeling, unleashed the rage, pouring every last drop on Lars in one mammoth surge.

A banshee-like screech shattered the cool night air. It reverberated through my soul and woke the forest. I saw Lars flinch. At first, his reaction seemed to be nothing more than surprise over the sound. But then, he looked toward me and on his bizarre face of faces was awareness. I was no longer someone to ignore.

For a fraction of a second, the world stood still. Lars and I stared at each other, eyes locked and wills clashing, until he stopped as well. All the movement that was inside him, all the movement that *was him,* simply ceased. And for one sweet moment, I could taste his fear.

I felt my lips pull up into a smile just before Lars exploded in a blinding burst of light that tore me off my feet and sent me hurtling through the air. I landed on my back with a breath-stealing thump and sat up immediately to look around.

Through the white spots in my vision, I could see that trees, even large trees, were flattened in a circle around where Lars had been. Dust and leaves were settling back to the earth in the aftermath of his brilliant disappearance and there was no sign of Lars, no sign that he'd ever stood in the woods across from me.

I scanned the forest, fully expecting him to pop back up somewhere else. I kept thinking that it was too easy, getting rid of him. For me—plain ol' me— to get rid of someone supposedly so old and powerful, it had been far, far too easy.

When several minutes had passed and it seemed that Lars wasn't coming back, I sprang into action, rushing to Bo's side. He was barely conscious and he was bleeding badly. I pulled at the stake in his right shoulder, but it wouldn't budge. I wasn't strong enough to move it even an inch.

"Bo," I whispered, stroking his cheek.

My heart sank when I got no response, so I tried a little more stimulation.

"Bo," I called more loudly, tapping his cheek with my hand.

I thought I heard a moan, but I couldn't be sure.

"Bo," I shouted near his ear, pinching his earlobe between my fingers.

"Ridley," he croaked.

I looked into his face and when I saw his eyelids flutter, my legs nearly gave out beneath me.

"Bo, I can't get the stakes out. What do I need to do?"

His lids trembled with his efforts to open them, but still they didn't rise.

"Follow the path to the cabin," he instructed, his breathing shallow and labored. "Bring Lucius."

Though I was afraid to meet a very old vampire like Lucius by myself, I was more afraid that Bo wouldn't make it. That fear trumped any leeriness of Lucius.

"But what about you? What if more vampires come? I can't leave you here alone."

It sounded ridiculous, even to my ears. Whatever bizarre thing had happened with Lars notwithstanding, what protection could I provide Bo? I was still nothing more than a weak, fragile human.

"No choice. You have to go."

Chewing my lip, I wrestled with indecision for a few seconds before Bo's voice spurred me into action.

"Now, Ridley."

Quickly, I bent and pressed my lips to his, promising, "I'll be right back." Not sparing myself even a brief glance behind me, I took off through the woods.

Turns out I didn't have to travel very far. Bo wasn't even out of sight yet when a man stepped in front of me, earning a startled yelp from me.

I didn't have to wonder what he was. Between a very pleasant honeysuckle smell and his uber pale skin, I knew he was a vampire.

I was instantaneously filled with a fright that froze my muscles and locked my heart in a vise grip. But before I could panic, he spoke.

"Don't be afraid, lass. I'm Lucius."

His silky voice put me at ease right away, like an auditory valium. I felt my muscles warm and relax and I had to purposely resist the smile that tugged at my lips.

Though I wouldn't have called Lucius handsome, I couldn't deny that he was incredibly appealing. He made me want to giggle like a silly ten year old, something I didn't do even when I *was* a silly ten year old.

Lucius had sparkling emerald green eyes and dark red hair that was parted in the middle and bound at his nape. Though his skin was alabaster white, it wasn't hard to imagine him with the ruddy, freckly complexion typical of an Irishman, which was what I imagined he once was. Though his accent had all but faded, there was still a lilt to his voice that gave away his European heritage. He was positively charming and attractive in an inexplicable way.

"Let me tend to Bo," he said, touching my arm with his cool fingers.

Lucius walked around me and made his way to Bo, with me fast on his heels.

I watched as he easily pulled the stakes from their place deep in the rock, freeing Bo's body.

When the last stake was removed, Bo slumped lifelessly to the ground and my heart lurched. Lucius bent and threw Bo over his shoulder and turned back to me.

"This way."

The cabin that had been our destination wasn't far from where we'd been accosted. It looked simple enough from the outside with its log walls and small front porch, but the inside was something entirely different.

The entry level of the cabin was innocuous enough with its one-room floor plan that consisted of a tiny kitchen, a living room with a fireplace and a bedroom that lay behind a folding metal partition. Not including the front door through which we entered, there were three other doors dotted throughout. I assumed one was a bathroom, since it was near the bedroom, and the other looked like a pantry beside the refrigerator.

It was the third door toward which Lucius headed. Curious and a little nervous, I followed.

The door led to a long flight of stairs that descended many feet into the earth. It ended at another door. This one had a sophisticated keypad that required biometrics to open.

Shifting Bo to better free his hand, Lucius pressed his thumb to the pad, punched in a series of numbers and, with a soft click, the door popped open. Lucius stepped through and held the door so that I could enter as well.

I stepped into a grand parlor that looked as if it was lifted out of a Victorian mansion and deposited beneath the cabin, beautiful and perfectly intact.

The walls were painted a rich dark cream and trimmed with wide crown molding and decorative corner pieces. A huge fireplace dominated one wall. Above it hung a mirror with an ornate, gilded frame that looked like it cost a fortune and weighed a ton.

The floors were hardwood and covered in thick rugs that were brown, rust and cream in color. Atop them sat several small delicately curved, Queen Ann-style sofas and chairs, upholstered in brocade of matching hues.

In the center of the high ceiling was a crystal chandelier, its base surrounded by a large plaster medallion. It shed a soft warm glow over the entire room.

The crackling of the fire and the smell of roses completed the surreal scene. I was speechless.

With no thought to the furniture, Lucius deposited Bo on one of the couches directly in front of the fire, arranging his limbs comfortably before he scrambled out, muttering a low, "I'll be right back."

I crossed the room and knelt beside Bo's head. I brushed the backs of my fingers over his clammy forehead and he stirred, wrinkling his brow and turning his face toward me. I saw his body tense and I stilled my hand.

Bo's nostrils flared as he tested my scent, and then, as if he was satisfied, his frown disappeared and his tension eased. With a weary sigh, he relaxed back into the cushions.

Lucius returned quickly, carrying a bag of blood and an opaque half gallon jug.

"I don't keep a very large supply of human blood on hand. I hope the one bag, coupled with the deer blood, will be enough to help him heal."

Setting the blood down beside the couch, Lucius looked over his shoulder at me.

"Come, lass," he said. "Lift his head."

I hurried to Bo's side, lifting his head while Lucius pierced the bag of human blood and waved it under Bo's nose.

He held the plastic packet to Bo's mouth and told Bo to drink. At first, Bo didn't respond, so Lucius rubbed the bag back and forth across Bo's lips until he finally opened his mouth and bit down on it.

Within seconds, Bo drained the bag. Beneath my hands, I could feel his body temperature warm a few degrees. I watched, fascinated, as life began to slowly seep back in to his features.

Next, Lucius held the sealed jug sideways against Bo's mouth. With a loud pop, Bo obediently sank his teeth into the rigid plastic. I watched his throat work as he pulled large gulps of liquid down his throat. He frowned as if it wasn't something he was enjoying.

When Bo had finished the animal blood, Lucius took the empty container and set it aside, turning to lean his back against the couch and stretch his legs out in front of him.

"Now, we wait," he announced.

"Alright." Though I agreed easily enough, I felt anxiety curl in my stomach, twisting it into a tight knot.

"I feel like I know you, Ridley, what with Bo talking about you so much." Lucius rolled his head toward me, a pleasant smile on his lips. "And of course, I'd like nothing better than to use this time to get to know you better, but I would imagine that you have even more questions than I. Is there anything you would like to know?"

Was there ever! With nothing but time on our hands, I knew I'd have the opportunity to get a few answers, but not to the million or so questions that started clamoring for attention all at once in my head. One drifted to the top, however, taking the position of top priority.

"Can Bo be saved? From the poison, I mean?"

Lucius sighed, a sad look coming to settle on his face. "You would ask that," he said. "No, lass, I'm afraid not."

My heart broke a little bit more with his answer, like he'd been the final word on the matter, the one tiny thread of hope to which I'd been clinging.

"How long does he have?" I smoothed my hand over Bo's brow, dreading the answer. Anything less than one hundred years was not enough.

"I can't be sure. There aren't very many vampires who try to kill themselves in this manner."

"It's not like that's the only reason he's doing it," I snapped. Then, shaking my head regretfully, I apologized. "Sorry. I'm just- I'm just frustrated."

"As am I, Ridley. As am I." Lucius looked morosely into the flames licking greedily at the wood inside the fireplace. "He's been like a son to me, a breath of fresh air in a long and lonely existence."

"He said you're four hundred years old."

"The brat," he chortled. "Telling a woman how old I am. And lying about it no less. I won't be four hundred for another nine years."

I couldn't help but grin. "What was he thinking? I mean, nine years makes a world of difference when you've lived nearly half a millennium."

Lucius smiled broadly up at me, apparently enjoying my sarcasm. "Oh, Ridley, what a joy you are." When he sobered, he continued. "Yes, I've lived a long, full life, but now—after all these years—it seems it was full of loss and heartache more than anything else."

I sat quietly for a moment, not knowing what to say to that. Finally, I asked, "Do you regret coming to America?"

"Good Lord, no! I love it here. It's been like watching a child grow up. I only hate that now they've infiltrated this continent."

"Who?"

"The Uccideres," he answered, the "r" rolling off his tongue.

"Who are they?"

"To best explain them, I must first give you a short history lesson about the vampire. Do you mind?"

"No, no. Please."

"It all started with the venom. It is said to have been given to man by the devil himself, a weapon through which he hoped to enslave the human race. According to legend, it nearly worked. But over time, as vampires learned to control themselves and learned the dangers of feeding off one human too often, we were able to settle down into a very peaceful existence.

"A code of sorts was adopted among that first small band of European vampires, who we now call the 'Elders'. Humans were rarely turned, usually only for the purpose of preserving one's mate. After all, it would be far too painful for a vampire to live without his mate, so not turning *anyone* was out of the question. Turning one's mate is really the only option in such cases."

Lucius paused, lost in thought, lost to something that took him from the present for a heartbeat. While he tarried elsewhere, a multitude of new questions rose to my mind. Before I could ask any one of them, however, he drifted back to the here and now to continue.

"Apologies, lass. I digress," he said, clearing his throat. "What you saw tonight was an Uccidere. They are aberrations that arose from one elder many, many years ago. His name was Constantine.

"For centuries, Constantine had never been satisfied with the low-key way of life the vampires had adopted. Though he'd had his missteps every now and again, none of the elders ever expected that he might defy The Tribunal so completely. But, alas, he did. When he left Rome, no one could have anticipated the havoc, the destruction, the slaughter that he would wreak upon the human race. By himself, he was quite the scourge. Some say it is as vampires were intended to be.

"Before Constantine could be stopped, he had turned hundreds, probably even thousands of humans into vampires. That, however, was not an issue in and of itself. It was the *kind* of people that he turned that posed such a problem. Criminals, prostitutes, drug addicts, sex fiends, masochists, killers, thieves, all from the distasteful company he kept. Unfortunately, when they turned, they not only brought along many of their own hedonistic habits, but learned the way of the vampire from Constantine himself. It was a bloody, bloody time."

"You said he was stopped, though, right?"

"Yes, but not before damage more than a thousand lifetimes could be done. Some of the world's most notorious murderers have been traced back to Constantine or one of his people. Jack the Ripper, Attila the Hun, Amelia Dyer, Darya Saltykova. There were even some Americans suspected of ties to Constantine's children, people like The Green River Killer and Son of Sam. The list is endless and spans hundreds of decades, but the vampire epidemic has never really been a confirmed threat in this country until recently."

"What does that mean?"

"It means that they must be stopped before another army, of Constantinian proportions, can be created. These days, it's easy to see why legend claims that the venom was born of the devil to destroy mankind. It is a power, a thirst that only the strong can contain, can manage without giving in to the euphoria of it, the thrill and the pleasure of it."

An odd look came over Lucius's face, a look that made the hairs on my arms prickle. I could tell he was lost again—somewhere, some place in time, in sensation—and for some reason, I was afraid to bring his attention back to me. Survival instinct maybe.

After a few tense moments, his expression cleared and he turned to me and smiled. I was glad to see that he had returned from…wherever.

"Honestly, I'm a little surprised that you wanted to use this time to learn about vampires. I just assumed that you would want to know what happened to you in the woods."

His statement puzzled me. "I'm sorry? I don't understand what you mean."

"My guess is that Bo has fed you, at least once. Is that right?"

"Yes, but how—"

"The poison affects humans differently."

"The poison?" I felt the blood drain from my face. I hadn't even thought of that. I wondered if Bo had. "How did you know?"

"Even if I hadn't seen what you did to that Uccidere, I would've known by your skin."

"My skin?"

"Yes. Standing in the forest, you looked just like Bo does after he ingests the poison."

In perfect clarity, the image of the gangrenous color spreading across Bo's nearly translucent, cracking skin came to mind. Reflexively, I looked down at my arms. I was incredibly relieved to see that they were the same medium olive tone that they always were.

"But- but—"

"Oh, you will only be able to see it when Bo's in danger. It's your body, your blood reacting to his. You share a common bond."

"When Lars exploded, is that how I- I did that?"

"Yes."

I struggled to wrap my mind around it, but I just couldn't get there. "But *how?*"

"Many strange and powerful things lie in the blood. The venom changes it, mutates it in various ways and, depending on the person, a broad spectrum of reactions can occur. For example, most vampires can affect a fair amount of influence over humans, an ability that only gets stronger with age. But some are so powerful, they can literally compel humans to do anything, even things that would bring pain and harm to themselves. It is a very dangerous ability."

"But I won't turn into a vampire from just drinking it, will I?"

"Oh, no. You have to be infected with venom for that to happen. But when you drink infected blood, its properties sort of *enhance* your human traits. You may experience better hearing, vision, healing, strength and speed, but it is usually short-lived unless you ingest blood regularly."

I shuddered. "Why would anyone want to do that?"

"Many humans like the augmentation, but even more, there are those vampires who would use it."

"Use it? How?"

"Unfortunately, in our history, some vampires have made a weapon of sorts out of humans. A vampire can turn several humans and feed them his own blood. His 'children' then go and feed their blood to any number of humans that they drink from, giving that one vampire—the father of them, if you will— control over the masses. Through his 'sons and daughters', he has access to the minds of all the humans they've bonded with."

While I was assimilating all that Lucius had revealed, I busied myself smoothing Bo's hair. It was then that I noticed his deteriorating condition.

His skin had begun to cool again and his gray-green pallor was deepening.

When I looked to Lucius, he was frowning.

"What's happening?"

"It appears the animal blood is not going to be enough to supplement the human blood."

"Can you give him more?"

"No. It's all I have."

"Is he going to get worse?"

His frown deepened. "That is a distinct possibility."

My mouth gaped open. While Lucius might be alright with that outcome, I certainly was not.

"Can't you get more?"

"I could hunt, but the animals can sense me, which means that they are scarce around here these days. I have to travel quite a ways to find prey."

That didn't sound very promising and I searched desperately for another option. And then I found one.

"Wh-what about me?"

Lucius cut his eyes to me in a look that gave me pause. "That's not an option."

"But why? It could save his life, right?"

"Yes, but it could risk yours."

"How so?"

"It's possible that he could accidentally inject you. In his current state, I'm not sure his control is completely intact."

Although that did cause a trickle of fear to ripple through me—living an existence like Bo's for eternity, only without Bo—I only hesitated for one short breath before I came to the conclusion that no cost was too high.

"I don't care. I'm willing to risk it to save him."

"Bo would never forgive me."

"Yes, he would. Eventually. Besides, he's worth it. He's worth anything."

Lucius eyed me, a smile curving his lips. "You love him."

It wasn't a question, it was an observation. A very good, very accurate observation. There was just no denying it anymore.

"Yes. And I can't lose him. Not yet."

"But there are other risks."

"You mean the bond?"

"No. I mean a risk to your life."

"What other risk? Bo didn't say anything about—"

"Bo doesn't know."

"What? Why?"

For the first time, I started to feel a little suspicious of Lucius. He was telling me that, after all this time, there were things Bo didn't know, things that Lucius himself hadn't told him. But why? Why wouldn't he have told Bo everything? That just didn't make any sense. It seemed to me that Lucius was trying to convince me to let Bo die, something I would never do.

"You know that Bo is dying," he said. When I nodded, he continued. "At first, he was so disgusted with what he'd become that he refused to drink human blood at all. It wasn't until revenge took hold that he began to use the blood bank supply to sustain himself. But only until he could find his father's killer. At that time, I saw no reason to tell him what he could do to humans. He had enough self-loathing without all the finer details. Since he began tracking and killing the Uccideres and draining them—poisoning himself—it hasn't been an issue simply because the poison affects the thirst, suppresses it, so that he doesn't crave fresh human blood like he would otherwise."

I nodded, resisting the urge to gloat when I told Lucius, "Bo told me that."

"What he didn't tell you, what he doesn't know, is that when a vampire drinks from a human, he feeds on more than just the blood. That is why animal blood cannot sustain us in an equal manner. We feed off of *life.* Each time a human is fed upon, it drains them of a portion of their essence, shortening their lifespan.

"I've seen humans, after having been fed on only twice, turn into something akin to the walking dead. They become decaying, mindless shells of the people they once were. Their lives, the minds and bodies, become dominated by a hunger of their own. They're insatiable, violent. Some, it only takes one feeding, some more. Again, it depends on the person. Stronger humans can take more…abuse than their weaker counterparts. But a vampire can never be sure which variety he's feeding upon. That's part of the risk."

I chewed my lip as I considered what Lucius was saying. What if he was telling the truth? Bo had admittedly already fed on me once, and, though many would probably argue the point, I seemed to be fine. But what would another feeding do to me? Make me some kind of zombie?

I thought of the recent reports of suspected mad cow disease and I wondered if they had anything to do with the rash of vampire attacks. Though I wanted to know, I refused to ask. I didn't want to be swayed, dissuaded from saving Bo for any selfish reason.

"I'm willing to take the risk, but I have one question. Why didn't you tell Bo? Whether he technically needed to know or not, he *deserved* to know."

Lowering his head, Lucius at least had the good grace to look contrite. "Bo was so devastated by what he'd become, by his father's death, by his own survival, I didn't have the heart to tell him what a danger he was. Not until it became necessary anyway. And, fortunately, it hasn't become a necessity."

"Until now," I clarified.

"Until now," he agreed with a somber nod.

With dread and anxiety gnawing insistently at my stomach, I took a deep breath and straightened my spine.

"Well, it doesn't matter. Bo's worth it. He's had too much pain and anguish in his life for it to end without him finding justice for his father, and he won't be able to do that dead, so…"

I thought I saw a flicker of admiration flash in the green eyes of Lucius, but it was gone as quickly as it had appeared.

"Alright then. Come," he said, offering me his hand.

On shaking legs, I rose, letting Bo's head fall gently back to the couch as I took Lucius's hand. I knelt beside him on the thick rug, my face right in front of Bo's grayish-green one.

I looked to Lucius for direction. His expression was one of sad resignation, but despite his reservations, he nodded toward Bo.

"Give him your throat."

Feeling the tremor in my fingertips, I released Lucius's hand, not wanting him to know how afraid I was. I looked at Bo's sweaty face and my resolve strengthened.

Scooting forward, I leaned over him, positioning my neck directly over his mouth.

"Is this good?"

"Perfect," Lucius replied quietly. "Now we need to stimulate him. Bo," he said, speaking sternly. "You need to feed."

I closed my eyes and waited. I had no idea what to expect, but I felt like I had a pretty good idea of what to fear. I just wanted Bo to hurry up and bite me so that I wouldn't start thinking of all the reasons I probably shouldn't be doing this.

"Bo," Lucius repeated, more harshly this time. "You need to feed. If you want to find your father's killer, you must feed." There was a hard edge to Lucius's voice, one I suspected he thought might infiltrate Bo's stupor and reach his foggy brain.

Still, there was no movement. I could feel the tickle of Bo's breath on my neck, but that was all.

Then Lucius shook him. Hard. "Bo!"

Nothing.

"Bo," I said, thinking that my pleas might jar him awake. "Please. You need to drink."

Nothing.

"Bo, please!"

Still nothing.

I leaned back and looked from Bo to Lucius and back again.

"He looks worse," I said of his shiny skin and generally unhealthy pallor.

"If we can't get him to respond, to drink, there will be no hope."

I whirled on Lucius. "Then do something!"

Lucius's jewel-like eyes bored into mine. "If I hunt, he could be gone by the time I get back," he warned.

"Then I guess you'd better hurry," I snapped coldly.

Reluctantly, Lucius stood, looked down at Bo for another few seconds then turned on his heel and he was gone. I didn't even see how he left the room. He was just gone. I didn't see or hear the door open. I didn't see or hear him running or moving. He was simply there one minute and not the next.

With a shudder, I turned my attention back to Bo.

"Bo, please wake up," I pleaded, stroking his cheek. "You can't leave me yet. I'm not ready. We haven't had enough time yet."

My voice broke on the last and I swallowed hard. I didn't want him to hear my upset. He needed my strength, not my weakness.

"Bo, if you ever had any feelings for me, open your eyes and look at me." When I got no response, I added, "Now!"

He was so still, he could already have been dead for all I knew.

I put my ear to his chest. In the quiet, I could make out the slow, steady thump of his heart. I knew that as long as I could hear that, there was still a chance to save him.

In repose, his usually animated mouth was relaxed. His lips were not too thick, not too thin; they were just right. Chiseled. Hard. Manly. Perfect.

I reached out and touched the tip of my finger to them, tracing the smooth contour. Impulsively, I leaned forward and pressed my mouth to his.

The intoxicating smell that was distinctively Bo's flooded my nostrils and washed over my senses. My throat clenched. The prospect of no longer smelling that scent was unthinkable.

I leaned back, just enough to lick my lips. I thought I might be able to taste him, but I couldn't. I wanted to take it in, take a part of him into myself, to hide it away for safekeeping. I wanted something of him that I never had to let go, something that would never fade or die.

I closed my eyes against the tears that threatened and pressed my lips to his once more.

A sob shook me and my lips moved against Bo's. When it passed, I still felt movement beneath me. I gasped. Bo's lips were stirring under mine, ever so slightly. I increased the pressure and, much to my relief, Bo responded, deepening the kiss.

By his fervor, or lack thereof, it was evident that he was still weak, but he was alive, alive enough to curl my toes and make me remember why I'd risk my life to save him, even for one more day.

My eyes flew open when the significance of his kiss fully penetrated my mind. He was *awake.* If he was awake, he could feed.

Pulling back just enough to break contact, I said, "Bo, you need to feed and I want you to drink from me."

Bo groaned and shook his head in one firm motion. He was resisting.

"Please, Bo. I want you to." I kissed him again, hoping to draw him in with passion. "Please," I sighed into his mouth.

His breathing increased, becoming more ragged, but still he resisted. "No," he whispered.

"Bo, you will die if you don't feed. I know it's going to happen eventually, but please don't leave me yet. Please. I'm begging you. I want you to drink from me. I want to be bonded with you forever. I want to feel you when you're gone. At least give me that. *Please."*

When I pressed my lips to Bo's this time, I was taking the proverbial gloves off. I put my hand on his chest and leaned up, sinking into the kiss. I let my tongue slide between his lips and glide over the silky interior of his mouth. I reveled in the sweet taste of him.

Again, he kissed me back. Not exactly vigorously, but it was enough to let me know that he was quickly coming back to the land of the living.

"Bo," I moaned, tearing my lips from his.

Scooting up over him, I straddled his hips, crushing my breasts to his chest and pressing my throat to his mouth.

"Bite me, Bo. Please. Take it."

My heart was booming inside me and I was suspended between desire and fear, a very heady combination. Every sense, every nerve, was tightly focused on Bo and his mouth.

When I felt his lips open and his tongue touch the flesh of my neck, I had to bite my lip to keep from crying out. My skin was hypersensitive and his cool tongue felt like ice—smooth, sensual, wet ice. My belly trembled with want.

"Please," I whimpered, shifting on top of him, craving the contact, the friction of his body against mine.

An instant before he gave in, I knew I'd won. I felt it somewhere deep inside me, like he was coming home, and I was his home. There was a flash of utter completion, of perfect peace right before I felt the sharp pinch of his teeth piercing my flesh.

CHAPTER TWELVE

Sweet pain swept through me, a hurt so good that I never wanted it to end. For a moment, it was as if Bo and I were one person. I could feel his pleasure—the thrill of the bite, the ecstasy of the blood—as if they were my own, and I gave myself over to it, sinking into him.

I wasn't aware of how I got onto the floor, onto my back, but when I opened my eyes, I saw the ceiling and Bo was on top of me. His body rested atop mine, his hips between my open thighs. His lips were at my neck and my hands were fisted in his hair. I held on tight, willing him not to stop, my body begging him for more.

Bo began to move, shifting and rubbing against me, pressing into me where our hips met. Husky noises of passion purred in his throat and tingled along my skin. Little pulses of electricity streaked through my body, setting my core on fire.

I was growing warmer by the second, melty, and my head was getting fuzzy. I opened my eyes and my vision swam in a hazy blur. I shut them to drown out the sights. I wanted only to concentrate on Bo and his mouth and all that he was making me feel.

Unbidden, the hair that I clutched at the back of his head slid through my fingers. My arms were falling, falling, falling until I heard the thump of them hitting the carpet at my side. They landed on a bed of cotton that cushioned them. It cradled my entire body, holding me in a sea of softness. I tried to lift my arms, to recapture Bo inside them, but they refused to obey my commands. The cotton, with its wispy fibers, held them firmly in place.

One delicate strand at a time, the cotton wove its way inside my head and around my body, stealing the air from the room, smothering it in flimsy filaments. It was growing harder and harder to breathe, but I was so comfortable, it was even harder to care.

More content than I could ever remember being, I stopped resisting. With a sigh, I relaxed back into the puffy cloud and let it take me, swallow me, consume me.

****

I awoke some time later with the sweet comfort of Bo's scent surrounding me. I opened my eyes and turned my head. I was lying in my bed and Bo was next to me. He was turned up on his side, his head in his hand, staring down at me. He was so close I could feel his body pressed along every inch of my left side.

We lay on top of the covers, but I had no need of them. Bo's body was feverish, more than enough to keep me warm in the cool of the night.

"Lucius said to tell you that he enjoyed meeting you. He was very impressed with you." Bo leaned forward and whispered conspiratorially. "Between us, I think he has a little bit of a crush."

"You're ok." All I could think about was the relief I felt that Bo was here with me, alive and well, talking to me in my bed.

"Thanks to you," he said, rubbing his finger across my brow. "You saved my life."

I shrugged. "It was my turn."

"You risked too much."

"Nothing's too much for you."

"Lucius told me everything."

"It doesn't matter."

"It does."

"No, it doesn't. I'd do it again."

"I wouldn't let you."

"You might not have a choice."

Bo rolled onto his back. His weary sigh cut through the silence. "That's why I'm leaving."

"What?" I bolted upright in the bed and turned toward Bo.

"I'm no good for you. I should've stayed away."

"How can you say that?"

"Because I care too much for you to stay, to continually put you in danger."

"Everyone's in danger, they just don't know it."

He nodded and rolled his eyes. "You're in more danger than most."

"You'll- ," I began, choking on the words as I tried to spit them out. "You'll be gone soon anyway. At least stay with me until then."

"Every day that I—"

"Please, Bo. Do this one thing for me. Stay until the end."

"Ridley—"

"I know it will hurt you to be away from me. But what about me? You don't know what it will do to *me* if you go. You don't know how the human half of a bond feels. But I do."

Bo stared into my eyes. I could see the war waging inside him. He was torn, not wanting to hurt me either way, but knowing it was going to happen regardless. I could also see his resolve weakening, so I pressed on.

"Don't deny me this, Bo. At least give me the rest of your life. It's not like I'm asking that much."

It was bizarre, using his imminent death as a valid point in an argument, but I'd use whatever I had to in order to get him to stay.

"I just don't—"

"And if you go, you'll never find out who killed your father."

Bo shot me a look that said *Dirty trick,* but I was not the least bit apologetic. If it would get him to stay, I'd remind him of his mission every day.

"Ridley," he started, sighing again.

When he didn't continue, I knew I'd won. At least for the time being.

"Plus," I said, snuggling back down beside him, resting my head on his chest. "You need to graduate."

Bo laughed and the rough rumble made my heart swell.

"Because school is so important at this stage in my life."

"I'm sure your mom would like to see you graduate. It's a maternal thing." Even as I mentioned it, I realized that I knew very little about their relationship.

"Actually, you're right. She's really the only reason that I enrolled in school to start with."

"See?"

"I think it's her way of retaining some semblance of normalcy. It got me out of Southmoore, too, which is what she wanted. She thought distance would make a difference, that I'd get interested in a new life and forget about finding Dad's killer."

"Sounds like she barely knows you," I quipped.

"She doesn't, not really. She was never home much before. She was a lot...different back then. She and Dad weren't exactly happy. I think she's got a lot of regrets."

"And if you left now, it would just hurt her even more. All the way around, it's just best for you to stay."

Hmm was Bo's only response.

****

By lunch on Friday, I was fully recovered and Bo was still in my life, so I was calling it a good day. Savannah was prattling on about our double date and even that didn't dampen my mood.

"We should totally go see that new scary movie. What's it called?" Before anyone could answer, Savannah got sidetracked, gasping excitedly. "Oh and then, we can go do something completely reckless like break into the marina and hijack a boat."

"What?" If I thought she wasn't serious, I'd have laughed. But, sadly, I knew she was dead serious. I was discovering that Savannah was fearless, too.

"You're frickin' nuts," Devon claimed. His tone said he was serious, but his eyes said he'd follow her to the ends of the earth.

"It doesn't have to be a yacht. It can be a little boat. A dingy or a blow-up raft. I don't care what it is, just as long as it will get us out into the water."

"Why?" This was Bo's question. He wasn't opposed to the idea, so long as there was a good reason behind it.

I rolled my eyes in exasperation. What kind of rebellious hoodlums had I inadvertently befriended?

"Because today's the fourth anniversary of my mother's drowning and I want to set a lantern out for her. She loved the water more than anything."

None of us had a comment for that and I knew that tonight we'd be breaking and entering. I felt a little bud of excitement unfurl in my stomach. Doing something completely crazy was out of character for me, but my character was changing pretty rapidly. I wanted to do as much living, reckless and otherwise, as I could squeeze in before Bo left me.

As always, thoughts of his condition sent a stab of pain through my heart. I slid a glance in Bo's direction as he talked with Savannah and Devon. He laughed and shifted his eyes to me. He winked and my stomach fluttered in response.

It seemed incongruous, a cruel twist of fate, that I could love someone more and more each day, and yet already be mourning his passing. As my love grew, so did the dark cancer of his illness. It was eating away at me, gnawing at my soul.

I'd begun to hate seeing lunch period come to an end. I'd found more genuine friendship and camaraderie at Savannah's table than I'd ever known, and Bo was always there. He was relaxed and happy and I basked in his unmasked affections. It was like a sun-drenched capsule of near-perfection that I never wanted to leave.

But I was coming to realize that all good things must end. And usually they ended badly.

Bo had just left, going in the opposite direction, toward his class, and I was closing my locker when Trinity approached.

She looked better, but only in a less-sick way. She looked more like a vampire than ever. Her skin was chalky white and her eyes held a viciousness that even I had never seen there before.

"I heard about the other night in the woods," she said without prelude.

"Trinity, I'm sorry. I know you had a thing for Lars, but—"

She laughed bitterly. "You two have no idea what you're doing, do you?"

"Trinity, I—"

"Of course you don't," she said, leaning in close to my face. "You know what the funny thing is?"

I sighed. "What, Trinity?" Something in her eyes creeped me out and I had to look away. I stared over her shoulder, trying to assume my most bored and unconcerned expression.

"All this was to find Bo's father's killer. At this rate, you'll never find her."

Her?

My eyes snapped back to Trinity's. "You know who was behind the attack?"

Trinity's smile was smug and self-satisfied. She'd gotten the reaction she wanted, so, with one more laugh in my face, she turned and walked away.

"Trinity!" I called after her, but she didn't even pause. "Trinity!"

For the rest of the day, I wrestled with when and how to tell Bo what she'd said. I decided to wait until after our double date. If I told him before, it would ruin the whole night. Besides, I was pretty sure he'd come to my room afterward and I could talk to him about it then.

****

Of all the terrible nights for my mother to stay home and get loaded, she chose that night, the night Bo came to get me. To add insult to injury, she even beat me to the door when he rang the bell.

I heard her shrill voice all the way back in my room, so I strapped on my wedge shoes, pulled the hem of my tunic down over my leggings and bolted for the door.

When I reached the foyer, Mom was already draped all over Bo. She was looking up into his face with doe eyes, smiling flirtatiously. I was mortified.

I hurried to Bo's side and took his other arm, the one she wasn't trying to tear off, and I tugged. "We'd better go. Savannah's going to kill us."

When I pulled, Bo shifted toward me and Mom stumbled drunkenly, grabbing Bo for support. She giggled, covering her lips with her fingertips.

"I'm so sorry. My balance is terrible today."

Mom put the coy in coy.

"What time does Dad's flight get in, Mom?"

Like magic, Mom sobered considerably at the mention of Dad. She always did. Straightening, she smoothed her hair.

"Not until morning."

"Oh, I thought it was tonight." That was not entirely true, but just mentioning him got the desired result.

"No, and you'd better be home at a decent hour, young lady. You know he'll want to spend some time with you tomorrow, so you can't be sleeping the day away."

"I'll have her home early, Mrs. Heller."

Mom turned her eyes to Bo and I could almost see her melt. For a moment, I sympathized with her. I knew exactly how that felt.

"Call me Becky," she oozed. "It's so nice to finally meet you, Bo."

"It's my pleasure, ma'am."

"Becky," she repeated.

Bo smiled graciously. "Becky."

Feeling disgusted and mortified, I tugged at Bo again. "Let's go."

As it turned out, Devon was driving. He'd picked up Savannah first then Bo, and then the trio had come for me. Bo opened the passenger door to Devon's Mazda and helped me in.

Savannah turned around in her seat and greeted me excitedly.

"Those shoes rock," she declared.

"Thanks. I got them for my birthday."

"Wish I got cool stuff like that for my birthday."

I didn't mention that I'd bought them for myself with the money that my parents had given me a month and a half later because it took them that long to remember that I even had a birthday.

Savannah's red hair was pulled up into a loose bun atop her head. Tendrils had already escaped the knot and were floating around her face like dancing flames. She wore a chic black gauzy top and a velvet choker around her throat, the tails trailing down over her collarbones and anchored with tiny metal crosses tied to the ends. Though her style wasn't necessarily "hip," Savannah was fashionable in her own way and she wore it flawlessly.

"You look great," I told her, and that was entirely true. I felt bland and monochromatic in comparison.

"So do you," Bo said, having climbed in beside me.

His eyes roved me from head to toe and shone with appreciation. The look he gave me when his eyes met mine again made me feel like a beautiful princess.

"Thank you." My smile was so wide, it was almost painful.

"Yeah, Ridley. I'm not the one who looks like a Vanessa Hudgens–Hayden Panettiere love child."

"What?" I turned my gaze to her where she leaned around the front seat. "I do not."

Savannah looked to Devon. "Tell her, Dev. She does, doesn't she?"

Devon craned his neck and looked back at me. "Yeah, you sorta do."

I looked to Bo. He was simply smiling. "A blend of two gorgeous people? Why complain?"

I rolled my eyes as Devon started the engine and pulled away from the curb.

The movie was awesome. Scarier than any movie had a right to be, but it was incredible. Savannah sat upright, wide-eyed and fascinated by the show. I spent the entire one hundred and two minutes scrunched down in my chair, trying to hide behind my hands.

By the time we got out, I was struggling not to be shaken. Truth be known, though, I was already dreading bedtime. I'd probably have some nasty nightmares.

Bo held the theater door open for me and as I passed by him, he whispered, "Looks like you might need some all-night company tonight."

He was grinning mischievously when I looked up at him. Warmth spread through me, radiating from my suddenly-steamy skin. I'd use any available excuse to get Bo to stay with me.

"I think you might be right."

My adrenaline was already sky high from the movie, so I was practically vibrating by the time we got to the car and headed for the marina.

Bo and I talked quietly in the back seat while Devon and Savannah occupied their own world in the front seat. For a second, my eyes were drawn to the gap between the seats where I could see that Devon held Savannah's hand on the console. He fiddled with her fingers in a casual, intimate way that made it seem like he'd been holding her hand his entire life.

As if by gravity, my attention was pulled back to Bo. His head was leaned back against the headrest and his eyes were closed as he told me about a dog he used to have. Listening to him, it was easy to see that he was an animal lover and I wondered at how hard it must've been for him, having to take the lives of so many to sustain himself for those first few weeks.

Bo was absently drawing circles on the inside of my wrist with his fingertips. His soothing touch coupled with the quiet timbre of his voice lulled my overwrought senses and I felt safer and more loved than I could ever remember feeling. I felt like I was as highly attuned to Bo as I was to my own body.

He stopped speaking and lifted his head, as if he could sense it as well. Reluctantly, I shifted my gaze from his mouth to his eyes. Without a word, he simply watched me. And I watched him back.

His shimmering eyes drew me in and held me. And in that moment, I knew—without a shadow of a doubt, I knew—that he loved me as much as I loved him, and that it wasn't a childish, fleeting crush. It was a real, true, deep love—the sacrificing kind that was excruciating; the transcendent kind that time and distance couldn't diminish; the eternal kind that even death couldn't weaken. It was ours and it was forever.

With a heartrending certainty, I knew that I would never love another person more than I loved Bo. Before long, he'd be taken from me and I'd live the rest of my life mourning the loss of the only person to ever walk the earth who could make me whole.

It was in that precious instant of perfect clarity that he found us.

CHAPTER THIRTEEN

Something heavy landed on the roof of the car with a loud and terrifying thump.

"What the—"

The car shook as if something was on top of it, wiggling it. But what was strong enough to move a car?

Alarm bells sounded in my head and I looked over at Bo. He was tight-lipped, his expression grave.

The car shuddered again and Devon swerved. The right front tire slid off into the gravel and we fish-tailed for a few nerve-racking seconds before he regained control of the car.

"Ohmigod, what is that?" Savannah had her feet braced against the dash and her knuckles were white where she gripped the handle above the door.

"Don't stop, Devon," Bo ordered sternly.

The engine whined as Devon pressed on the gas. We lurched forward and all four of us looked back, anxious to see if whatever had assailed us had fallen off in the road.

I was the first to turn back around.

"Devon, look out!"

Up ahead, shining brilliantly in the headlights, was a person standing in the middle of the road.

"Devon, don't stop," Bo said again.

"What? There's someone in the road. I can't just—"

"Devon, don't stop."

"Devon, you have to stop," Savannah screamed as we bore down on the figure in the road.

With a squeal of tires, Devon mashed on the brakes. We came to a screeching halt that threw all of us forward in the car.

When we were once more settled in our seats, our attention was drawn to the person standing in the center of the dark, country lane.

It was Trinity.

Dressed in a solid white baby doll dress and wearing no shoes, Trinity's hair was a tangled mess that hung wildly about her shoulders. Her skin was only a shade darker than her dress and her eyes were a washed out green. It was her lips that stood out the most, though. They were blood red and curled back from her teeth, teeth that now included four elongated canines.

"Is that Trinity?" Savannah's voice was low and breathy, laced with fear and confusion.

"Stay in the car," Bo said, as he opened the door.

In a flash that was too fast for us to see, Trinity was at the car, holding Bo's door closed.

With one sharp extension of his arm, Bo pushed Trinity out of the way and got out of the car. She stumbled back and began stepping away from him.

"What's wrong with her?" It was Savannah that spoke again.

I didn't answer and Devon didn't say a word. Though I could only see him in profile, his expression was full of both shock and disgust.

I scooted over into Bo's seat and rolled down the window so I could hear.

"Trinity, don't make this mistake. Go home and leave them alone."

Trinity laughed, a maniacal sound that made my skin crawl.

"Oh, no. I've waited too long for this. Besides, they're my gift. How rude would it be to turn down a gift?"

"Your gift?" Bo asked what we were all thinking, only he came up with an answer before everyone else.

Bo turned a circle, scanning the road and the woods beyond, looking for something. Or someone.

He tipped his chin up and I saw his nostrils flare. He whipped his head around, his gaze focused on a spot over the top of the car in the forest. It was another few seconds before I could smell anything, but when the scent finally reached my nose, my stomach clenched in fear as my mind spun in disbelief.

"It can't be," I whispered.

"What?" Devon's voice was equally quiet.

A fraction of a second later, another thump sounded on the roof of the car. Devon and I jumped. Savannah yelped.

Another thump toward the back of the car had us all turning toward the trunk. Out the back window, a pair of jeans-clad legs came into view.

As they hopped gracefully down off the car, I felt the change in Bo and, like dominos, I felt the change in me.

It was the fire, the consuming flames of something that I couldn't control and didn't understand, but something I recognized from that night in the woods. The same night I faced the man that stood only feet from me now. It was Lars, in his fully human form. I didn't want to believe my eyes, but how could I not? He was standing only a few feet away.

How could that be? I thought, but then I remembered thinking that killing him was far too easy. Apparently I'd been right—it wasn't that easy.

A deep growl rumbled in Bo's throat, sending chills down my arms and legs. Like a predator, he moved around Lars, as if to flank him. A hiss sounded from the rear, no doubt coming from Lars.

"Come and get it, pup," he taunted Bo.

Bo made a low, vicious roaring sound that triggered a reaction in Trinity.

She laughed, albeit a bit nervously, and said, "You can't kill him, Bo. If you do, you'll never know who was behind your father's death."

I saw Bo stiffen as his stalking motion stilled. He neither moved nor made a single sound.

"Now, it's time to join him," Lars said.

His words poured through me like gasoline, turning the low-burning embers of anger into a raging wild fire of fury.

Breathing heavily and moving numbly, I opened the car door and stepped out. In that same instant, Lars put his foot on the rear bumper.

"Here, darling," he called to Trinity.

With a quick flick of his leg, the car was ripped away from me as Lars sent Devon and Savannah careening down the road toward Trinity.

I looked to my right and watched it happen in slow motion. The smoke of burning tires curled into the air. The acrid stench of it stung my nostrils. I was frantically trying to think of how I could help my friends and help Bo at the same time. When Lars moved, my attention shifted completely back to him and a choice was made. I couldn't leave Bo.

He took one step toward me and Bo sprang into action. With a crazed bellow that pierced the night like a sword, Bo launched himself at Lars.

They tumbled into the grass along the side of the road, grappling and struggling for the upper hand. I watched, breathless and terrified, as they bit and tore at each other. I heard the snap and crunch of bones breaking, the coarse crackle of clothes tearing. But it wasn't until I heard Bo cry out in pain that I felt the agony begin inside my own body.

The knives sliced through my skin, tearing across my face and chest. They made their way down my arms, freeing the fury inside me, letting it pour out to consume the object of my wrath.

The next tortured moan that I heard was not Bo's; it came from Lars. Satisfaction washed through me, but it did nothing to dampen the flames of my rage. It simply propelled me forward, leading me to the two bodies that wrestled in the darkness.

I concentrated on the form of Lars and I let the burn and the pain of my fear for Bo take hold. I used it, directed it, focused it. On Lars. It flowed through me, out of me, around me until every nerve, every inch of skin, every fiber of muscle was saturated with it.

I couldn't contain the cry. It tore through me and burst out of my throat with a life of its own. I closed my eyes to it, gave my soul to it, until I heard an answering cry from Lars.

I felt the shift in power. I felt the surge as Bo overtook him. When I opened my eyes, Bo had pinned Lars to the ground and, with a howl of victory, he bore his teeth and drilled them into the soft tissue of Lars's neck.

Triumph—Bo's, mine, ours—flooded me, eclipsing everything else. It was heady, intoxicating, all-encompassing. It washed over me, wave after delicious wave, until it hit me with a blast of weakness that sent me staggering to the ground.

It was then that I realized what was happening. Bo was draining Lars. And it was killing him.

"Bo, stop!" My breath was not enough to make much sound.

Bo continued.

I felt the poison, the death of it, creeping through my chest as if I'd taken it in as well. I struggled to my knees, desperate to make my way to Bo.

"Bo, please!"

On all fours, I put one shaky limb in front of the other, never taking my eyes off Bo. I couldn't move fast enough to get to him, the frailty was so debilitating. I felt it sinking further and further into my body and I knew Bo didn't have long.

"Bo," I panted, desperate to reach him.

My heart raced frantically until I saw Bo slump onto Lars's chest and then roll lifelessly onto his side. Terror ripped a gaping hole in my heart.

"Bo," I cried, dragging my knees through the gravel.

I felt the cool air dry the tears that were streaming down my face, but they were too fast, too many. They dripped from my chin, hitting the ground in a delicate patter, as I pushed myself toward Bo.

Somewhere in the distance, I could hear someone calling Bo's name over and over and over. It was my own voice, but it was hard to hear over the frenzied pounding of my heart as it drummed in my ears.

When I reached Bo, I gently pushed him onto his back. Every inch of visible skin was that unhealthy greenish black and it was all cracked like the Nevada desert. His mouth and his shirt were stained with blood the color of tar. I didn't need to be told that it was the poisonous, memory-rich blood that Bo had sought for so long. I didn't need to be told the power of it. And the devastation. I'd felt it.

As he looked up at me, I could see that the blackness of it even invaded the whites of his eyes. But still, when he looked at me with those liquid brown orbs, my heart melted.

Bo coughed and drops of inky blood spewed from his mouth, dotting his face like paint spatter.

I couldn't speak past the lump in my throat. Even if I could've, my chest was so tight, I doubted air could flow in and out.

Bo was dying and my heart was breaking over and over again. As I watched him, each jagged piece splintered into tinier pieces until I felt like there was nothing left in my chest but sand.

"I know who did it," he breathed feebly.

Tears fell from my cheeks in a steady stream, washing Bo's face clean, one drop at a time. With trembling fingers, I lifted my hand to wipe at his mouth and chin, tenderly ridding it of all evidence of the price he'd paid for knowledge, for revenge, for justice.

"Tell Lucius 'Heather'," he wheezed, gasping for enough air to fill his deteriorating lungs.

I felt the sob bubble up in my throat before it erupted, spilling out in one syllable. "Bo," I cried.

Though he was obviously fighting for his breath, he inhaled as deeply as he could and spoke.

"I've never loved anyone more."

I squeezed my eyes shut, praying that this was all a dream, that when I opened them again, I'd be in my bedroom and Bo would be beside me. Alive.

"Bo, please," I wept.

"Thank you," he panted.

My eyes opened at the touch of his cool fingers to my lips and then his arm fell back to his chest with a hollow thud.

"Bo!" I shook his shoulder, but he didn't move. "Bo!" I tapped my fingers against his cheek, but still got no response.

I looked into his face, the face that had haunted my dreams, the face that was etched onto my heart. I searched his dark eyes, but they were empty. They stared blankly past me, looking into a world that I couldn't see.

"Bo, don't go," I cried. "Please don't leave me."

As I watched, his form began to fade. As his body's last efforts to fight metabolized the remainder of the blood, I lost sight of him. Though I could still feel the ever-cooling shape beneath my hands, I could no longer see Bo. He disappeared right before my eyes.

"Bo!" I wailed, the last bits of my heart exploding in a spray of emotional shrapnel that left me dead and lifeless inside.

The crunch of metal drew my attention away from Bo and I remembered that my friends were stranded down the road, at the mercy of Trinity. But I didn't want to leave Bo. Not yet. I couldn't bear to let him go.

More noises reached my ears, the sounds of struggling, scuffling. What if there was still time to help them? How could I not at least try?

Guilt, sharp and poignant, seared my soul. I was so torn. I wanted nothing more to stay with Bo, but deep down, I knew that the only right thing to do was to help the living. They still had a chance for happiness, even if I did not.

I leapt to my feet and ran as fast as my stiff muscles would carry me. As I reached the car, I saw that the doors had been ripped off, the windshield was broken and the hood was up, the radiator steaming and hissing in the dying glow of the headlights.

I heard a faint rustling and I saw a flash of red in the forest. I raced forward to Savannah. She was jerking spasmodically where she lay at the base of a tree. There was a dark stain on the bark, blood that ran down to where she was crumpled on the ground. The right side of her face was covered in it and her hair was wet with it.

"Savannah?"

There was no response; she just continued to twitch. She was making a gurgling sound in the back of her throat that made me nauseous. Whatever Trinity had done to her, I knew Savannah was in trouble.

Pulling my cell phone from my pocket, I dialed 911. When I'd reported the accident to the operator and hung up, I cradled Savannah's head in my lap and listened for sounds of Trinity or Devon. After a few minutes, when still I had not heard the sounds of other people, I realized that I was alone in the night. It was absolutely silent but for the suffering of Savannah and the tick of the car's engine where it was slowly dying on the road behind me.

****

Three numb days later, I lay in my bed, reliving the nightmare of the previous seventy-some hours.

After the ambulances had come and one of them had taken Savannah away, one of the responding policemen attempted to question me as an EMT checked me out. To his questions, I said nothing. There was nothing to say.

Another officer tried to get through to me, but the pain I was feeling was too consuming to allow my brain enough function to manufacture a believable story, so still I said nothing.

I heard the word "catatonic" bandied about in hushed whispers, probably because all I could manage during the entire ordeal were bouts of staring off into the distance alternating with crying jags where I sobbed so violently my ribs ached.

On the ride home, that's what I did the most of—cry. After that, for hours and hours each day and all through every sleepless night, I cried. I mourned a loss so great, I wasn't sure I could survive it, didn't think I wanted to. I prayed many times for death, not wanting to see another sunrise and face another day without Bo in it. But each day, despite my pleas for relief, dawn came and I got up and went about pretending it was business as usual, that I was whole and human. Only I wasn't. Even now, I'm not sure what I am. Half dead. Half human. Nothing complete, and I never would be again.

Late the night Bo died, I ventured to see Lucius, to carry out Bo's last wishes and deliver the message "Heather." When Lucius answered the door, I knew by the look on his face that he knew, that I need not explain that Bo was gone. Whether it was the gaping hole in my heart that gave it away, or something less subtle like my puffy red eyes and absolute silence, I don't know. But he knew.

After I gave him the message, I turned and left. I could tell he wanted to talk, to help me, to comfort me, but I had no interest in anything but the grief that was tearing me apart. There would be no solace, no relief for me. Though my physical life continued, my inner life had been extinguished. It had disappeared with Bo.

Besides, I had to conserve what little spark I had left in me. There was one more stop I had to make before I could collapse in the blessed peace and solitude of my bedroom—Bo's house.

Barely able to get the words out, I told Denise what had happened as best I could. Her grief seemed nearly a match of my own, but where I had the regret of not having had enough time with Bo, she seemed to have an ocean of regrets of another sort. Though I was curious about them, I was glad that she didn't want to talk about it. I doubted I could've listened. It was all I could do to be in the house, where I smelled Bo as if he still lived there, as if he still lived anywhere. As if he still lived at all.

She sent word to me that she was having a small service for him on Sunday, and by small I mean only me and Denise. Since no body was recovered, Bo was officially listed as a missing person, but we knew better. That's why the memorial was so small. Devon had disappeared and no one else knew the truth, no one conscious anyway.

I wasn't sure what Savannah knew, what she'd seen. She'd suffered brain damage when Trinity had thrown her into a tree and she had slipped into coma only hours after she'd been rescued. It was with her in mind that I took a lantern to the river to join Denise Bowman in remembering her son, the love of my life.

Even now, as I lay in my bed with the cloak of midnight all around me and the night singing right outside my open window, I can't imagine enduring anything more gut-wrenchingly painful than that service by the water.

The sun was setting across the river, its orangey glow reflected in every ripple of the water, a silent tribute to the memory of the dying day. It seemed apropos; we'd come in memory of the dead, too.

I could hear the creak and groan of the trees as they swayed in the wind, and just below that, there was the soft whisper of the leaves rustling, their gilded tips fluttering and twisting on the breeze.

From the road, I could see Denise standing at the water's edge, her back to me. Before I descended the bank, I closed my eyes and took a deep breath. The tangy scent of citrus filled my nostrils and my thoughts went immediately to Bo, as they always did.

When I opened my eyes and looked around, searching the dappled woods for him, my heart squeezed painfully with the realization that my mind was just playing tricks on me. Bo was nowhere around. He was gone.

Denise had asked an old family friend, a minister, to come and say a few words, to give Bo a ceremony even if no one else knew of it. When he was finished, Denise opened a jar and spread some sort of ashy substance across the water. I wasn't sure what it was, but it wasn't Bo. The chalky mist that drifted down river was just a symbol of him, carried quietly away by the wind.

I put my arm around Denise's shoulders, each of us drawing what little comfort could be had from each other's grief. She squeezed my hand and thanked me with her bloodshot eyes. And then she walked away with the minister, leaving me alone on the bank, staring into the water.

My legs held strong until I heard their engines start and then I collapsed, my knees sinking into the mud at the river's edge. Digging the lighter I'd brought from my pocket, I lit the lantern and set it onto the water and gave it a little push.

I watched Bo's lantern drift steadily down stream, away from me. The further it got from my view, the harder I cried. I closed my eyes once more, drawing in the scent of Bo that still clung to the heavy air, breathing him in.

How long I stayed like that, I have no idea. The constant ache in my soul that seemed only to worsen with each passing minute drowned out life and most everything in it, including time.

When night had fallen and there were no more tears to cry, no more moisture left to shed, and I had only the company of crickets to see me home, I finally left. It occurred to me that no matter how long I knelt there, crying by the river, Bo wasn't coming back, and since I was no closer to saying goodbye than I ever had been, I might as well go home.

Closing my eyes against that excruciating memory, I drifted off to sleep for the first time in three days. Fatigue had finally won.

I hadn't been asleep very long when I woke. Only forty minutes if my clock was telling the truth. At first, I wasn't sure what had stirred me. I was still hovering in that place between wakefulness and sleep, suspended between the two. I was so exhausted—emotionally and physically— that I felt as if I'd been drugged, my head thick and fuzzy.

I listened closely for sounds, for what had roused me. Outside my open window, I heard nothing but the sounds of nature, the same nighttime lullaby as always.

An agonizingly familiar tangy scent assailed me. Again. I felt the sting of tears at the backs of my eyes and a sob clogged my throat. It was all in my head. It had to be. Bo was gone. I was just imagining his smell.

As I lay there, breathing him in, I realized that, this time, my treacherous body didn't even seem to know the difference. It was reacting to him, to the magnetism of him, as if he was near, even though he was no longer with me. It just felt like he was. Just a feeling. Nothing more. Emotional trickery.

I gave in to the urge to cry—again—the damn breaking as his scent swirled through the air and his presence swirled in my blood.

"Bo," I groaned, turning to bury my face in the pillow, wishing that it could drown out the bittersweet memory of him, the smell of him, or that it would swallow me whole so that I could find peace, find relief, find *him* in death.

A soft, familiar voice hushed me.

"I'm here," it said.

The voice was Bo's. I'd know it anywhere. My ears were confirming what my body already knew. Bo was near.

I sat up and looked around my moonlit room, inspecting the darkness. Desperately, I searched the shadows for some indication that I wasn't imagining him, but I found none. No matter how much I wished it otherwise, I was still painfully, achingly alone.

I flopped back onto the bed, tears streaming down across my temples, collecting in a warm pool just inside my ears. I closed my eyes and lay perfectly still, drinking in the still-strong aroma, basking in it.

It startled me when a cool finger touched my cheek. My skin tingled in recognition when it brushed away a tear as it slid from my eye.

Slowly, I opened my eyes. In my gut, I knew I'd see nothing. And I was right, but that didn't stop the electricity that shot through my body when the finger traced a path to my lips.

"Shhh," the voice said.

My soul soared despite my mind's unwillingness to consider the possibility. I knew that voice. I knew that touch. Even on my deathbed, I'd remember it, crave it, need it. And this was no trick of my mind. It was real.

It was Bo. It had to be.

The murmur of death, a dark shadow overcast,

Ringing long and eternal as life slips slowly past,

It breeds the unthinkable and touts the unknown,

It begins at the end, on a whisper, a moan.

EPILOGUE

The next day, I woke with traces of Bo all around me, even inside me. He swam in my blood, alive and well. Though I couldn't see him and I really had no reason to believe that he could've survived that last fatal poisoning, I knew, somewhere in the bottom of my soul, that he lived.

Rather than driving to school, I headed to the forest, to Lucius, trying my best to remember the way. He'd been ready and anxious to talk to me when I'd given him Bo's final message. I was curious to see what he had to say now.

Getting to the right spot along the road to stop and enter the forest wasn't the difficult part of my journey. Bo had parked just beyond a sign about littering that someone had spray painted obscene symbols all over. I wasn't likely to forget that marker. No one probably did.

No, it was the forest itself that gave me a fit. I couldn't imagine how I'd found it so easily the night of Bo's death, because today I felt like I was walking in circles. Everything looked the same. Just when I thought I was making progress, I'd run into something that I'd already seen once or twice.

Finally, just before I was about to give up, I widened my path further to the right and came upon the huge boulder that Lars had staked Bo to. It still gave me chills to look at it, although it wasn't as devastating now that I believed Bo was alive. Twenty-four hours ago, I wouldn't have been able to stand the sight of it.

Within ten minutes of finding the rock, I found the cabin that was my destination. I hesitated before walking up on the small porch. I was just about to reconsider my impulsive visit, a tiny doubt niggling at my brain, telling me I was wrong, that Bo wasn't alive. I was suddenly afraid that Lucius would tell me that Bo was never coming back, rather than confirm that what I'd felt had been real. I didn't think I could survive that soul-crushing loss again.

Turning back was no longer an option, however, when a quiet *whoosh* broke into my musing. The cabin door opened and Lucius stood just inside. We stared at each other for a couple of long, tense minutes before he stepped aside and swept one arm in front of him, beckoning me in.

Taking a deep breath, I walked into the tiny above-ground living area, the one I liked to think of as a decoy, and turned to look back at Lucius.

"You know," he said simply.

I felt like crying again, but this time for joy. Those two words, they said all that needed to be said, all that I needed so desperately to hear. Bo was alive.

I nodded.

"That's why I wanted to talk to you the night it happened. There are things you need to know."

"What kinds of things?"

"Things about Bo, about who he is."

"What do you mean? I know who Bo is."

"No, I'm afraid you don't."

"Lucius, what are you trying to say?"

He paused. "Bo's not who you think he is. Bo's doesn't even know who he really is."

I had no idea what to say to that. I had only questions, hundreds of questions.

Lucius looked at me and nodded, as if in understanding. "Come with me," he said, walking to the door that led to the cabin's luxurious basement. "I'll tell you everything I know."

TO BE CONTINUED IN BOOK 2

BLOOD LIKE POISON: DESTINED FOR A VAMPIRE

ABOUT THE AUTHOR

M. Leighton is a native of Ohio, but she relocated to the warmer climates of the South, where she can be near the water all summer and miss the snow all winter. Possessed of an overactive imagination from early in her childhood, Michelle finally found an acceptable outlet for her fantastical visions: writing fiction. Five of Michelle's novels can now be found on Amazon, as well as several other sites. She's currently working on sequels, though her mind continues to churn out new ideas, exciting plots and quirky characters. Pick one up and enjoy a wild ride through the twists and turns of her vivid imagination.

OTHER BOOKS BY M. LEIGHTON

Caterpillar
Madly
The Reaping
Wiccan

WHERE TO FIND MICHELLE

Blog: http://mleightonbooks.blogspot.com
Facebook: M. Leighton Author Page
Twitter: mleightonbooks
Goodreads: M. Leighton, Author

CONTACT ME

m.leighton.books@gmail.com

10690006R00175

Made in the USA
Charleston, SC
23 December 2011